ESSAYS AN

ᴏ̣ꜰ

GIACOMO LEOPARDI

BY GIACOMO LEOPARDI

TRANSLATED

BY

CHARLES EDWARDES

"Manure with Despair, but let it be genuine, and you will have a noble harvest."—
RAHEL.

The name of Giacomo Leopardi is not yet a household word in the mouths of
Englishmen. Few of us have heard of him; still fewer have read any of his writings. If
known at all, he is probably coupled, in a semi-contemptuous manner, with other foreign
representatives of a phase of poetic thought, the influence of which has passed its zenith.
As a contemporary of Byron, Leopardi is perhaps credited with a certain amount of
psychological plagiarism, and possibly disregarded as a mere satellite of the greater planet.
But if this be so, it is unjust. His fame is his own, and time makes his isolation and grand
individuality more and more prominent. What Byron and Shelley, Millevoye, Baudelaire
and Gautier, Heine and Platen, Pouchkine and Lermontoff, are to England, France,
Germany, and Russia respectively, Leopardi is, in a measure, to Italy. But he is more than
this. The jewel of his renown is[Pg viii] triple-faceted. Philology, poetry, and philosophy
were each in turn cultivated by him, and he was of too brilliant an intellect not to excel in
them all. As a philologist he astonished Niebuhr and delighted Creuzer; as a poet he has
been compared with Dante; as a philosopher he takes high rank among the greatest and
most original men of modern times. One of his biographers (Dovari: "Studio di G.
Leopardi," Ancona, 1877) has termed him "the greatest philosopher, poet, and prose-
writer of the nineteenth century." Though such eulogy may be, and doubtless is,
excessive, the fact that it has been given testifies to the extraordinary nature of the man
who is its subject.

In Germany and France, Leopardi is perhaps as well known and highly appreciated
as in Italy. His poems have been translated into the languages of those countries; and in
France, within the last year, two more or less complete versions of his prose writings have
appeared. Biographies, reviews, and lighter notices of the celebrated Italian are of
repeated and increasing occurrence on the Continent. England, however, knows little of
him, and hitherto none of his writings have been made accessible to the English reading
public. The following brief outline of his life may in part help to explain the peculiarly
sombre philosophical views which he held, and of which his works are chiefly an
elaboration.

Giacomo Leopardi was born at Recanati, a small town about fifteen miles from
Ancona, on the[Pg ix] 29th June 1798. He was of noble birth, equally on the side of his
father and mother. Provided with a tutor at an early age, he soon left him far behind in
knowledge; and when only eight years old, he discarded the Greek grammar he had
hitherto used, and deliberately set himself the task of reading in chronological order the
Greek authors of his father's library. It was due to his own industry, and his father's care,
that later he acquired a perfect acquaintance with classical literature. In 1810 he received
his first tonsure, in token of his dedication to the Church; but this early promise was not
destined to be fulfilled. Before he was eighteen years of age Leopardi had attained
recognised distinction for the amount and matter of his erudition. The mere catalogue of
his writings—chiefly philological—by that time is of sufficient length to excite wonder,
and their nature is still more surprising. Latin commentaries and classical annotations
were apparently child's play to him. Writing in 1815 to the Roman scholar Cancellieri,
who had noticed one of these classical productions, Leopardi says: "I see myself secured
to posterity in your writings.... Commerce with the learned is not only useful, but
necessary for me." He was only seventeen when he completed a task which represented
the sum of all his early study. This was an "Essay on the Popular Errors of the Ancients,"
of considerable length (first published posthumously), in the course of which he cites

more than four hundred authors, ancient and modern. A single extract will suffice to show[Pg x] that his youthful powers of expression were as precocious as his learning, though his judgment was doubtless at fault. He thus reviews the wisdom of the Greeks:

"The philosophy of the ancients was the science of differences; and their academies were the seats of confusion and disorder. Aristotle condemned what Plato had taught. Socrates mocked Antisthenes; and Zeno scandalised Epicurus. Pythagoreans, Platonians, Peripatetics, Stoics, Cynics, Epicureans, Sceptics, Cyrenaics, Megarics, Eclectics scuffled with and ridiculed one another; while the truly wise laughed at them all. The people, left to themselves during this hubbub, were not idle, but laboured silently to increase the vast mound of human errors."

He ends this Essay with a eulogy of the Christian religion: "To live in the true Church is the only way to combat superstition." Shortly afterwards, increasing knowledge, which Goethe has called "the antipodes of faith," enabled him to perceive that Roman Catholicism, the antidote which he then prescribed for superstition, was itself full charged with the poison he sought to destroy.

In 1817 Leopardi made acquaintance by letter with Pietro Giordani, one of the leading literary men of the day, and a man of varied experience and knowledge. In his first letter Leopardi opens his heart to his new friend:

"I have very greatly, perhaps immoderately, yearned for glory ... I burn with love for Italy, and thank Heaven that I am an Italian. If I live, I will live for[Pg xi] literature; for aught else, I would not live if I could."

(21st March 1817.)

A month later, from the same source we are able to discern traces of that characteristic of Leopardi's temperament which by certain critics is thought to explain his philosophy. Writing to Giordani, he expatiates on the discomforts of Recanati and its climate; and proceeds:—

"Added to all this is the obstinate, black, and barbarous melancholy which devours and destroys me, which is nourished by study, and yet increases when I forego study. I have in past times had much experience of that sweet sadness which generates fine sentiments, and which, better than joy, may be said to resemble the twilight; but my condition now is like an eternal and horrible night. A poison saps my powers of body and mind."—

In the same letter he gives his opinion on the relative nature of prose and poetry.

"Poetry requires infinite study and application, and its art is so profound, that the more you advance in proficiency, so much the further does perfection seem to recede.... To be a good prose writer first, and a poet later, seems to me to be contrary to nature, which first creates the poet, and then by the cooling operation of age concedes the maturity and tranquillity necessary for prose."

(30th April 1817.)

The correspondence between Leopardi and Giordani lasted for five years, and it is from their published letters that we are able to form the best possible estimate of Leopardi's character and aspirations. His own letters serve as the index of[Pg xii] his physical and mental state. In them we trace the gradual failure of his health, the growth of sombreness in his disposition, and the change which his religious convictions underwent. During his twentieth year he suffered severely in mind and body. Forced to lay aside his studies, he was constantly a prey to ennui, with all its attendant discomforts. He thus writes to Giordani of his condition, in August 1817:

"My ill-health makes me unhappy, because I am not a philosopher who is careless of life, and because I am compelled to stand aloof from my beloved studies.... Another thing that makes me unhappy, is thought. I believe you know, but I hope you have not experienced, how thought can crucify and martyrise any one who thinks somewhat differently from others. I have for a long time suffered such torments, simply because thought has always had me entirely in its power; and it will kill me unless I change my condition. Solitude is not made for those who burn and are consumed in themselves."

(1st August 1817.)

His mental activity was numbed by his physical incapacity; the two combined reduced him to a state of despair. There is a noble fortitude in the following words of another letter addressed to Giordani:—

"I have for a long time firmly believed that I must die within two or three years, because I have so ruined myself by seven years of immoderate and incessant study.... I am conscious that my life cannot be other than unhappy, yet I am not frightened; and if I could in any way be useful, I would endeavour to bear my condition without losing heart. I have passed years so[Pg xiii] full of bitterness, that it seems impossible for worse to succeed them; nevertheless I will not despair even if my sufferings do increase ... I am born for endurance."

(2d March 1818.)

Leopardi was now of age, and at the time of life when mans aspirations are keenest. He had repeatedly tried to induce his father to let him go forth into the world, and take his place in the school of intellect; but all his endeavours were in vain. Though seconded by Giordani, who some months before had become personally acquainted with his young correspondent during a visit of a few days to Casa Leopardi, the Count was resolute in refusing to grant his son permission to leave Recanati. Giacomo, driven to desperation, conceived a plan by which he hoped to fulfil his desire in spite of the paternal prohibition. The following extract from the Count's diary furnishes the gist of the matter, and also gives us some small insight into his own character:—

"Giacomo, wishing to leave the country, and seeing that I was opposed to his doing so, thought to obtain my consent by a trick. He requested Count Broglio to procure a passport for Milan, so that I might be alarmed on hearing of it, and thus let him go. I knew about it, because Solari wrote unwittingly to Antici, wishing Giacomo a pleasant journey. I immediately asked Broglio to send me the passport, which he did with an accompanying letter. I showed all to my son, and deposited the passport in an open cupboard, telling him he could take it at his leisure. So all ended."

Thus the plot failed, and Giacomo was constrained to resign himself, as best he could, to a[Pg xiv] continuance of the "life worse than death" which he lived in Recanati. Two letters written in anticipation of the success of his scheme, one to his father, and the other to Carlo, his brother, are of most painful interest. They suggest unfilial conduct on his part, and unfatherly treatment of his son on the part of Count Monaldo.

"I am weary of prudence," he writes in the letter to Carlo, "which serves only as a clog to the enjoyment of youth ... How thankful I should be if the step I am taking might act as a warning to our parents, as far as you and our brothers are concerned! I heartily trust you will be less unhappy than myself. I care little for the opinion of the world; nevertheless, exonerate me if you have any opportunity of doing so.... What am I? a mere good-for-nothing creature. I realise this most intensely, and the knowledge of it has determined me to take this step, to escape the self-contemplation which so disgusts me. So long as I possessed self-esteem I was prudent; but now that I despise myself, I can only find relief by casting myself on fortune, and seeking dangers, worthless thing that I am.... It were better (humanly speaking) for my parents and myself that I had never been born, or had died ere now. Farewell, dear brother."

The letter to his father is in a different key. It is stern and severe, and contains reproofs, direct and inferential, for his apparent indifference to his sons' future prospects. Giacomo upbraids him with intentional blindness to the necessities of his position as a youth of generally acknowledged ability, for whom Recanati could offer no scope, or chance of renown. He goes on to say:

[Pg xv]

"Now that the law has made me my own master, I have determined to delay no longer in taking my destiny on my own shoulders. I know that man's felicity consists in contentment, and that I shall therefore have more chance of happiness in begging my bread than through whatever bodily comforts I may enjoy here.... I know that I shall be deemed mad; and I also know that all great men have been so regarded. And because the career of almost every great genius has begun with despair, I am not disheartened at the same commencement in mine. I would rather be unhappy than insignificant, and suffer than endure tedium.... Fathers usually have a better opinion of their sons than other people; but you, on the contrary, judge no one so unfavourably, and therefore never imagined we might be born for greatness.... It has pleased Heaven, as a punishment, to ordain that the only youths of this town with somewhat loftier aspirations than the Recanatese should belong to you, as a trial of patience, and that the only father who would regard such sons as a misfortune should be ours."

The relationship between Giacomo and his parents has been a vexed question with all his biographers, who, for the most part, are of the opinion that they had little sympathy with him in the mental sufferings he underwent. The Count has been called "despota sistematico" in the administration of his household; and the most favourably disposed writers have agreed to regard him as somewhat of a Roman father. But there does not seem to be sufficient evidence to support the theory that he was intentionally harsh and repressive to the extent of cruelty in his treatment of his children. He was an Italian of the old school, and as such his conduct was probably different from[Pg xvi] that of more modern Italian fathers; but that was all.

In 1819, when his whole being was in a turmoil of disquiet, Leopardi made his début as a poet, with two Odes—the one addressed to Italy, and the other on the monument to Dante, then recently erected in Florence. The following literal translation of the first stanza of the Ode to Italy gives but a faint echo of the original verse:—

"O my country, I see the walls and arches, the columns, the statues, and the deserted towers of our ancestors; but their glory I see not, nor do I see the laurel and the iron which girt our forefathers. To-day, unarmed, thou showest a naked brow and naked breast. Alas! how thou art wounded! How pale thou art, and bleeding! That I should see thee thus! O queen of beauty! I call on heaven and earth, and ask who thus has humbled thee. And as a crowning ill, her arms are weighed with chains; her hair dishevelled and unveiled; and on the ground she sits disconsolate and neglected, her face hid in her knees, and weeping. Weep, Italia mine, for thou hast cause, since thou wert born to conquer 'neath Fortune's smiles and frowns.

> O patria mia, vedo le mura e gli archi
> E le colonne e i simulacri e l' erme
> Torri degli avi nostri,
> Ma la gloria non vedo,
> Non vedo il lauro e il ferro ond' eran carchi
> I nostri padri antichi. Or fatta inerme,
> Nuda la fronte e nudo il petto mostri.
> Oimè quante ferite,

Che lividor, che sangue! oh qual ti veggio,
Formosissima donna! Io chiedo al cielo,
E al mondo: dite, dite:
Chi la ridusse a tale? E questo è peggio,
Che di catene ha carene ambe le braccia.
[Pg xvii]Si che sparte le chiome e senza velo
Siede in terra negletta e sconsolata,
Nascondendo la faccia
Tra le ginocchia, e piange.
Piangi, che ben hai donde, Italia mia,
Le genti a vincer nata
Et nella fausta sorte e nella ria."

These odes, which represent the first fruits of his muse, ring with enthusiasm. They are the expression of a soul fired with its own flame, which serves to illumine and vivify a theme then only too real in his country's experience, the sufferings of Italy. Patriotism pervades his earliest verse; sadness and hopelessness that of later times. For these two odes Giordani bestowed unsparing eulogy on his young protégé. Before their appearance he had begun to regard Leopardi as the rising genius of Italy, and had not hesitated to say to him, "Inveni hominem!" Now, however, his admiration was unbounded; he thus apostrophised him: "O nobilissima, e altissima, e fortissima anima!" He referred to the reception of his poems at Piacenza in these terms: "They speak of you as a god."

In 1822 Leopardi first left home. Repeatedly, year after year, he had besought his father to permit him to see something of the world. He longed to associate with the men who represented the intellect of his country. With his own fellow-townsmen he had little sympathy, and they on their part regarded him as a phenomenon, eccentric rather than remarkable. They gave him the titles of "little pedant," "philosopher," "hermit," &c., in half ironical appreciation of his learning. As[Pg xviii] he was naturally very sensitive, these petty vexations became intensified to him, and were doubtless one of the chief reasons of his unfailing dislike for his native place. In one of his essays, that of "Parini on Glory," we discover a reference to Leopardi's life at Recanati, which place is really identical with the Bosisio of the essay. Yet the prophet who is not a prophet in his own country when living, seldom fails of recognition after death. A statue is now raised to Leopardi in the place that refused to honour him in life. The appreciative recognition he failed to attract in Recanati, he hoped to obtain at Rome. But Count Monaldo, his father, long maintained his resistance to his son's wishes. Himself of a comparatively unaspiring mind, content with the fame he could acquire in his own province, he saw no necessity why his son should be more ambitious. Probably also his paternal love made him fearful of the dangers of the world, to which his son would be exposed. Of these hazards he knew nothing from experience; and they were doubtless magnified to him by his imagination. Yet, though naturally a man rather deficient in character than otherwise, Count Monaldo was, as we have seen, in his own household, a stern not to say unreasonable disciplinarian. Only after repeated solicitations from his son, and remonstrances from his friends, did he give Giacomo the desired permission, chiefly in the hope that at Rome he might be induced to enter the Church, towards which he had latterly manifested some signs of repugnance. The five months[Pg xix] spent by Leopardi in Rome sufficed to disenchant him of his ideas of the world of life. A day or two after his arrival he writes to Carlo his brother:

"I do not derive the least pleasure from the great things I see, because I know that they are wonderful, without feeling that they are so. I assure you their multitude and grandeur wearied me the first day."

(25th November 1822.)

Again, to Paulina his sister: "The world is not beautiful; rather it is insupportable, unless seen from a distance."

Ever prone to regard the real through the medium of the ideal, he was bitterly disappointed with his first experience of men. The scholar, whom he was prepared to revere, proved on acquaintance to be—

"a blockhead, a torrent of small talk, the most wearisome and afflicting man on earth. He talks about the merest trifles with the deepest interest, of the greatest things with an infinite imperturbability. He drowns you in compliments and exaggerated praises, and does both in so freezing a manner, and with such nonchalance, that to hear him one would think an extraordinary man the most ordinary thing in the world."

(25th November 1822.)

The stupidest Recanatese he termed wiser and more sensible than the wisest Roman. Again, to his father he complains of the superficiality of the so-called scholars of Rome.

"They all strive to reach immortality in a coach, as bad Christians would fain enter Paradise. According to them, the sum of human wisdom, indeed the only true science of man, is antiquity. Hitherto I have not[Pg xx] encountered a lettered Eoman who understands the term literature as meaning anything except archæology. Philosophy, ethics, politics, eloquence, poetry, philology, are unknown things in Rome, and are regarded as childish playthings compared to the discovery of some bit of copper or stone of the time of Mark Antony or Agrippa. The best of it is that one cannot find a single Eoman who really knows Latin or Greek; without a perfect acquaintance with which languages, it is clear that antiquity Cannot be Studied."

(9th December 1822.)

He was disheartened by the depraved condition of Roman literature. Everywhere he saw merit disregarded or trodden under foot. The city was full of professional poets and poetesses, and literary cliques formed for the purpose of the self-laudation of their members. Illustrious names of the past were insulted by the pseudo-great men of the day, whose fame was founded on writings of the most contemptible nature. These circumstances made Leopardi confess, in a letter to his brother, that had he not

"the harbour of posterity, and the conviction that in time all would take its proper place (illusory hope, but the only, and most necessary one for the true scholar),"

(16th December 1822.)

he would abandon literature once for all. But it was only during moments of depression that such words as these escaped him. He loved study for its own sake; fame was, after all, but a secondary consideration. Nor were men of genuine worth entirely wanting in Rome. Niebuhr, then Prussian ambassador at the Papal Court, Reinhold, the Dutch ambassador, Mai, subsequently a cardinal, were[Pg xxi] noble exceptions to the general inferiority. By them Leopardi was highly esteemed. Niebuhr especially was profoundly struck with his genius. "I have at last seen a modern Italian worthy of the old Italians and the ancient Romans," was his remark to De Bunsen after his first interview with the young scholar. Both he and De Bunsen became firm friends with Leopardi. They endeavoured their utmost to procure for him some official appointment from Cardinal Consalvi, then Secretary of State, and his successor; but owing to the intrigues, prejudices, and disturbances of the Papal Court they were unable to effect anything on his behalf. It was an unfulfilled intention of De Bunsen's, later in life, to write a memoir of Leopardi, for whom he always felt the highest esteem and admiration.

Count Monaldo's wish that his son should become an ecclesiastic was never realised. Leopardi was of too honest a nature to profess what was not in accordance with his convictions. The secular employment that he sought, he could not obtain, so perforce he seems to have turned his mind towards literary work—the drudgery of letters as distinct from the free, untrammelled pursuit of literature. He obtained the charge of cataloguing the Greek manuscripts of the Barberine Library, and his spirits rose in anticipation of some discovery he hoped to make which might render him famous. "In due time we will astonish the world," he writes to his father. He was indeed successful in finding a fragment of Libanius hitherto[Pg xxii] unpublished; but the glory seems to have been stolen from him, since the manuscript was ushered forth to the world by alien hands. Poor Leopardi! all his hopes seemed destined to be proved illusive. It was time for him to leave a place that could furnish him with no other pleasure than that of tears. "I visited Tasso's grave, and wept there. This is the first and only pleasure I have experienced in Rome" (Letter to Carlo, February 15, 1823). Already he had begun to steel himself to the shocks of fortune; suffering and misfortune he could bear; mental agony and despair were too strong for him. In a long letter to his sister Paulina, he tries to impart to her a little of the philosophy of Stoicism which he had taken to himself. She was distressed about the rupture of a matrimonial arrangement contracted by the Count between her and a certain Roman gentleman of position and fortune. Leopardi thus consoles her:

"Hope is a very wild passion, because it necessarily carries with it very great fear.... I assure you, I Paolina mia,' that unless we can acquire a little indifference towards ourselves, life is scarcely possible, much less can it be happy. You must resign yourself to fortune, and not hope too deeply.... I recommend this philosophy to you, because I think you resemble me in mind and disposition."

(19th April 1823.)

Four years later Leopardi confesses the insufficiency of his own remedies. Writing to Dr. Puccinotti in 1827, he says:

"I am weary of life, and weary of the philosophy of indifference which is the only cure for misfortune and[Pg xxiii] ennui, but which at length becomes an ennui itself. I look and hope for nothing but death."

(16th August 1827.)

In May 1823, he left Rome, and returned to Recanati.

The succeeding ten years of Leopardi's life were, during his intervals of health, devoted to poetry and literature. He had passed the Rubicon of his hopes; henceforth he studied to expound to the world the uselessness of its own anticipations, and its essential unhappiness. His bodily infirmities increased with years. His frame, naturally weak, suffered from the effects of early over-application; his eyes and nerves were a constant trouble to him. To obtain what relief was possible from change of air, and to remove himself from Recanati, which he detested increasingly, Leopardi went to Bologna, Florence, Milan, and Pisa, wintering now at one place, now at another. From family reasons, his father was unable to supply him with sufficient money to secure his independence. Consequently he was obliged to turn to literature for a livelihood. The publisher Stella, of Milan, willingly engaged his services, and for several years Leopardi was in receipt of a small but regular payment for his literary labours. He compiled Chrestomathies of Italian prose and poetry, and made numerous fragmentary translations from the classics. A commentary on Petrarch, to which he devoted much time and care, is, in the words of Sainte-Beuve, "the best possible guide through such a charming labyrinth." As he said of himself,[Pg xxiv] "mediocrity is not for me," so in all that he undertook the mark of his genius appeared. At Florence Leopardi was honoured by the representatives of Italian literature and culture, who there formed a brilliant coterie. Colletta was desirous of his co-operation in the "History of Naples," with which he was occupying the last years of his life. The "Antologia" and "Nuove Ricoglitore" reviews were open to contributions from his pen. Giordani, Niccolini, Capponi, and Gioberti, amongst others, welcomed him with open arms. To these his Tuscan friends he dedicated his "Canti" in 1830, with the following touching letter:—

"MY DEAR FRIENDS,—Accept the dedication of this book. Herein I have striven, as is often done in poetry, to hallow my sufferings. This is my farewell (I cannot but weep in saying it) to literature and studies. Once I hoped these dear resources would have been the support of my old age: pleasures of childhood and youth might vanish, I thought, and their loss would be supportable if I were thus cherished and strengthened. But ere I was twenty years of age, my physical infirmities deprived me of half my powers; my life was taken, yet death was not bestowed on me. Eight years later I became totally incapacitated; this, it seems, will be my future state. Even to read these letters you know that I make use of other eyes than mine. Dear friends, my sufferings are incapable of increase; already my misfortune is too great for tears. I have lost everything, and am but a trunk that feels and suffers." ...

It is scarcely wonderful that, under such circumstances, his philosophy should fail him. A code of ethics, however admirable intrinsically, has but[Pg xxv] cold consolation to offer to one whose life is prolonged pain. Leopardi at one time allowed the idea of suicide to rest, and almost take root, in his mind. He describes the incident: "A great desire comes into my mind to terminate once for all these wretched years of mine, and to make myself more completely motionless." But he was of a nature noble and strong enough to resist such temptation.

He left Recanati for the last time in 1830. The next two years were passed in Florence, Rome, and Pisa. Whilst in Rome, Leopardi received substantial proof of his fame in being elected an Academician of the Crusca. At length the doctors recommended him to try Naples, from the mild air and general salubrity of which place they anticipated much improvement in his condition. Thither he went in company with a young friend, Antonio Ranieri, whose acquaintance he had made in Florence. In the house of Ranieri he stayed from 1833 until his death in 1837, tended by him and his sister Paulina (his second Paulina, as he used to call her) with a devotedness and affection as rare as it was noble. Posterity will couple together the names of Ranieri and Leopardi as naturally as we associate together those of Severn and Keats. All that could be done for the unfortunate poet, Ranieri did. His condition was a singular one. Before he left Florence for Naples, the doctor said of him that his frame did not possess sufficient vitality to generate a mortal illness; yet he was seldom, if ever, free from[Pg xxvi] suffering. He died on the 14th June 1837, as he and his friend were on the point of setting out from Naples to a little villa that Ranieri possessed on one of the slopes of Vesuvius. On the night of the 15th he was buried, in the church of St. Vitale, near the reputed grave of Virgil. His tomb is marked by a stone erected at the expense of Ranieri, bearing the signs of the cross, and the owl of Minerva, together with an inscription from the pen of Giordani. The few following lines from his own verse would form a suitable epitaph for one whose life was spent in bodily and mental disquietude:—

"O weary heart, for ever shalt thou rest
Henceforth. Perished is the great delusion
That I thought would ne'er have left me. Perished!

8

Nought now is left of all those dear deceits;
Desire is dead, and not a hope remains.
Rest then for ever. Thou hast throbbed enough;
Nothing here is worth such palpitations.
Our life is valueless, for it consists
Of nought but ennui, bitterness, and pain.
This world of clay deserveth not a sigh.
Now calm thyself; conceive thy last despair,
And wait for death, the only gift of Fate."

(Poem "A Se Stesso.")

These words might have been an echo of Çâkyamuni's utterance beneath the sacred fig-tree of Bôdhimanda, when, according to the legend, he was in process of transformation from man to Buddha: the resemblance is at any rate a remarkable one.

In 1846, the Jesuits made an impudent attempt to convince the public that Leopardi died[Pg xxvii] repenting of his philosophical views, and that he had previously expressed a desire to enter the Society of Jesus. A long letter from a certain Francesco Scarpa to his Superior, giving a number of pretended details of Leopardi's history, conversion, and death, appeared in a Neapolitan publication, entitled "Science and Faith." Ranieri came forward to show the entire falsity of these statements; and to give a more authoritative denial to them, he engaged the willing help of Vicenzo Gioberti. The latter in his "Modern Jesuit" contested their truth in every respect. He said: "The story put forward in this letter is a tissue of lies and deliberate inventions; it is sheer romance from beginning to end." It is thought by some people that Leopardi's father was concerned in this Jesuit manifesto. But, although the Count was doubtless shocked beyond measure that his son did not hold the same beliefs as himself, it is scarcely credible that he should concoct a series of such absurdities as were contained in Scarpa's letter.

Leopardi anticipated that posterity, and even his contemporaries, would endeavour to explain the pessimism of his philosophy by his personal misfortunes and sufferings. Accordingly, in a letter to the philologist Sinner, he entered a protest against such a supposition:

"However great my sufferings may have been, I do not seek to diminish them by comforting myself with vain hopes, and thoughts of a future and unknown happiness. This same courage of my convictions has led me to a philosophy of despair, which I do not hesitate to[Pg xxviii] accept. It is the cowardice of men, who would fain regard existence as something very valuable, that instigates them to consider my philosophical opinions as the result of my sufferings, and that makes them persist in charging to my material circumstances that which is due to nothing but my understanding. Before I die, I wish to make protest against this imputation of weakness and trifling; and I would beg of my readers to burn my writings rather than attribute them to my sufferings."

(24th May 1832.)

Ranieri thus describes Leopardi's personal appearance:

"He was of middle height, inclined to stoop, and fragile; his complexion was pale; his head was large, and his brow expansive; his eyes were blue and languid; his nose was well formed (slightly aquiline), and his other features were very delicately chiselled; his voice was soft and rather weak; and he had an ineffable and almost celestial smile."

His friend here scarcely even suggests what others have perhaps unduly emphasised, that is, Leopardi's deformity. He was slightly humpbacked; doubtless the consequence of those studies which simultaneously ruined him and made him famous.

9

It were an omission not to refer to the influence which love exerted over Leopardi's life. So strong was this, in the opinion of one of his critics, that he even ascribes his philosophy to an "infelicissimo amore." Another writer says of him that "his ideal was a woman." Ranieri asserts that he died unmarried, after having twice felt the passion of love as violently as it was ever realised by any[Pg xxix] man. His poems also testify how omnipotent at one time was this bitter-sweet sensation.

"I recall to mind the day when love first assaulted me; when I said, Alas! if this be love, how it pains me!"

(The First Love.)

Again:

"It was morning, the time when a light and sweeter sleep presses our rested lids. The sun's first grey light began to gleam across the balcony, through the closed windows into my still darkened chamber. Then it was that I saw close by, regarding me with fixed eyes, the phantom form of her who first taught me to love, and left me Weeping."

(The Dream.)

His poem to Aspasia is a frank confession of love, and the humiliation he suffered in its rejection. It is a noble, yet a terrible poem. Opening with a description of the scene that met his eye as he entered the room where his charmer sat, "robed in the hue of the melancholy violet, and surrounded by a wondrous luxury," pressing "tender and burning kisses on the round lipsé" of her children, and displaying "her snowy neck," he saw as it were "a new heaven, and a new earth, and the lustre of a celestial light."

"Like a divine ray, O woman, thy beauty dazzled my thought. Beauty is like such music as seems to open out to us an unknown Elysium. He who loves is filled with the ecstasy of the phantom love conceived by his imagination. In the woman of his love he seeks to discover the beauties of his inspired vision; in his words and actions he tries to recognise the personality of his dreams. Thus when he strains her to his bosom, it is not[Pg xxx] the woman, but the phantom of his dream that he embraces."

Then comes the awakening. He vituperates the reality for not attaining to the standard of his ideal.

"Rarely the woman's nature is comparable with that of the dream image. No thought like ours can dwell beneath those narrow brows. Vain is the hope that man forges in the fire of those sparkling eyes. He errs in seeking profound and lofty thoughts in one who is by nature inferior to man in all things. As her members are frailer and softer, so is her mind more feeble and confined."

He betrays his position, and gives the key to his unjust censure of woman's powers.

"Now, boast thyself, for thou canst do so. Tell how thou art the only one of thy sex to whom I have bent my proud head, and offered my invincible heart. Tell how thou hast seen me with beseeching brows, timid and trembling before thee (I burn with indignation and shame in the avowal), watching thy every sign and gesture, beside myself in adoration of thee, and changing expression and colour at the slightest of thy looks. The charm is broken; my yoke is on the ground, sundered at a single blow." (Aspasia.)

Who were the real objects of Leopardi's affection, is not at all clear. Certain village girls of Recanati, immortalised in his verse as Nerina and Silvia, were the inspirers of his first love; but his brother Carlo bears witness to the superficial nature of his affection in their cases. They merely served as the awakeners of the sensation; his own mind and imagination magnified it into a passion. True it is[Pg xxxi] that his nature was one that yearned and craved for love in no ordinary degree. When at Rome, isolated from his family, he wrote to Carlo: "Love me, for God's sake. I need love, love, love, fire, enthusiasm, life." He addressed similar demands to Giordani and others with whom he was on the most intimate terms. Indeed we are tempted to conjectures as to what might have been the fruit of Leopardi's life had he found a helpmate and a consoler in his troubles.

A brief consideration of the general nature of Leopardi's poetry and prose may not be out of place in this short summary.

His poems are masterpieces of conception and execution. Their matter may be open to criticism; but their manner is beyond praise. His odes are of the nobler kind. Full of fire and vigour, they reach the sublime where he stimulates his fellow-countrymen to action, and urges them to aspire to a freedom, happily now obtained. His elegies breathe out an inspired sorrow. They are the pro-duct of a mind filled with the sense of the misery that abounds on earth, and unable, though desirous, to discern a single ray of light in the gloom of existence. His lyrical pieces are the most beautiful and emotional of his poems. The following, entitled "The Setting of the Moon," though pervaded with the spirit of sadness that is so predominant a characteristic of Leopardi's verse, contains some charming imagery:—

[Pg xxxii]

"As in the lonely night, over the silvered fields and the waters where the zephyrs play, where the far-off shades take a thousand vague appearances and deceitful forms, amid the tranquil waves, the foliage and the hedges, the hill-slopes and the villages, the moon arrived at heaven's boundary descends behind the Alps and Apennines into the infinite bosom of the Tyrrhenian Sea; whilst the world grows pale, and the shadows disappear, and a mantle of darkness shrouds the valley and the hills; night alone remains, and the carter singing on his way salutes with a sad melody the last reflection of that fleeing light which hitherto had led his steps: So vanishes our youth, and leaves us solitary with life. So flee away the shadows which veiled illusive joys; and so die too the distant hopes on which our mortal nature rested. Life is left desolate and dark, and the traveller, trying to pierce the gloom, looks here and there, but seeks in vain to know the way, or what the journey yet before him; he sees that all on earth is strange, and he a stranger dwelling there.... You little hills and strands, when falls the light which silvers in the west the veil of night, shall not for long be orphaned. On the other side of heaven the first grey light of dawn shall soon be followed by the sun, whose fiery rays shall flood you and the ethereal fields with a luminous stream. But mortal life, when cherished youth has gone, has no new dawn, nor ever gains new light; widowed to the end it stays, and on life's other shore, made dark by night, the gods have set the tomb's dark seal."

In his interpretation of nature he is literal, but withal truly poetic: he worships her in the concrete, but vituperates her in the abstract, as representative to him of omnipresent Deity, creative, but also destructive. The two or three poems that may be termed satirical, are at the same time half elegiac. In them he ridicules and censures the folly of his[Pg xxxiii] contemporaries, and mourns over the mystery of things. To these, however, there is one exception, the longest of all his poems. This is known as the "Continuation of the Battle of the Frogs and Mice," It consists of eight cantos, comprising about three thousand lines, and was first published posthumously. The abruptness of its ending gives the idea, erroneous or not, of incompleteness. Leopardi had, several years before, translated and versified Homer's "Batrachomyomachia," and this satire takes up the story where Homer ends. It is exclusively a ridicule of the times, with especial reference to his own country and her national enemy, Austria. In style and treatment it has been compared with Byron's "Don Juan," from which, however, it totally differs in its intrinsic character. It abounds in beauties of description, sentiment, and expression, and well deserves to be considered his chef d'oeuvre. Leopardi thus describes his method of poetic composition:—

"I compose only when under an inspiration, yielding to which, in two minutes, I have designed and organised the poem. This done, I wait for a recurrence of such inspiration, which seldom happens until several weeks have elapsed. Then I set to work at composition, bub so slowly that I cannot complete a poem, however short, in less than two or three weeks. Such is my method; without inspiration it were easier to draw water from a stone than a single verse from my brain."

Leopardi's reputation was firmly established by the appearance of his "Operette morali," as his prose writings were termed. Monti classed them[Pg xxxiv] as the best Italian prose compositions of the century. Gioberti compared them to the writing of Machiavelli. Giordani, with his usual tendency to extravagance, gives his friend the following pompous panegyric:—"His style possesses the conciseness of Speroni, the grandiloquence of Tasso, the smoothness of Paruta, the purity of Gelli, the wit of Firenzuola, the solidity and magnificence of Pallavicino, the imagination of Plato, and the elegance of Cicero." Leopardi has been aptly termed an aristocrat in his writing. Too much of a reasoner to be very popular with the masses, who do not care for the exertion of sustained thought, his logic is strikingly clear to the intelligent. His periods are occasionally as long as those of Machiavelli or Guicciardini, but their continuity and signification are never obscure. Ranieri bears witness to the fact that his prose was the fruit of very great labour.

The subject and tendency of Leopardi's writings will be evident to the reader of the following dialogues. Framed on the model of Lucian, they will compare favourably with the writings of the Greek satirist in subtlety and wit, in spite of their sombre tone. They cannot be said to possess much originality, save in treatment. The subjects discussed, and even the arguments introduced, are mostly old. Every acute moraliser since the world began has, in more or less degree commensurate with his ability, debated within himself the problems here considered. Facts, beliefs, opinions, theories, may be marshalled to produce[Pg xxxv] an infinite number of diverse harmonies; but no one such combination formed by the mind of man may be put forward as the true and ultimate explanation of the mystery of life. Leibnitz, with his harmony of universal good, is as fallible as Leopardi or Schopenhauer with their harmonies of evil. In either case the real is sacrificed to the ideal, whether of good or evil. Either from temperament or circumstances, these philosophers were predisposed to give judgment on life, favourably or adversely, without duly considering the attributes of existence. As M. Dapples, in his French version of Leopardi, has remarked, he early withdrew from actual life, i.e., life with all those manifold sensations which he himself defines to be the only constituents of pleasure in existence. His body proved little else than the sensation of suffering. All his vitality was concentrated in his mind; so that he was scarcely a competent and impartial judge of the ordinary pleasures and ills of life. He could not be otherwise than prejudiced by his own experiences, or rather lack of experiences. Yet, though Leopardi was physically incapable of many of life's pleasures, he none the less passionately yearned for them. Strength and desire struggled within him, and the former only too frequently proved weaker than the latter. Thus he was innately adapted for pessimism.

We consider Leopardi to have been a man of the grandest intellectual powers, capable originally of almost anything to which the human mind could attain; but that his reason, later in life, became[Pg xxxvi] somewhat perverted by his sufferings. Were human life as absolutely miserable a thing as he represents it to be, it would be insupportable. That he should so regard it does not seem remarkable when we consider his circumstances; he was poor, seldom free from pain, and unsupported by a creed. For the sufferings of his life, he could see no shadow of atonement or compensation: a future state was incomprehensible to him. He bestows much gratuitous pity on the human race, which we, though revering his genius, may return to him as more deserving of it than ourselves. His heart was naturally full of the most lively affection; but he could never sufficiently satisfy the yearnings of his nature. Like Ottonieri, whose portrait is his own to a great extent, his instincts were noble; like him also he died without effecting much in proportion to his powers.

The conclusions of Leopardi's philosophy may be thus summed up. The universe is an enigma, totally insoluble. The sufferings of mankind exceed all good that men experience, estimating the latter in compensation for the former. Progress, or, as we call it, civilisation, instead of lightening man's sufferings, increases them; since it enlarges his capacity for suffering, without proportionately augmenting his means of enjoyment.

How far are these conclusions refutable? It may be regarded as indubitable that the first two cannot be refuted without the aid of revelation. Science is incompetent to explain the "why" and the "wherefore" of the universe; it is yet groping to discover[Pg xxxvii] the "how." Still less can any satisfactory explanation be given of the purpose for which suffering exists, unless we rely on revelation. Religion, which modern philosophers somewhat contemptuously designate as "popular metaphysics," can alone afford an explanation of these problems. Çâkyamuni, nearly 2500 years ago, asked, "What is the cause of all the miseries and sufferings with which man is afflicted?" He himself gave what he considered to be the correct answer: "Existence;" and then he traced existence to the passions and desires innate in man. These last were to be conquered in the condition of insensibility to all material things called "Nirvana," Truly his remedy was a radical one, and had he succeeded in procuring universal acceptance for his doctrines, the human race would have become extinct a few generations later than his own time. But "Nirvana" is unnatural if it be nothing else; unnatural in itself and in the steps that lead up to it. And although it is due to Schopenhauer, and his more or less heterodox disciples, that this Buddhistic dogma is regarded theoretically by some people with a certain amount of favour, we think the instincts of life are strong enough within them all to resist any decided inclination on their part to carry it into effect.

As for the third conclusion, it must be admitted that man's susceptibilities of suffering are enlarged with increasing culture. Leopardi has shown us that the more vividly we realise the evils that surround and affect us, so much the more keenly do they arouse in us sensations of pain. Knowledge[Pg xxxviii] of them makes us suffer from them. The bliss of ignorance is rudely dispelled by the cold hand of science. But must this necessarily continue? May not the same progress which exposes the wound find the salve to heal it? We trust and think so, in spite of all assertions to the contrary. There is nothing in the near future of humanity that need alarm us: men will not work less because they think more; nor is there any sufficient reason to show that increasing knowledge must represent increasing sorrow. As Johnson has said: "The cure for the greatest part of human miseries is not radical but palliative." For the material means of palliation we look to science. We hope and think that there is good to be gained from these writings of Leopardi, in spite of the tone of despair that rings throughout them. His theory of the "infelicità" of things, cheerless though it be, often suggests ideas, sublime in themselves and noble in their effect; and the very essence of his philosophy resolves itself into a recommendation to act, rather than by contemplation to lose the power of action; for, as he says, "A life must be active and vigorous, else it is not true life, and death is preferable to it."

A brief reference to the most recent publications on Leopardi may be interesting as tending to throw light on his domestic relationships, and as giving us an idea of his own habits in private life. Antonio Ranieri (now in his seventy-sixth year) in a book[1] published at Naples in 1880 gives many interesting details of the poet's life. He first met him at Florence, and was touched with compassion for his unfortunate state. Ill and helpless, he was incapable of doing anything but weep in despair at the thought of being obliged to return to his native place. "Recanati and death are to me one and the same thing," he exclaimed through his tears. Ranieri in a generous moment replied: "Leopardi, you shall not return to Recanati. The little that I possess is enough for two. As a benefit to me, not to yourself, we will henceforth live together." This was the beginning of what Ranieri calls his "vita nuova." He conducted Leopardi from Florence to Rome; thence back to Florence; and finally from Florence to Naples. The doctors everywhere shrugged their shoulders at his case, and suggested, as delicately as possible, the mortal nature of his maladies. At Naples Ranieri and his sister Paulina did all they could for Leopardi, and from 1833 to his death in 1837 supplied all his wants. He could seldom see to read or write. "We used to read to him constantly and regularly, and were fortunately conversant with the languages he knew," says Ranieri. Occasionally he was able to go to the theatre, and[Pg xl] enjoyed it greatly. In his habits he seems to have tried his friend's temper and patience considerably. He was wont to turn night into day, and day into night. Ranieri and his sister often did the same in order to read, work, and talk with him. He breakfasted between three and five o'clock in the afternoon, and dined about midnight. Like Schopenhauer, he delighted in after-dinner conversation, which he termed "one of the greatest pleasures of life." He was very obstinate in personal matters, disobeying the doctors in his diet and everything else. His fondness for his old clothes was remarkable; he loved them for their associations. Ranieri mentions "a certain very ancient overcoat which for seven years" had tormented him, and which he used to entreat Leopardi to lay aside, but which he clung to with an incredible affection, preferring it to a new one that he allowed the moths to destroy. The mere names of wind, cold, and snow were enough to pale him. He could not bear fire, and formerly used to pass the winters three parts submerged in a sack of feathers, reading and writing thus the greater part of the day. He was very terrified when the cholera appeared at Naples, to avoid which he and Ranieri went to a country house of the latter's on one of the slopes of Vesuvius. Here Leopardi wrote his poem "La Ginestra," inspired by the desolate scenes at the foot of the mountain. He died suddenly at Naples, as he and Ranieri's household were about to set off again for the country. The Neapolitan Journal "Il Progresso,"[Pg xli] in an article on Lis death, remarked of him that "such brilliancy is not allowed to illumine the earth for long."

"Notes Biographiques sur Leopardi et sa Famille" (Paris, 1881). This is a book of considerable value. Written by the widow of Count Carlo Leopardi, Giacomo's younger brother, and his "other self," it is most valuable as delineating the characters of Leopardi's father and mother. A softer light is shed on the character of Leopardi's mother. We learn that she was not passionless, hard, and unsympathetic, as we had previously supposed her to be. On the contrary, she was a good woman, of deep affection, who made it the aim of her married life to work for the welfare of the family of which she became a member. Weighted with debt almost to the point of exhaustion, the estates of Casa Leopardi needed a skilful and vigorous administrator, if they were to continue in the hands of their old owners. Count Monaldo Leopardi was not such an administrator. He was a man devoted "tout entier à science," and occupying himself more with bibliology and archæology than with the finances of his estate. The Jews of Perousa, Milan, and the March towns would, sooner or later, have tightened their hold on the Leopardi patrimony to such a degree that the ancient family could only have continued to exist as proprietors on sufferance. But, in the words of the authoress of this book, Providence watched over the house "en lui envoyant dans la jeune marquise Adelaide Antici l'ange qui[Pg xlii] devait la sauver." The young bride accepted her position with an entire knowledge of the responsibilities that would accompany it. She took the reins of the neglected administration, and set herself the task of restoring the fortunes of Casa Leopardi. By her exertions the Pope was made acquainted with their difficulties, and by his intervention an arrangement was made between the creditors and the Leopardi family, whereby the former were restrained from demanding the amount of their debt for forty years, receiving thereon in the mean time interest at 8 per cent, per annum. This was the life-work of Countess Leopardi. During forty years she administered the finances of Casa Leopardi, and by the end of that time succeeded in freeing the family from the burden with which it had been long encumbered. She died in 1857, ten years after her husband, and twenty years later than her eldest son, Giacomo.

ST. MARK'S PLACE, WOLVERHAMPTON,

December, 1881.

[1] Sette anni di Sodalizio con Giacomo Leopardi.

[Pg xliii]

The following works, amongst others, have been made use of in the preparation of this volume:—

Opere Leopardi. 6 vols. Firenze, 1845.

Opere inedite Leopardi. Cugnoni: Halle, 1878.

Studio di Leopardi. A. Baragiola: Strasburg, 1876.

Traduction complète de Leopardi. F. A. Aulard: Paris, 1880.

Opuscules et Pensées de Leopardi. A. Dapples: Paris, 1880.

G. Leopardi: sa Vie et ses Oeuvres. Bouché Leclercq: Paris, 1874.

Le Pessimisme. E. Caro: Paris, 1878.

Pessimism. Jas. Sully: London, 1877.

La Philosophie de Schopenhauer. Th. Ribot: Paris, 1874.

Il Buddha, Confucio, e Lao-Tse. C. Puini: Firenze, 1878.

Article in Quarterly Review on Leopardi. 1850.

Article in Fraser's Magazine, Leopardi and his Father: a Study, by L. Villari. November 1881.

[Pg xliv]

[Pg 1]

HISTORY OF THE HUMAN RACE.

It is said that the first inhabitants of the earth were everywhere created simultaneously. Whilst children they were fed by bees, goats, and doves, as the poets say the infant Jove was nourished. The earth was much smaller than it is at present, and devoid of mountains and hills. The sky was starless. There was no sea; and the world as a whole was far less varied and beautiful than it now is.

Yet men were never weary of looking at the sky and the earth, which excited within them feelings of wonder and admiration. They considered them both to be of infinite extent, majesty, and magnificence. Their souls were filled with joyous hopes, and every sensation of life gave them inexpressible pleasure. Their contentment daily increased, so that they at length thought themselves supremely happy. In this peaceful state of mind they passed their infancy and youth.

Arrived at a mature age, their feelings began to experience some alteration. As their early hopes, to which they had perseveringly adhered, failed of realisation, they no longer put faith in them. But, on the other hand, present happiness isolated from anticipation of the future, did not suffice them; especially seeing that, either from habit or because the charm of a first acquaintanceship had worn off, nature and all the incidents of[Pg 2] life gave them much less pleasure than at first. They travelled over the earth, and visited the most distant lands. This they could easily do, because there were neither seas, mountains, nor obstacles of any kind to oppose them. After a few years, most men had proved the finite nature of the earth, the boundaries of which were by no means so remote as to be unattainable. They found too, that all countries of the world, and all men, with but slight differences, were alike. These discoveries I so greatly increased their discontent, that a weariness of life became prevalent among men even before they had passed the threshold of manhood. And as men grew older, this feeling gradually transformed itself into a hatred of existence, so that at length, seized by despair, they in one way or another hesitated not to abandon the light and life once so beloved.

It seemed to the gods a shocking thing that living creatures should prefer death to life, and should destroy themselves for no other reason than that they were weary of existence. It also amazed them beyond measure to find their gifts held in such contempt, and so unequivocally rejected by men. They thought the world had been endowed with sufficient beauty, goodness, and harmony to make it not merely a bearable, but even a highly enjoyable place of residence for every living thing, and especially for man, whom they had fabricated with peculiar care, and a marvellous perfection. At the same time, touched with a deep feeling of compassion for the distress men exhibited, they began to fear lest the renewal and increase of these deplorable actions might not soon result in the extinction of the human race, contrary to destiny, and they would thus lose the most perfect work of their creation, and be deprived of the honours they received from men.

Jove determined therefore to improve the condition of men, since it seemed necessary, and to increase the means whereby they might obtain happiness. They complained of the deceitfulness of things; which were[Pg 3] neither as great, beautiful, perfect, nor varied as they at first imagined them to be; but were, on the contrary, small, imperfect, and monotonous. They derived no pleasure from their youth; still less were they satisfied with the times of maturity, and old age. Their infancy alone gave them pleasure, and yearning for the sweetness of their early days, they besought Jove to make their condition one of perpetual childhood. But the god could not satisfy them in this matter; for it was contrary to the laws of nature, and the divine decrees and intentions. Neither could he communicate his own infinity to mortal creatures, nor the world itself, any more than he could bestow infinite happiness and perfection on men and things. It seemed best to him to extend the limits of creation, at the same time increasing the world's diversity and beauty. In fulfilment of this intention, he enlarged the earth on all sides; and made the sea to flow as a separation between inhabited places, so that it might vary the aspect of things, and by severing their roads, prevent men from easily discovering the confines of the world. He also designed the sea to serve as a vivid representation of the infinity which they desired. Then it was that the waters covered the island Atlantis, as well as many other vast tracts of country; but the remembrance of this island alone has survived the multitude of centuries that have passed since that time.

16

Jove formed valleys by lowering certain places; and by exalting others he created hills and mountains. He bespread the night with stars; purified the atmosphere; increased the brilliancy and light of day; intensified the colours of the sky and the country, and gave them more variety. He also mixed the generations of men, so that the aged of one generation were contemporaneous with the children of another. Above all, Jove determined to multiply resemblances of that infinity for which men so eagerly craved. He could not really satisfy them, but wishing to soothe and appease their imagination, which[Pg 4] he knew had been the chief source of their happiness in childhood, he employed many expedients like that of the sea. He created the echo, and hid it in valleys and caverns, and gave to the forests a dull deep whispering, conjoined with a mysterious undulation of their tree-tops. He created also the gorgeous land of dreams, and gave men power to visit it in their sleep. There they could experience such perfect happiness as could not in reality be accorded to them. This served as a substitute for the vague unrealisable conception of felicity formed by men within themselves, and to which Jove himself could not have given any real expression, had he desired to do so.

By these means the god infused new strength and vigour into the minds of men, and endeared life to them again, so that they were full of admiration for the beauty and immensity of nature. This happy state lasted longer than the previous one. Its duration was chiefly due to the diversity of ages among men, whereby those who were chilled and wearied with their experience of the world, were comforted by the society of others full of the ardency and hopefulness of youth.

But in process of time this novelty wore off, and men again became discontented and wearied with life. So despondent did they become, that then is said to have originated the custom attributed by history to certain ancient nations; the birth of a child was celebrated with tears, and the death of a parent was the occasion of rejoicing for his deliverance.[1] At length wickedness became universal. This was either because men thought that Jove disregarded them, or because it is the nature of misfortune to debase even the noblest minds.

It is a popular error to imagine that man's misfortunes are the result of his impiety and iniquity. On the contrary, his wickedness is the consequence of his misfortunes.

The gods avenged themselves for their injuries, and[Pg 5] punished mortals for their renewed perverseness, by the deluge of Deucalion. There were only two survivors of this shipwreck of the human race, Deucalion and Pyrrha. These unhappy ones were filled with the sense of their wretchedness, and far from regretting the loss of all their fellows, themselves loudly invoked death from the summit of a rock. But Jove commanded them to remedy the depopulation of the earth, and seeing that they had not the heart to beget a new generation, directed them to take stones from the hill-sides, and cast them over their shoulders. From these stones men were created, and the earth was again peopled.

The history of the past had enlightened Jove as to the nature of men, and had shown him that it is not sufficient for them, as for other animals, merely to live in a state of freedom from sorrow and physical discomfort. He knew that whatever their condition of life, they would seek the impossible, and if unpossessed of genuine evils, would torment themselves with imaginary ones. The god resolved therefore to employ new means for the preservation of the miserable race. For this purpose he used two especial artifices. In the first place, he strewed life with veritable evils; and secondly, instituted a thousand kinds of business and labour, to distract men as much as possible from self-contemplation, and their desires for an unknown and imaginary happiness.

He began by sending a multitude of diseases, and an infinite number of other calamities among them, with the intention of varying the conditions of life so as to

17

obviate the feeling of satiety which had resulted before, and to induce men to esteem the good things they possessed so much the more by contrast with these new evils. The god hoped that men would be better able to bear the absence of the happiness they longed for, when occupied and under the discipline of suffering. He also determined by means of these physical infirmities and exertions, to reduce the vigour of men's[Pg 6] minds, to humble their pride, to make them bow the head to necessity, and be more contented with their lot. He knew that disease and misfortune would operate as a preventive to the committal of those acts of suicide which had formerly been rife; for they would not only make men cowardly and weak, but would help to attach them to life by the hope of an existence free from such sufferings. For it is a characteristic of the unfortunate that they imagine happiness will wait on them as soon as the immediate cause of their present misfortune is removed.

Jove then created the winds and the rain-clouds, prepared the thunder and lightning, gave the trident to Neptune, launched comets, and arranged eclipses. By means of these and other terrible signs, he resolved to frighten mortals from time to time, knowing that fear and actual danger would temporarily reconcile to life, not only the unhappy, but even those who most detested and were most disposed to put an end to their existence.

As a cure for the idleness of the past, Jove gave to men a taste and desire for new foods and drinks, unprocurable, however, without the greatest exertions. Previous to the deluge men had lived on water, herbs, and such fruits as were yielded by the earth and the trees, just as certain people of California and other places live even in the present day. He assigned different climates to different countries, and appointed the seasons of the year. Hitherto there had been no diversity of temperature in any place, but the atmosphere was uniformly so equable and mild that men were ignorant of the use of clothing. Now, however, they were obliged to exert themselves industriously to remedy the inclemency and changeability of the weather.

Jove gave Mercury command to lay the foundations of the first cities, and to divide men into different races, nations, and languages, separated by feelings of rivalry and discord. He was also commissioned to teach them[Pg 7] music and those other arts, which, owing to their nature and origin, are still called divine. Jove himself distributed laws and constitutions to the new nations. Finally, as a supreme gift, he sent among men certain sublime and superhuman Phantoms, to whom he committed very great influence and control over the people of the earth. They were called Justice, Virtue, Glory, Patriotism, &c. Among these Phantoms was one named Love, which then first entered the world. For previous to the introduction of clothes, the sexes were drawn towards one another by merely a brute instinct, far different from love. The feeling was comparable to that which we experience towards articles of food and such things, that we desire, but do not love.

By these divine decrees the condition of man was infinitely ameliorated, and rendered easier and pleasanter than before; in spite of the fatigues, sufferings, and terrors which were now inseparable from humanity. And this result was chiefly due to the wonderful chimeras, whom some men regarded as genii, others as gods, and whom they followed with an intense veneration and enthusiasm for a very long time. To such a pitch was their ardour excited by the poets and artists of the times, that numbers of men did not hesitate to sacrifice their lives to one or other of these Phantoms. Far from displeasing Jove, this fact gratified him exceedingly, for he judged that if men esteemed their life a gift worthy of sacrifice to these fine and glorious illusions, they would be less likely to repudiate it as before. This happy state of affairs was of longer duration than the preceding ages. And even when after the lapse of many centuries, a tendency to decline became apparent, existence, thanks to these bright illusions, was still easy and bearable enough, up to a time not very far distant from the present. This decline was chiefly due to the facility with which men were able to satisfy their wants and desires; the growing inequality between men in their[Pg 8] social and other conditions, as they receded farther and farther from the republican models founded by Jove; the reappearance of vanity and idleness as a consequence of this retrocession; the diminishing interest with which the variety of life's incidents inspired them; and many other well-known and important causes. Again men were filled with the old feeling of disgust for their existence, and again their minds clamoured for an unknown happiness, inconsistent with the order of nature.

But the total revolution of the fortunes of men, and the end of that epoch which we nowadays designate as the "old world," was due to one especial influence. It was this. Among the Phantoms so appreciated by the ancients was a certain one called Wisdom. This Phantom had duly contributed to the prosperity of the times, and like the others received high honour from men, a number of whom consecrated themselves to her service. She had frequently promised her disciples to show them her mistress, the Truth, a superior spirit who associated with the gods in heaven, whence she had never yet descended. The Phantom assured them that she would bring Truth among men, and that this spirit would exercise so marvellous an influence over their life, that in knowledge, perfection, and happiness they would almost rival the gods themselves. But how could a shadow fulfil any promise, much less induce the Truth to descend to earth? So after a long confiding expectancy, men perceived the falseness of Wisdom. At the same time, greedy of novelty because of the idleness of their life, and stimulated partly by ambition of equalling the gods, and partly by the intensity of their yearning for the happiness they imagined would ensue from the possession of Truth, they presumptuously requested Jove to lend them this noble spirit for a time, and reproached him for having so long jealously withheld from men the great advantages that would follow from the presence of Truth. They with one accord expressed dissatisfaction with their[Pg 9] lot, and renewed their former hateful whinings about the meanness and misery of human things. The Phantoms, once so dear to them, were now almost entirely abandoned, not that men had discerned the unreality of their nature, but because they were so debased in mind and manners as to have no sympathy with even the appearance of goodness. Thus they wickedly rejected the greatest gift of gods to men, and excused themselves by saying that none but inferior genii had been sent on earth, the nobler ones, whom they would willingly have worshipped, being retained in heaven.

Many things long before this had contributed to lessen the goodwill of Jove towards men, especially the magnitude and number of their vices and crimes, which were far in advance of those punished by the deluge. He was out of patience with the human race, the restless and unreasonable nature of which exasperated him. He recognised the futility of all effort on his part to make men happy and contented. Had he not enlarged the world, multiplied its pleasures, and increased its diversity? Yet all things were soon regarded by men (desirous and at the same time incapable of infinity) as equally restricted and valueless. Jove determined therefore to make a perpetual example of the human race. He resolved to punish men unsparingly, and reduce them to a state of misery far surpassing their former condition. Towards the attainment of this end, he purposed sending Truth among men, not for a time only as they desired, but for eternity, and giving her supreme control and dominion over the human race, instead of the Phantoms that were now so greatly despised.

The other gods marvelled at this decision of Jove, as likely to exalt the human race to a degree prejudicial to their own dignity. But he explained to them that all genii are not beneficial, and that apart from this, it was not of the nature of Truth to produce the same results among men as with the gods. For whereas to the gods[Pg 10] she unveiled the eternity of their joy, to mortals she would expose the immensity of their unhappiness, representing it to them not as a matter of chance, but as an inevitable and perpetual necessity. And since human evils are great in proportion as they are believed to be so by their victims, it may be imagined how acute an affliction Truth will prove to men. The vanity of all earthly things will be apparent to them; they will find that nothing is genuine save their own unhappiness. Above all, they will lose hope, hitherto the greatest solace and support of life. Deprived of hope, they will have nothing to stimulate them to any exertions; consequently work, industry, and all mental culture will languish, and the life of the living will partake of the inertness of the grave. Yet in spite of their despair and inactivity, men will still be tormented by their old longing for happiness intensified and quickened, because they will be less distracted by cares, and the stir of action. They will also be deprived of the power of imagination, which in itself could mysteriously transport them into a state of happiness comparable to the felicity for which they long.

"And," said Jove, "all those representations of infinity which I designedly placed in the world to deceive and satisfy men, and all the vague thoughts suggestive of happiness, which I infused into their minds, will yield to the doctrines of Truth. The earth, which formerly displeased them for its insignificance, will do so increasedly when its true dimensions are known, and when all the secrets of nature are made manifest to them. And finally, with the disappearance of those Phantoms that alone gave brightness to existence, human life will become aimless and valueless. Nations and countries will lose even their names, for with Patriotism will vanish all incentive to national identities. Men will unite and form one nation and one people (as they will say), and will profess a universal love for the race. But in[Pg 11] reality there will be the least possible union amongst them; they will be divided into as many peoples as there are individuals. For having no special country to love, and no foreigners to hate, every man will hate his neighbour, and love only himself. The evil consequences of this are incalculable. Nevertheless, men will not put an end to their unhappiness by depriving themselves of life, because under the sway of Truth they will become as cowardly as miserable. Truth will increase the bitterness of their existence, and at the same time bereave them of sufficient courage to reject it."

These words of Jove moved the gods to compassion for the human race. It seemed to them that so great inflictions were inconsistent with the divine attribute of mercy.

But Jove continued: "There will remain to humanity a certain consolation proceeding from the Phantom Love, which alone I purpose leaving among men. And even Truth, in spite of her almost omnipotence, will never quite prevail over Love, nor succeed in chasing this Phantom from the earth, though the struggle between them will be perpetual. Thus the life of man, divided betwixt the worship of Truth and Love, will consist of two epochs, during which these influences will respectively control his mind and actions. To the aged, instead of the solace of Love, will be granted a state of contentment with their existence, similar to that of other animals. They will love life for its own sake, not for any pleasure or profit they derive from it."

Accordingly, Jove removed the Phantoms from earth, save only Love, the least noble of all, and sent Truth among men to exercise over them perpetual rule. The consequences foreseen by the god were not long in making themselves manifest. And strange to say, whereas the spirit before her descent on earth, and when she had no real authority over men, was honoured by a multitude of temples and sacrifices, her presence had the[Pg 12] effect of cooling their enthusiasm on her behalf. With the other gods this was not so; the more they made themselves manifest, the more they were honoured; but Truth saddened men, and ultimately inspired them with such hatred that they refused to worship her, and only by constraint rendered her obedience. And whereas formerly, men who were under the especial influence of any one of the ancient Phantoms, used to love and revere that Phantom above the others, Truth was detested and cursed by those over whom she gained supreme control. So, unable to resist her tyranny, men lived from that time in the complete state of misery, which is their fate in the present day, and to which they are eternally doomed.

But not long ago, pity, which is never exhausted in the minds of the gods, moved Jove to compassionate the wretchedness of mortals. He noticed especially the affliction of certain men, remarkable for their high intellect, and nobility, and purity of life, who were extraordinarily oppressed by the sway of Truth. Now in former times, when Justice, Virtue, and the other Phantoms directed humanity, the gods had been accustomed at times to visit the earth, and sojourn with men for awhile, always on such occasions benefiting the race, or particular individuals, in some especial manner. But since men had become so debased, and sunk in wickedness, they had not deigned to associate with them. Jove therefore, pitying our condition, asked the immortals whether any one of them would visit the earth as of old, and console men under their calamities, especially such as seemed undeserving of the universal affliction. All the gods were silent. At length Love, the son of celestial Venus, bearing the same name as the Phantom Love, but very different in nature and power, and the most compassionate of the immortals, offered himself for the mission proposed by Jove. This deity was so beloved by the other gods, that hitherto they had never allowed him to[Pg 13] quit their presence, even for a moment. The ancients indeed imagined that the god had appeared to them from time to time; but it was not so. They were deceived by the subterfuges and transformations of the Phantom Love. The deity of the same name first visited mankind after they were placed under the empire of Truth.

Since that time the god has rarely and briefly descended, because of the general unworthiness of humanity, and the impatience with which the celestials await his return. When he comes on earth he chooses the tender and noble hearts of the most generous and magnanimous persons. Here he rests for a short time, diffusing in them so strange and wondrous a sweetness, and inspiring them with affections so lofty and vigorous, that they then experience what is entirely new to mankind, the substance rather than the semblance of happiness. Sometimes, though very rarely, he brings about the union of two hearts, abiding in them both simultaneously, and exciting within them a reciprocal warmth and desire. All within whom he dwells beseech him to effect this union; but Jove forbids him to yield to their entreaties, save in very few instances, because the happiness of such mutual love approaches too nearly to the felicity of the immortals.

The man in whom Love abides is the happiest of mortals. And not only is he blessed by the presence of the deity, but he is also charmed by the old mysterious Phantoms, which, though removed from the lot of men, by Jove's permission follow in the train of Love, in spite of the great opposition of Truth, their supreme enemy. But Truth, like all the other genii, is powerless to resist the will of the gods. And, since destiny has granted to Love a state of eternal youth, the god can partially give effect to that first desire of men, that they might return to the happiness of their childhood. In the souls he inhabits, Love awakens and vivifies, so long as ha stays there, the boundless hopes, and the sweet and fine[Pg 14] illusions of early life. Many persons, ignorant and incapable of appreciating Love, vituperate and affront the god, even to his face. But he disregards these insults, and exacts no vengeance for them, so noble and compassionate is his nature.

21

Nor do the other gods any longer trouble themselves about the crimes of men, being satisfied with the vengeance they have already wrought on the human race, and the incurable misery which is its portion. Consequently, wicked and blasphemous men suffer no punishment for their offences, except that they are absolutely excluded from being partakers of the divine favours.

[1] See Herodotus, Strabo, &c.

[Pg 15]

DIALOGUE BETWEEN HERCULES AND ATLAS.

Hercules. Father Atlas, Jove's compliments, and in case you should be weary of your burden, I was to relieve you for a few hours, as I did I don't know how many centuries ago, so that you may take breath, and rest a little.

Atlas. Thanks, dear Hercules, and I am very much obliged to Jove. But the world has become so light, that this cloak which I wear as a protection against the snow, incommodes me more. Indeed, were it not Jove's will that I should continue to stand here, supporting this ball on my back, I would put it under my arm, or in my pocket, or suspend it from a hair of my beard, and go about my own affairs.

Hercules. How has it become so light? I can easily see it has changed shape, and has become a sort of roll, instead of being round as when I studied cosmography in preparation for that wonderful voyage with the Argonauts. But still I cannot see why its weight should have diminished.

Atlas. I am as ignorant of the reason as you are. But take the thing for a moment in your hand, and satisfy yourself of the truth of my assertion.

Hercules. Upon my word, without this test, I would not have believed it. But what is this other novelty that I discover? The last time I bore it, I felt a strong pulsation on my back, like the beat of an animal's heart;[Pg 16] and I heard a continuous buzzing like a wasp's nest. But now, it throbs more like a watch with a broken spring, and as for the buzzing, I don't hear a sound of it.

Atlas. I know nothing of this either, except that long ago, the world ceased making any motion, or sensible noise. I even had very great suspicions that it was dead, and expecting daily to be troubled by its corruption, I considered how and where I should bury it, and what epitaph I should place on its tomb. But when I saw that it did not decompose, I came to the conclusion that it had changed from an animal into a plant, like Daphne and others; and this explained its silence and immobility. I began to fear lest it should soon wind its roots round my shoulders, or bury them in my body.

Hercules. I am rather inclined to think it is asleep, and that its repose is like that of Epimenides,[1] which lasted more than half a century. Or perhaps it is like Hermotimus,[2] whose soul used to leave his body when it pleased, and stay away many years, disporting itself in foreign lands. To put an end to this game, the friends of Hermotimus burned the body; so that the spirit returning, found its home destroyed, and was obliged to seek shelter in another body, or an inn. So, to prevent the world from sleeping for ever, or lest some friend, thinking it were dead, should set it on fire, let us try to arouse it.

Atlas. I am willing. But how shall we do it?

Hercules. I would give it a good blow with this club, if I were not afraid of smashing it, and were I not sure that it would crack under the stroke like an egg. Besides, I fear lest the men, who in my time used to wrestle with lions, but are now only a match for fleas,

22

should faint from so sudden a shock. Suppose I lay aside my club, and you your cloak, and we have a game at ball with the poor little sphere. I wish I had brought the rackets[Pg 17] that Mercury and I use in the celestial courts, but we can do without them.

Atlas. A likely thing indeed! So that your father seeing our game, may make a third, and with his thunderbolt precipitate us both I do not know where, as he did Phaeton into the Po!

Hercules. That might be, if, like Phaeton, I were the son of a poet, and not his own son; and if there were not this difference between us, that whereas poets formerly peopled cities by the melody of their art, I could depopulate heaven and earth by the power of my club. And as for Jove's bolt, I would kick it hence to the farthest quarter of the empyrean. Be assured that even if I wished to appropriate five or six stars for the sake of a game, or to make a sling of a comet, taking it by the tail, or even to play at ball with the sun, my father would make no objection. Besides, our intention is to do good to the world, whereas Phaeton simply wished to show off his fleetness before the Hours, who held the steps for him when he mounted his chariot. He also wanted to gain reputation as a skilful coach-man, in the eyes of Andromeda, Callisto, and the other beautiful constellations, to whom, it is said, he threw, in passing, lustre bonbons, and comfits of light; and to make a fine parade of himself before the celestial gods during his journey that day, which chanced to be a festival. In short, don't give a thought to the possibility of my father's wrath. In any case, I will bear all the blame; so throw off your cloak, and send me the ball.

Atlas. Willingly or not, I must do as you wish; since you are strong and armed, whereas I am old and defenceless. But do take care lest it fall, in which case it will have fresh swellings, or some new fracture, like that which separated Sicily from Italy, and Africa from Spain. And if it should get chipped in any way, there might be a war about what men would call the detachment of a province or kingdom.

[Pg 18]

Hercules. Rely on me.

Atlas. Then here goes. See how it quivers on account of its altered shape!

Hercules. Hit a little harder; your strokes scarcely reach me.

Atlas. It is the fault of the ball. The south-west wind catches it, because of its lightness.

Hercules. It is its old failing to go with the wind.

Atlas. Suppose we were to inflate the ball, since it has no more notion of a bounce than a melon.

Hercules. A new shortcoming! Formerly it used to leap and dance like a young goat.

Atlas. Look out! Run quickly after that. For Jove's sake, take care lest it fall! Alas! it was an evil hour when you came here.

Hercules. You sent me such a bad stroke that I could not possibly have caught it in time, even at the risk of breaking my neck. Alas, poor little one!... How are you? Do you feel bad anywhere? I don't hear a sigh, nor does a soul move. They are all still asleep.

Atlas. Give it back to me, by all the horns of the Styx, and let me settle it again on my shoulders. And you, take your club, and hasten to heaven to excuse me with Jove for this accident, which is entirely owing to you.

Hercules. I will do so. For many centuries there has been in my father's house a certain poet, named Horace. He was made court poet at the suggestion of Augustus, who has been deified by Jove for his augmentation of the Eoman power. In one of his songs, this poet says that the just man would stir not, though the world fell. Since the world has now fallen, and no one has moved, it follows that all men are just.

23

Atlas. Who doubts the justice of men? But do not lose time; run and exculpate me with your father, else I shall momentarily expect a thunderbolt to transform me from Atlas into Etna.

[1] See Pliny, Diogenes Laertius, Apollonius, Varrò, &c.

[2] See Apollonius, Pliny, Tertullian, &c.

[Pg 19]

DIALOGUE BETWEEN FASHION AND DEATH.

Fashion. Madam Death, Madam Death!

Death. Wait until your time comes, and then I will appear without being called by you.

Fashion. Madam Death!

Death. Go to the devil. I will come when you least expect me.

Fashion. As if I were not immortal!

Death. Immortal?

"Already has passed the thousandth year,"

since the age of immortals ended.

Fashion. Madam is as much a Petrarchist as if she were an Italian poet of the fifteenth or eighteenth century.

Death. I like Petrarch because he composed my triumph, and because he refers so often to me. But I must be moving.

Fashion. Stay! For the love you bear to the seven cardinal sins, stop a moment and look at me.

Death. Well. I am looking.

Fashion. Do you not recognise me?

Death. You must know that I have bad sight, and am without spectacles. The English make none to suit me; and if they did, I should not know where to put them.

Fashion. I am Fashion, your sister.

Death. My sister?

[Pg 20]

Fashion. Yes. Do you not remember we are both born of Decay?

Death. As if I, who am the chief enemy of Memory, should recollect it!

Fashion. But I do. I know also that we both equally profit by the incessant change and destruction of things here below, although you do so in one way, and I in another.

Death. Unless you are speaking to yourself, or to some one inside your throat, raise your voice, and pronounce your words more distinctly. If you go mumbling between your teeth with that thin spider-voice of yours, I shall never understand you; because you ought to know that my hearing serves me no better than my sight.

Fashion. Although it be contrary to custom, for in France they do not speak to be heard, yet, since we are sisters, I will speak as you wish, for we can dispense with ceremony between ourselves. I say then that our common nature and custom is to incessantly renew the world. You attack the life of man, and overthrow all people and nations from beginning to end; whereas I content myself for the most part with influencing beards, head-dresses, costumes, furniture, houses, and the like. It is true, I do some things comparable to your supreme action. I pierce ears, lips, and noses, and cause them to be torn by the ornaments I suspend from them. I impress men's skin with hot

24

iron stamps, under the pretence of adornment. I compress the heads of children with tight bandages and other contrivances; and make it customary for all men of a country to have heads of the same shape, as in parts of America and Asia. I torture and cripple people with small shoes. I stifle women with stays so tight, that their eyes start from their heads; and I play a thousand similar pranks. I also frequently persuade and force men of refinement to bear daily numberless fatigues and discomforts, and[Pg 21] often real sufferings; and some even die gloriously for love of me. I will say nothing of the headaches, colds, inflammations of all kinds, fevers—daily, tertian, and quartan—which men gain by their obedience to me. They are content to shiver with cold, or melt with heat, simply because it is my will that they cover their shoulders with wool, and their breasts with cotton. In fact, they do everything in my way, regardless of their own injury.

Death. In truth, I believe you are my sister; the testimony of a birth certificate could scarcely make me surer of it. But standing still paralyses me, so if you can, let us run; only you must not creep, because I go at a great pace. As we proceed you can tell me what you want. If you cannot keep up with me, on account of our relationship I promise when I die to bequeath you all my clothes and effects as a New Year's gift.

Fashion. If we ran a race together, I hardly know which of us would win. For if you run, I gallop, and standing still, which paralyses you, is death to me. So let us run, and we will chat as we go along.

Death. So be it then. Since your mother was mine, you ought to serve me in some way, and assist me in my business.

Fashion. I have already done so—more than you,—imagine. Above all, I, who annul and transform other customs unceasingly, have nowhere changed the custom of death; for this reason it has prevailed from the beginning of the world until now.

Death. A great miracle forsooth, that you have never done what you could not do!

Fashion. Why cannot I do it? You show how ignorant you are of the power of Fashion.

Death. Well, well: time enough to talk of this when you introduce the custom of not dying. But at present, I want you, like a good sister, to aid me in rendering[Pg 22] my task more easy and expeditious than it has hitherto been.

Fashion. I have already mentioned some of my labours which are a source of profit to you. But they are trifling in comparison with those of which I will now tell you.

Little by little, and especially in modern times, I have brought into disuse and discredit those exertions and exercises which promote bodily health; and have substituted numberless others which enfeeble the body in a thousand ways, and shorten life. Besides, I have introduced customs and manners, which render existence a thing more dead than alive, whether regarded from a physical or mental point of view; so that this century may be aptly termed the century of death. And whereas formerly you had no other possessions except graves and vaults, where you sowed bones and dust, which are but a barren seed, now you have fine landed properties, and people who are a sort of freehold possession of yours as soon as they are born, though not then claimed by you. And more, you, who used formerly to be hated and vituperated, are in the present day, thanks to me, valued and lauded by all men of genius. Such an one prefers you to life itself, and holds you in such high esteem that he invokes you, and looks to you as his greatest hope.

But this is not all. I perceived that men had some vague idea of an after-life, which they called immortality. They imagined they lived in the memory of their fellows, and this remembrance they sought after eagerly. Of course this was in reality mere fancy, since what could it matter to them when dead, that they lived in the minds of men? As well might they dread contamination in the grave! Yet, fearing lest this chimera might be prejudicial to you, in seeming to diminish your honour and reputation, I have abolished the fashion of seeking immortality, and its concession, even when merited. So that now, whoever dies may assure himself that he is dead altogether, and that every bit of him goes[Pg 23] into the ground, just as a little fish is swallowed, bones and all.

These important things my love for you has prompted me to effect. I have also succeeded in my endeavour to increase your power on earth. I am more than ever desirous of continuing this work. Indeed, my object in seeking you to-day was to make a proposal that for the future we should not separate, but jointly might scheme and execute for the furtherance of our respective designs.

Death. You speak reasonably, and I am willing to do as you propose.

[Pg 24]

PRIZE COMPETITION ANNOUNCED BY THE ACADEMY OF SILLOGRAPHS.

The Academy of Sillographs, ardently desiring to advance the common welfare, and esteeming nothing more conformable to this end than the promotion of the progress

"Of the happy century in which we live,"

as says an illustrious poet, has taken in hand the careful consideration of the nature and tendency of our time. After long and mature consultation, the Academy has resolved to call our era the age of machines; not only because the men of to-day live and move perhaps more mechanically than in past times, but also on account of the numerous machines now invented and utilised for so many different purposes. To such an extent indeed is this carried, that machines and not men may be said to manage human affairs, and conduct the business of life. This circumstance greatly pleases the said Academy, not so much because of the manifest convenience of the arrangement, as for two reasons, which it thinks very important, although ordinarily they are not so regarded. The one is the possibility that in process of time the influence and usefulness of machines may extend to spiritual as well as material things. And as by virtue of these machines and inventions, we are already protected from lightning, storms, and other such evils and terrors; similarly there may be discovered some cure for envy,[Pg 25] calumny, perfidy, and trickery; some safety-cord or other invention to deliver us from egotism, from the prevalence of mediocrity, from prosperous fools, bad and debased persons, from the universal spirit of indifference, from the wretchedness peculiar to the wise, the cultivated, the noble-minded, and from other discomforts which for many centuries have been more invincible than either lightning or tempests. The other and chief reason concerns the unhappy condition of the human race. Most philosophers despair of its improvement, or the cure of its defects, which probably equal or exceed in number its virtues. They believe it would be easier to entirely re-create the race in another way, or to substitute a different "genus" altogether, than to amend it. The Academy of Sinographs is therefore of opinion that it is very expedient for men to withdraw from the business of life as much as possible, and gradually to resign in favour of machines. And being resolved to support with all its might the progress of this new order of things, it now begs to offer three prizes for the inventors of the three following machines.

The aim of the first machine must be to represent a friend warranted not to abuse or ridicule his absent friend; nor forsake his friend when he hears him made the subject of jest; nor to seek the reputation of acuteness, sarcasm, and the power of exciting men's laughter at his friend's expense; nor to divulge or boast of secrets confided to him; nor to take advantage of his friend's intimacy and confidence in order to supplant and surpass him; nor to envy his friend's good fortune. But it must be solicitous for his friend's

26

welfare, join issue with him against his misfortunes, and assist him in deeds as well as words. Reference to the treatises of Cicero and the Marquise of Lambert on "Friendship" may be advantageously made for further suggestions as to the manufacture of this automaton. The Academy thinks the invention of this machine ought not to be regarded as either[Pg 26] impossible, or even very difficult, seeing that besides the automata of Regiomontano, Vaucanson, and others, and the one in London which drew figures and portraits, and wrote from dictation, there are machines that can even play chess unassisted. Now in the opinion of many "savants," human life is a game, and some assert it to be a thing even more frivolous. They say that the game of chess is a more rationally conceived thing, and its hazards are less uncertain than those of life. Besides, Pindar has called life a thing of no more substance than the dream of a shadow; in which case it ought not to be beyond the capacity of a vigilant automaton. As to speech, there is no reason why men should not be able to communicate this to machines of their manufacture. For amongst examples of manufactures so endowed, we may number the statue of Memnon, and the head formed by Albertus Magnus; this latter was so loquacious that St. Thomas Aquinas, irritated at its incessant tittle-tattle, broke it in pieces. And if the parrot of Nevers (though certainly this was an animal, however small a one) could converse, how much more credible that a machine, conceived by the mind of man, and constructed by his hands, should be able to acquire such attainments? The machine ought not to be so talkative as the parrot of Nevers, and other similar ones, which we see and hear everywhere; nor as the head made by Albertus Magnus; for it must not weary its friend, thereby inciting him to its destruction.

The inventor of this machine shall receive a reward of a gold medal weighing four hundred sequins, which on the one side shall have a representation of the figures of Pylades and Orestes, and on the other side the name of the person rewarded, together with the inscription, "First verifier of the ancient fables."

The second machine must be an artificial man worked by steam, adapted and constructed for virtuous and magnanimous actions. The Academy is of opinion[Pg 27] that since no other method appears to exist, steam ought to be capable of directing an animated automaton in the paths of virtue and glory. Candidates for this competition are referred to books of poems and romances for suggestions as to the qualities and powers with which to endow the figure. The reward to be a gold medal weighing four hundred and fifty sequins, stamped on the one side with some fanciful design significative of the age of gold, and on its reverse the name of the inventor of the machine, together with this inscription from the fourth eclogue of Virgil: "Quo ferrea primum desinet ac toto surget gens aurea mundo."

The third machine should be empowered to act as a woman, realising the conception formed partly by Count Baldassar Castiglione, who describes his idea in the book of the "Cortegiano," and partly by others, easily discoverable in various writings which must be consulted and combined with those of the Count. Nor ought the invention of this machine to appear impossible to men of our times, when it be remembered that Pygmalion long ago, in an age far from scientific, was able to fabricate a spouse with his own hands, who was considered to be the best woman that had ever existed. To the originator of this machine a gold medal weighing five hundred sequins is assigned, on the one side of which shall be represented the Arabian Phoenix of Metastasio, perched on a tree of some European species, and on the other side shall be written the name of the recipient, with the inscription, "Inventor of faithful women, and conjugal happiness." The Academy decrees that the cost of these prizes must be defrayed with what was discovered in the satchel of Diogenes, late Secretary of this Academy, or by means of one of the three golden asses that belonged to three Sillographic Academicians, Apuleius, Firenzuola, and Macchiavelli; all which property passed to the Sillographists by will of the deceased, as may be read in the Chronicles of the Academy.

[Pg 28]

DIALOGUE BETWEEN A GOBLIN AND A GNOME.

Goblin. You here, son of Beelzebub! where are you going?

Gnome. My father has sent me to find out what these rascals of men are doing. He is inclined to suspect something, because it is so long since they gave us any trouble, and in all his realms there is not a single one to be seen. He wonders whether any great change has taken place, and thinks perhaps they have returned to the primitive system of barter, whereby they use sheep instead of gold and silver; or the civilised people have become dissatisfied with paper notes for money, as they have often been, or have taken to cowrie shells such as savages use; or the laws of Lycurgus have been re-established. The last possibility seems to him the least likely.

Goblin. "You seek them in vain, for they are all dead," as said the survivors in a tragedy where the principal personages died in the last act.

Gnome. What do you mean?

Goblin. I mean that men are all dead, and the race is lost.

Gnome. My word! what news for the papers! But how is it they have not already mentioned it?

Goblin. Stupid. Do you not see that if there are no men there will be no more newspapers?

[Pg 29]

Gnome. Yes, that is true. But how shall we know in future the news of the world?

Goblin. News! what news? That the sun rises and sets? That it is hot or cold? That here or there it has rained or snowed, or been windy?

Since men disappeared, Fortune has unbandaged her eyes, put on spectacles, and attached her wheel to a pivot. She sits with arms crossed, watching the world go round without troubling herself in the least as to its affairs. There are no more kingdoms nor empires to swell themselves, and burst like bubbles, for they have all vanished. There is no more war; and the years are as like one another as two peas.

Gnome. No one will know the day of the month, since there will be no more calendars printed!

Goblin. What a misfortune! Nevertheless, the moon will continue her course.

Gnome. And the days of the week will be nameless!

Goblin. What does it matter? Do you think they will not come unless you call them? Or, that once passed, they will return if you call out their names?

Gnome. And no one will take any count of the years!

Goblin. We shall be able to say we are young when we are old; and we shall forget our cares when we cannot fix their anniversary. Besides, when we are very old, we shall not know it, nor be expecting death daily.

Gnome. But how is it these rogues have disappeared?

Goblin. Some killed themselves with fighting; others were drowned in the sea. Some ate each other. Not a few committed suicide. Some died of ennui in idleness; and some turned their brains with study. Debauch, and a thousand other excesses, put an end to many more. In short, they have arrived at their end, by endeavouring, as long as they lived, to violate the laws of nature, and to go contrary to their welfare.

Gnome. Still, I do not understand how an entire race[Pg 30] of animals can become extinct without leaving any trace behind it.

Goblin. You who are a specialist in geology ought to know that the circumstance is not a new one, and that many kinds of animals lived anciently, which to-day are nowhere to be found except in the remains of a few petrified bones. Moreover, these poor creatures employed none of the means used by men for their destruction.

Gnome. It may be so. I should dearly like to resuscitate one or two of the rascals, just to know what they would think when they saw all going on as before, in spite of the disappearance of the human race. Would they then imagine that everything was made and maintained solely for them?

Goblin. They would not like to realise that the world exists solely for the use of the Goblins.

Gnome. You are joking, my friend, if you mean what you say.

Goblin. Why? Of course I do.

Gnome. Go along with you, buffoon! who does not know that the world is made for the Gnomes?

Goblin. For the Gnomes, who live underground! That is one of the best jokes I have ever heard. What good are the sun, moon, air, sea, and country to the Gnomes?

Gnome. And pray of what use to the Goblins are the mines of gold and silver, and the whole body of earth, except the outer skin?

Goblin. Well, well: suppose we abandon the discussion. It is unimportant after all. For I imagine even the lizards and gnats think the whole world was created for their exclusive service. Let each of us believe what we please, for nothing will make us change our opinion. But, between ourselves, if I had not been born a Goblin, I should be in despair.

Gnome. And I, had I not been born a Gnome. But I should like to know what men would say of their[Pg 31] impertinence in former times, when, besides other misdeeds, they sank thousands of underground shafts, and stole our goods from us by force, asserting that they belonged to the human race. Nature, they said, concealed and buried the things down below, as a sort of game at hide and seek, just to see if they could discover and abstract them.

Goblin. I do not wonder at that, since they not only imagined the things of the world were at their service, but they also regarded them as a mere trifle compared to the human race. They called their own vicissitudes "revolutions of the world;" and histories of their nations, "histories of the world;" although the earth contained about as many different species of animals as living individual human beings. Yet these animals, though made expressly for the use of men, were never conscious of the so-called revolutions of the world!

Gnome. Then even the fleas and gnats were made for the service of men?

Goblin. Just so. To exercise their patience, men said.

Gnome. As if, apart from fleas, man's patience were not tried sufficiently!

Goblin. And a certain man named Chrysippus termed pigs pieces of meat expressly prepared by nature for man's table. Their souls, he said, served the purpose of salt, in preserving them from decay.

Gnome. In my opinion, if Chrysippus had had a little sense (salt) in his brain, instead of imagination (soul), he would never have conceived such an idea.

Goblin. Here is another amusing circumstance. An infinite number of species of animals were never seen, nor heard of by men their masters, either because they lived where man never set foot, or because they were too small to be observed. Many others

29

were only discovered during the last days of the human race. The same may be said of plants, minerals, &c. Similarly, from time to time, by means of their telescopes, they[Pg 32] perceived some star or planet, of the existence of which hitherto, during thousands and thousands of years, they had been ignorant. They then immediately entered it on the catalogue of their possessions; for they regarded the stars and planets as so many candles placed up above to give light to their dominions, because they were wont to transact much business in the night.

Gnome. And in summer, when they saw those little meteor flames that rush through the air at night, they imagined them to be sprites employed in snuffing the candles for the good of mankind.

Goblin. Yet now that they are all gone, the earth is none the worse off. The rivers still flow, and the sea, although no longer used for navigation and traffic, is not dried up.

Gnome. The stars and planets still rise and set; nor have they gone into mourning.

Goblin. Neither has the sun put on sackcloth and ashes, as it did, according to Virgil, when Cæsar died; about whom I imagine it concerned itself as little as Pompey's Pillar.

[Pg 33]
DIALOGUE BETWEEN MALAMBRUNO AND FARFARELLO.

Malambruno. Spirits of the deep, Farfarello, Ciriatto, Raconero, Astarotte, Alichino, or whatever else you are called, I adjure you in the name of Beelzebub, and command you by virtue of my art, which can unhinge the moon, and nail the sun in the midst of the heavens, come one of you with your prince's permission, to put all the powers of hell at my disposal.

Farfarello. Here I am.

Mal. Who are you?

Far. Farfarello, at thy service.

Mal. Have you the mandate of Beelzebub?

Far. I have; and can thus do for thee all that the king himself could do, and more than lies in the power of all other creatures together.

Mal. It is well. I wish to be satisfied in but one desire.

Far. Thou shalt be obeyed. What is it? Dost thou wish for majesty surpassing that of the Atrides?

Mal. No.

Far. More wealth than shall be found in El Dorado, when it is discovered? Mal. No.

Far. An empire as large as that of which Charles V. dreamt one night?

Mal. No.

[Pg 34]
Far. A mistress chaster than Penelope?

Mal. No: methinks the devil's aid were superfluous for that.

Far. Honours and success, however wicked thou mayst be?

Mal. I should rather more need the devil, if I wished the contrary, under such circumstances.

Far. Then what dost thou want?

Mal. Make me happy for a moment.

Far. I cannot.

Mal. Why?

Far. I give you my word of honour—I cannot do it.

Mal. The word of honour of a good demon?

Far. Yes, to be sure. Thou shouldest know that there are good devils as well as good men.

Mal. And you must know that I will hang you by the tail to one of these beams if you do not instantly obey me without more words.

Far. It were easier for you to kill me, than for me to satisfy your demands.

Mal. Then return with my malediction, and let Beelzebub come himself.

Far. Beelzebub and the whole army of hell would be equally powerless to render you or any of your race happy.

Mal. Not even for a single moment?

Far. As impossible for a moment, half a moment, or the thousandth part of a moment, as for a lifetime.

Mal. Well, since you cannot make me happy in any way, at least free me from unhappiness.

Far. On condition that you no longer love yourself above everything else.

Mal. I shall only cease doing that when I die.

Far. But as long as you live you will be unable to do it. Your nature would tolerate anything rather than that.

Mal. So it is.

[Pg 35]

Far. Consequently, loving yourself above everything, you desire your own happiness more than anything. But because this is unattainable, you must necessarily be unhappy.

Mal. Even when engaged in pleasure; since no gratification can make me happy, or satisfy me.

Far. Truly none.

Mal. And because pleasure cannot satisfy my soul's innate desire for happiness, it is not true pleasure, and during its continuance I shall still be unhappy.

Far. As you say: because in men and other living beings, the deprivation of happiness, even though pain and misfortune be wanting, implies express unhappiness. This, too, during the continuance of so-called pleasures.

Mal. So that from birth to death our unhappiness never ceases for an instant.

Far. Yes, it ceases whenever you sleep dreamlessly, or when, from one cause or another, you are deprived of your senses.

Mal. But never, so long as we are sensible that we live.

Far. Never.

Mal. So that in fact it were better not to live than to live.

Far. If the absence of unhappiness be better than unhappiness itself.

Mal. Then?

Far. Then if you would like to give me your soul before its time, I am ready to carry it away with me.

[Pg 36]

DIALOGUE BETWEEN NATURE AND A SOUL.

Nature. Go, my beloved child. You shall be regarded as my favoured one for very many centuries. Live: be great and unhappy.

Soul. What evil have I done before beginning to live, that you condemn me to this misery?

Nature. What misery, my child?

Soul. Do you not ordain that I am to be unhappy?

Nature. Yes; but only so far as to enable you to be great, which you cannot become without unhappiness. Besides, you are destined to animate a human body, and all men are of necessity unhappy from their birth.

Soul. It were more reasonable that you made happiness a necessity; or this being impossible, it were better not to bring men into the world.

Nature. I can do neither the one thing nor the other, because I am subordinate to Destiny, who decrees the contrary. The reason of this is as much a mystery to myself as to you. Now that you are created and designed to animate a human being, no power in the world can save you from the unhappiness common to men. Moreover, your infelicity will be especially great, owing to the perfection with which I have fashioned you.

Soul. I know nothing yet, because I have only just begun to live. Doubtless this is why I do not understand you. But tell me, is greatness the same thing as[Pg 37] extreme unhappiness? If, however, they are different, why could not the one be separated from the other?

Nature. In the souls of men, and proportionately in those of all animals, they are inseparable, because excellence of soul implies great capacity for knowledge, which in exposing to men the unhappiness of humanity may be termed unhappiness itself. Similarly, a life of greater intensity involves a greater love of self, manifested in different ways. An increased desire for happiness is a consequence of this self-love and increased unhappiness, because of the impossibility of satisfying this desire, and as the unfortunate condition of humanity becomes realised. All this is decreed from the beginning of creation, and is unalterable by me.

Moreover, the keenness of your intellect and the strength of your imagination will lessen considerably your power of self-control. Brute animals readily adapt all their faculties and powers to the attainment of their ends; but men rarely do so, being usually prevented by their reason and imagination, which give birth to a thousand doubts in deliberation, and a thousand hindrances in execution. The less men are inclined or accustomed to deliberate, the more prompt are they in decision, and the more vigorous in action. But such souls as yours, self-contained, and proudly conscious of their greatness, are really powerless for self-rule, and often succumb to irresolution both in thought and action. This temperament is one of the greatest curses of human life.

Added to this, although by your noble talents you will easily and quickly excel most men in profound knowledge and works of the greatest difficulty, you will yet find it almost impossible to learn, or put in practice, a host of things, trivial enough, but very essential, for your intercourse with others. At the same time, you; will see your inferiors, and even men of scarcely any intelligence, perfectly at home with these things. Such difficulties and miseries as these occupy and surround[Pg 38] great souls; but they are amply atoned for by fame, praise, and honours paid to their greatness, and by the lasting memory they leave behind them.

Soul. Whence will come these praises and honours,—from heaven, from you, or from whom?

Nature. From men, who alone can dispense them.

Soul. But I thought my ignorance of those things necessary for the intercourse of life, which intellects inferior to mine so easily comprehend, would cause me to be despised and shunned, not praised by men. I thought too that I should surely live unknown to most of them, because of my unfitness for their society.

Nature. I have not the power to foresee the future, so I cannot say exactly how men will behave to you whilst you are on earth. But judging from past experience, I think they will probably be jealous of you. This is another misfortune to which great minds are peculiarly liable. Perhaps too, they will despise you, and treat you with indifference. Fortune herself, and even circumstances, are usually unfriendly to such as you.

But directly after your death, as happened to one named Camoens, or a few years later, like Milton, you will be eulogised and lauded to the skies, if not by every one, at any rate by the few men of noble minds. Perhaps the ashes of your body will be deposited in a magnificent tomb, and your likeness reproduced in many different forms, and passed about from hand to hand. Men will also study your life and writings, and at length the world will ring with your name. Always provided you are not hindered by evil fortune, or even by the very excess of your genius, from leaving undoubted testimonies of your merit; instances are not wanting of such unfortunates, known only to myself and Destiny.

Soul. O mother, I care not if I be deprived of all knowledge, so long as I obtain what I most desire, happiness. And as for glory, I know not whether it be a good or evil thing, but I do know that I shall only[Pg 39] value it in so far as it procures me happiness, directly or indirectly. Now, on your own showing, the excellence with which you have endowed me, though it may be fruitful of glory, is also productive of the greatest unhappiness. Yet even this paltry glory I may not gain until I am dead, when I fail to see how I shall benefit by it. And besides, there is the probability that this phantom glory, the price of so much suffering, may be obtained neither in life nor after death.

In short, from what you yourself have said, I conclude that far from loving me with peculiar affection, as you affirmed, you bear me greater malice than that of which I can be the victim, either at the hands of men or Destiny. Why else should you have endowed me with this disastrous excellence, about which you boast so much, and which will be the chief stumbling-block in the road to happiness, the only thing for which I care?

Nature. My child, all men are destined to be unhappy, as I have said, without any fault of mine. But in the midst of this universal misery, and amid the infinite vanity of all their pleasures and joys, glory is by most men considered to be the greatest good of life, and the worthiest object of ambition and fatigue. Therefore, not hatred but a feeling of especial kindliness, has prompted me to assist you as far as I could in your attainment of this glory.

Soul. Tell me: among the animals you mentioned, are there any of less vitality and sensibility than men?

Nature. All are so, in more or less degree, beginning with plants. Man, being the most perfect of them all, has greater life and power of thought than all other living beings.

Soul. Then if you love me, place me in the most imperfect thing existing, or that being impossible, at least deprive me of this terrible excellence, and make me like the most stupid and senseless soul you have ever created!

[Pg 40]

Nature. I can satisfy your second request, and will do so, since you reject the immortality I would have given you.

Soul. And instead of the immortality, I beseech you to hasten my death as much as possible.

Nature. I will consult Destiny about that.

[Pg 41]

DIALOGUE BETWEEN THE EARTH AND THE MOON

Earth. Dear Moon, I know that you can speak and answer questions like a human being, for I have heard so from many of the poets. Besides, our children say you have really a mouth, nose, and eyes like every one else, and that they see them with their own eyes, which at their time of life ought to be very sharp. As for me, no doubt you know

33

that I am a person; indeed, when I was young, I had a number of children; so you will not be surprised to hear me speak. And the reason, my fine Moon, why I have never uttered a word to you before, although I have been your neighbour for I don't know how many centuries, is that I have been so occupied as to have no time for gossip. But now my business is so trifling that it can look after itself. I don't know what to do, and am ready to die of ennui. So in future, I hope we may often have some talk together; and I should like to know all about your affairs, if it does not inconvenience you to recount them to me.

Moon. Be easy on that score. May the Fates never trouble me more than you are likely to! Talk as much as you please, and although, as I believe you know, I am partial to silence, I will willingly listen and reply, to oblige you.

Earth. Do you hear the delightful sound made by the heavenly bodies in motion?
[Pg 42]
Moon. To tell you the truth, I hear nothing.

Earth. Nor do I; save only the whistling of the wind, which blows from my poles to the equator, and from the equator to the poles, and which is far from musical. But Pythagoras asserts that the celestial spheres make an incredibly sweet harmony, and that you take part in the concert, and are the eighth chord of this universal lyre. As for me, I am so deafened by my own noise that I hear nothing.

Moon. I also am doubtless deafened, since I hear no more than you. But it is news to me that I am a chord.

Earth. Now let us change the subject. Tell me; are you really inhabited, as thousands of ancient and modern philosophers affirm—from Orpheus to De Lalande? In spite of all my efforts to prolong these horns of mine, which men call mountains and hills, and from the summits of which I look at you in silence, I have failed to discern a single one of your inhabitants. Yet I am told that a certain David Fabricius, whose eyes were keener than those of Lynceus, at one time observed your people extending their linen to be dried by the sun.

Moon. I know nothing about your horns. I will admit that I am inhabited.

Earth. What colour are your men?

Moon. What men?

Earth. Those that you contain. Did you not say you were inhabited?

Moon. Yes, what then?

Earth. Does it not follow that all your inhabitants are animals?

Moon. Neither animals nor men, though I am really in ignorance as to the nature of either the one or the other. As for the men you speak of, I have not an idea what you mean.

Earth. Then what sort of creatures are yours?
[Pg 43]
Moon. They are of very many different kinds, as unknown to you, as yours are to me.

Earth. This is so strange that if you yourself had not informed me of it, I would never have believed it. Were you ever conquered by any of your inhabitants?

Moon. Not that I know of. But how? And for what reason?

Earth. Through ambition and jealousy; by means of diplomacy and arms.

Moon. I do not know what you mean by arms, ambition, and diplomacy. Indeed, I understand nothing of what you say.

Earth. But surely if you do not understand the meaning of arms, you know something of war; because, not long ago, a certain doctor discovered through a telescope, which is an instrument for seeing a long distance, that you possessed a fine fortress with

34

proper bastions. Now this is certain proof that your races are at any rate accustomed to sieges and mural battles.

Moon. Pardon me, Mother Earth, if I reply to you a little more at length than would be expected from one so subjugated as it seems I am. But in truth, you appear to me more than vain to imagine that everything in the world is conformable to your things; as if Nature had no other intention than to copy you exactly in each of her creations. I tell you I am inhabited, and you jump to the conclusion that my inhabitants are men. I assert that they are not, and whilst admitting that they may be another race of beings, you endow them with qualities and customs similar to those of your people. You also speak to me about the telescope of a certain doctor. But it seems to me the sight of these telescopes is about as good as that of your children, who discover that I have eyes, a mouth, and a nose, all of which I am ignorant of possessing.

Earth. Then it is not true that your provinces are intersected by fine long roads, and that you are cultivated;[Pg 44] which things are clearly discernible with a telescope from Germany.[1]

Moon. I do not know whether I am cultivated, and I have never observed my roads.

Earth. Dear Moon, you must know that I am of a coarse composition, and very simple-minded. No wonder therefore that men easily deceive me. But I can assure you that if your own inhabitants do not care to conquer you, you are by no means free from such danger; for at different times many people down here have thought of subduing you, and have even made great preparations for doing so. Some have tried to reach you by going to my highest places, standing on tiptoe, and stretching out their arms. Besides, they have made a careful study of your surface, and drawn out maps of your countries. They also know the heights of your mountains, and even their names. I warn you of these things out of pure goodwill, so that you may be prepared for any emergency.

Now, permit me to ask you another question or two. Are you much disturbed by the dogs that bay at you? What do you think of those people who show you another moon in a well? Are you masculine or feminine[2]—because anciently there was a difference of opinion. Is it true that the Arcadians came into the world before you?[3] Are your women, or whatever I should call them, oviparous, and did one of their eggs fall down to us, once upon a time?[4] Are you perforated like a bead, as a modern philosopher believes?[5] Are[Pg 45] you made of green cheese, as some English say? Is it true that Mahomet one fine night cut you in two like a water melon, and that a good piece of your body fell into his cloak? Why do you like to stay on the tops of minarets? What do you think of the feast of Bairam?

Moon. You may as well go on. I need not answer such questions, nor depart from my accustomed habit of silence. If you wish to be so frivolous, and can find nothing else to talk to me about except matters incomprehensible to me, your people had better construct another planet to rotate round them, which they can design and populate as they please. You seem unable to talk of anything but men, and dogs, and such things, of which I know as much as of that one great being round which I am told our sun turns.

Earth. Truly the more I determine not to touch on personal matters, the less I succeed in my resolution. But for the future I will be more careful. Tell me; do you amuse yourself by drawing up my sea-water, and then letting it fall again?

Moon. It may be. But if I have done this, or other such things, I am unaware of it. And you, it seems to me, do not consider what you effect here, which is of so much the more importance as your size and strength are greater than mine.

Earth. I know nothing of these effects, except that from time to time I deprive you of the sun's light, and myself of yours, and that I illumine you during your nights, as is sometimes evident to me.

But I am forgetting one thing, which is the most important of all. I should like to know if Ariosto is correct in saying that everything man loses, such as youth, beauty, health, the vigour and money spent in the pursuit of glory, in the instruction of children, and founding or promoting useful institutions, flies to you; so that you possess all things pertaining to man, except[Pg 46] folly, which has never left mankind. If this be true, I reckon you ought to be so full as to have scarcely any space unoccupied, especially since men have recently lost a great many things (such as patriotism, virtue, magnanimity, righteousness), not merely in part, or singly, as in former times, but completely, and without exception. And certainly if you have not got these things, I do not know where else they can be. But supposing you have them, I wish we could come to an agreement whereby you might soon return the lost things to me; for I imagine you must be greatly encumbered, especially with common sense, which I understand crowds you very much. In return for this, I will see that men pay you annually a good sum of money.

Moon. Men again! Though folly, as you say, has not left your domains, you wish nevertheless to make an utter fool of me, by depriving me of what reason I possess, to supply the deficiency in your people. But I do not know where this reason of yours is, nor whether it can be found in the universe. I know well that it is not here, any more than the other things you mention.

Earth. At least, you can tell me if your inhabitants are acquainted with vices, misdeeds, misfortunes, suffering, and old age; in short, evils? Do you understand these names?

Moon. Yes, I understand these well enough, and not only the names. I am full of them, instead of the other things.

Earth. Which are the more numerous among your people, virtues or vices?

Moon. Vices, by a long way.

Earth. Does pleasure or pain predominate?

Moon. Pain is infinitely more prevalent.

Earth. And your inhabitants, are they mostly happy or unhappy?

Moon. So unhappy that I would not exchange my lot with the happiest of them.
[Pg 47]
Earth. It is the same here. I wonder why we differ so much in other things, yet agree in this.

Moon. I am also like you in shape, I rotate like you, and am illumined by the same sun. It is no more wonderful that we should resemble each other in these things, than that we should possess common failings; because evil is as common to all the planets of the universe, or at least of the solar system, as rotundity, movement, and light. And if you could speak loud enough for Uranus or Saturn, or any other planet, to hear you, and were to ask them if they contained unhappiness, and whether pleasure or pain predominated, each would answer as I have done. I speak from experience, for I have already questioned Venus and Mercury, to whom I am now and then nearer than you. I have also asked certain comets which have passed by me; they all replied to the same effect. I firmly believe even the sun and every star would make the same response.

Earth. Still I am very hopeful. In future I trust men will permit me to experience much happiness.

Moon. Hope as much as you please. I will answer for it you may hope for ever.

Earth. Ha! Did you hear that? These men and animals of mine are making an uproar. It is night on the side from which I am speaking to you, and at first they were all asleep. But, thanks to our conversation, they are now wide awake, and very frightened.

Moon. And here, on the other side, you see it is day.

Earth. Yes. Now I do not wish to terrify my people, or interrupt their sleep, which is the best thing they possess; so let us postpone conversation until another opportunity. Adieu, and good-day to you.

Moon. Adieu. Good-night.

[1] See German newspapers of March 1824, for particulars of the discoveries attributed to Gruithuisen.

[2] See Macrobius, Saturnal: lib. 3. cap. 8; Tertullian, Apolog., cap. 15. The moon was also honoured as the god moon. In the German language moon is masculine.

[3] See Menander, lib. 1. cap. 15, in Rhetor, graec. veter.

[4] Athen: lib. 2. ed. Casaub. p. 57.

[5] Antonio di Ulloa. See Carli, Lettere Americane, par. 4. lett. 7. Milan, 1784.

[Pg 48]

THE WAGER OF PROMETHEUS.

In the year 833,265 of the reign of Jove, the College of the Muses caused certain notices to be printed and affixed in the public places of the city and suburbs of Hypernephelus. These notices contained an invitation to all the gods, great and small, and the other inhabitants of the city, who had recently or anciently originated some praiseworthy invention, to make representation thereof, either actually, or by model or description, to certain judges nominated by this College. And, regretting that its well-known poverty prevented it from displaying the liberality it would have liked to show, the College promised to reward the one whose invention should be judged the finest or most useful, with a crown of laurel. In addition to the prize itself, the College would give the victor permission to wear the crown, day and night, in public and private life, and both in the city and outside it; he might also be painted, sculptured, or modelled in any manner or material whatever, with the emblem of victory on his brow.

Not a few of the gods contested the prize, simply to kill time, a thing as necessary for the citizens of Hypernephelus, as for the people of other towns. They had no wish for the crown, which was about as valuable as a cotton night-cap; and as for the glory, if even men despise it as soon as they become philosophers, it may be imagined in what esteem the phantom was held by the[Pg 49] gods, who are so much wiser than the wisest of men, if indeed they are not the sole possessors of wisdom, as Pythagoras and Plato affirm.

The prize was awarded with an unanimity hitherto unheard of in cases of reward bestowed on the most meritorious. Neither were there any unfair influences exercised, such as favouritism, underhand promises, or artifice. Three competitors were chosen: Bacchus, for the invention of wine; Minerva, for that of oil, with which the gods were daily wont to be anointed after the bath; and Vulcan, for having made a copper pot of an economical design, by which cooking could be expeditiously conducted with but little fire. It was necessary to divide the prize into three parts, so there only remained a little sprig of laurel for each of the victors. But they all three declined the prize, whether in part or the whole. Vulcan said, that since he was obliged to stand the greater part of his time at the forge fire, perspiring and considerably exerting himself, the encumbrance on his brow would be a great annoyance to him; added to which, the laurel would run risk of being scorched or burnt, if some spark by chance were to fall on its dry leaves and set it on fire. Minerva excused herself on the ground of having to wear a helmet large enough, as Homer says, to cover the united armies of a hundred cities; consequently any increase of this weight would be very inconvenient, and out of the question. Bacchus did not wish to change his mitre and chaplet of vine leaves for the laurel, which, however, he would willingly have accepted, had he been allowed to put it up as a sign outside his tavern; but the Muses declined to grant it for that purpose. Finally, the wreath remained in the common treasury of the College.

None of the competitors for the prize envied the three successful gods; nor did they express vexation at the award, nor dispute the verdict—with one exception, Prometheus. This god brought to the contest the clay[Pg 50] model he had used in the formation of the first man. Attached to the model was some writing which explained the qualities and office of the human race, his invention. The chagrin displayed by Prometheus in this matter caused no little astonishment; since all the other gods, whether victors or vanquished, had regarded the whole affair as a joke. But on further inquiry it transpired that what he especially desired, was not the honour, but rather the privilege accompanying success. Some thought he meant to use the laurel as a protection for his head against storms; as it is said of Tiberius that whenever he heard thunder, he donned his crown, esteeming the laurel proof against thunderbolts. But this suggestion was negatived by the fact that the city of Hypernephelus never experienced either thunder or lightning. Others, more rationally, affirmed that Prometheus, owing to age, had begun to lose his hair, and being greatly troubled at this misadventure, as are many mortals in similar circumstances (and either not having read Synesius' eulogy on baldness, or being unconvinced by it), wished, like Julius Cæsar, to hide the nakedness of his head beneath the leafy diadem.

But to turn to facts. One day Prometheus, talking with Momus, bitterly complained of the preference given to the wine, oil, and copper-pot, in comparison with the human race, which he said was the finest achievement of the immortals that the universe had ever seen. And not being able sufficiently to convince Momus, who gave various reasons against this assertion, they made a wager on the subject. Prometheus proposed that they should descend together to the earth, and alighting by chance in the first place they should discover inhabited by man in each of the five parts of the world, they might find out whether or not there were in all or most of these parts conclusive evidence that man is the most perfect creature of the universe. Momus accepted the wager; and having settled the amount, they began without delay[Pg 51] to descend towards the earth. First of all they directed themselves to the New World, which, from its name, and the fact that as yet none of the immortals had set foot in it, greatly excited their curiosity.

They touched ground towards the north of Popuyan, not far from the river Cauca, in a place which showed many signs of human habitation. There were traces of cultivation, level roads broken and impassable in places, trees cut and strewn about, appearances of what might be graves, and here and there human bones were scattered. But the celestials could neither hear the voice, nor see the shadow of a living man, though they listened acutely, and looked all around them. They proceeded, walking and flying, for the distance of many miles, passing mountains and rivers, and finding everywhere the same traces of human habitation, and the same solitude.

"How is it these countries are now deserted," said Momus to Prometheus, "though they were evidently once inhabited?"

Prometheus mentioned the inundations of the sea, earthquakes, storms, and heavy rains, which he knew were ordinary occurrences in the tropics. Indeed, as if in confirmation of his words, they could distinctly hear in the neighbouring forests the incessant patter of rain-drops falling from the branches of trees agitated by the wind.

But Momus was unable to understand how that locality could be affected by inundations of the sea, which was so distant as not to be visible on any side. Still less could he comprehend why the earthquakes, storms, and rains should have destroyed the human beings of the country, sparing however, the jaguars, apes, ants, eagles, parrots, and a hundred other kinds of animals and birds which surrounded them.

At length, descending into an immense valley, they discovered a little cluster of houses, or wooden cabins, covered with palm leaves, and environed on all sides by[Pg 52] a fence like a stockade. Before one of these cabins, many persons, some standing, some sitting, were gathered round an earthen pot suspended over a large fire.

The two celestials, having taken human form, drew near, and Prometheus, courteously saluting them all, turned to the one who seemed to be their chief, and asked him what they were doing.

Savage. Eating, as you see.

Prom. What savoury food have you got?

Savage. Only a little bit of meat.

Prom. Of a domestic, or wild animal?

Savage. Domestic, in truth, since it is my own son.

Prom. What! Had you then, like Pasiphaë, a calf for your son?

Savage. Not a calf, but a child like every one else.

Prom. Do you mean what you say? Is it your own flesh and blood that you are eating?

Savage. My own? No. But certainly that of my son. Why else did I bring him into the world, and nourish him?

Prom. What! To eat him?

Savage. Why not? and I will also eat his mother when she can have no more children.

Momus. As one eats the hen after her eggs.

Savage. And I will likewise eat my other women, when they can no longer have children. And why also should I keep these slaves of mine alive, if it were not that from time to time they give me children to eat? But when they are old, I will eat them all one after the other, if I live.[1]

Prom. Tell me, do these slaves belong to your tribe or to another?

Savage. Another.

Prom. Far from here?

Savage. A very long way. A river divides their huts from ours. And pointing with his finger to a hillock, he[Pg 53] added: They used to live there, but our people have destroyed their dwellings.

By this time it seemed to Prometheus that many of the savages were standing looking at him with the sort of appreciative gaze that a cat gives to a mouse. So, to avoid being eaten by his own manufactures, he rose suddenly on the wing, and Momus followed his example. And such was their fright that in setting out they unconsciously behaved as did the Harpies towards the Trojans when at meat. But the cannibals, more hungry, or less dainty, than the companions of Æneas, continued their horrid repast.

Prometheus, very dissatisfied with the New World, turned immediately towards Asia, the older one. Having traversed almost in an instant the space which lies between the East and West Indies, they both descended near Agra, in a field where they saw a number of people. These were all gathered round a funeral pyre of wood, by which men with torches were standing, ready to set it on fire; and on a platform was a young woman very sumptuously attired, and wearing a variety of barbaric adornments, who, dancing and shouting, displayed signs of the liveliest joy. Prometheus, seeing her, imagined that a second Lucretia or Virginia, or some imitator of the children of Erectheus, of Iphigenia, Codrus, Menecius, Curtius, or Decius, was about to sacrifice herself voluntarily on behalf of her country, in obedience to the decree of some oracle. Learning however that the woman was about to die because her husband was dead, he supposed that, like Alcestis, she wished at the cost of her own life to reanimate her husband. But, when they informed him that she was only induced to burn herself because it was customary for widows of her caste to do so, and that she had always hated her husband, that she was drunk, and that the dead man, instead of being resuscitated, was to be burnt in the same fire, he abruptly turned his back on the spectacle, and set out for Europe. On their way[Pg 54] thither, Prometheus and his companion held the following conversation.

Momus. Did you think, when at so great a hazard you stole fire from heaven to give to men, that some of them would make use of it to cook one another in pots, and others voluntarily to burn themselves?

Prom. No, indeed! But consider, dear Momus, that the men we have hitherto seen are barbarians; and one must not judge of human nature from barbarians, but rather from civilised people, to whom we are now going. I have a strong conviction that among these latter we shall see things, and hear words, which will astonish as much as delight you.

Momus. I for my part do not see, if men are the most perfect race of the universe, why they need be civilised in order not to burn themselves, or eat their own children. Other animals are all uncivilised, and yet none of them deliberately burn themselves, except the phoenix, which is fabulous; rarely they eat their own kind; and much more rarely make food of their own offspring by any chance whatever; neither do they specially give birth to them for that purpose. I also understand that of the five divisions of the world, only the smallest possesses even incompletely the civilisation that you praise. To this may be added minute portions of other parts of the world. And you yourself will not venture to assert that the civilisation of the present day is such that the men of Paris or Philadelphia have reached the highest possible state of perfection. Yet, to enable them to attain to their present imperfect state of civilisation, how much time has had to elapse? Even as many years as the world can number from its origin to the existing age. Again, almost all the inventions which have been of greatest use or importance in the advancement of civilisation have originated rather fortuitously than rationally. Hence, human civilisation is a work of chance rather[Pg 55] than nature, and where opportunity has been lacking, the people are still barbarians, though on the same level of age as civilised people.

Consequently I make the following deductions: that man in the savage state is many degrees inferior to every other animal; that civilisation as compared with barbarism is only possessed even in the present day by a small portion of the human race; that these privileged people have only reached their existing state of culture after the lapse of many ages, and more by chance than anything else; and finally, that the present state of civilisation is imperfect. Consider, therefore, whether your opinion about the human race would not be better expressed in saying, that it is chief among races, but supreme rather in imperfection than perfection. It does not affect the case that men themselves, in talking and reasoning, continually confuse perfection and imperfection, arguing as they do from certain preconceived notions, which they take for palpable truths. It is certain that the other races of creatures were each from the very beginning in a state of perfection. And, since it is clear that man in a savage state compares unfavourably with other animals, I do not understand how beings, naturally the most imperfect among the races, as it seems men are, come to be esteemed superior to all others.

Added to which, human civilisation, so difficult to acquire, and almost impossible to perfect, is not so immutable that it cannot relapse. In fact, we find it has done so several times, among people who once possessed a high degree of culture.

In conclusion, I think your brother Epimetheus would have gained the prize before you, had he brought to the judges his model of the first ass, or first frog. I will, however, quite agree with you as to the perfection of man, if you on your part will admit that his excellence is of the kind attributed to the world by Plotinus. This[Pg 56] philosopher says the world in itself is supremely perfect, but containing as it does every conceivable evil, it is in reality as bad as can be. From the same point of view, I might perhaps agree with Leibnitz, that the present world is the best of all possible worlds.

There can be no doubt that Prometheus had prepared a concise and crushing reply to all this reasoning; but it is very certain he did not give it expression, for just then they found themselves over the city of London. The gods descended, and seeing a great many people rushing to the door of a private house, they mixed with the crowd, and entered the building. Within, they found a dead man, who had been shot in the breast, laid out on a bed. He had a pistol clenched in his right hand, and by his side lay two children, also dead. There were several people of the house in the room, who were being questioned by magistrates, while an official wrote down their replies.

Prom. Who are these unfortunate beings?

Servant. My master and his children.

Prom. Who has killed them?

Servant. My master himself.

Prom. What! Do you mean to say he killed his children and himself?

Servant. Yes.

Prom. Alas! Why did he do that? Surely some great misfortune must have befallen him.

Servant. None that I know of.

Prom. Perhaps he was poor, or despised by every one, unfortunate in love, or in disgrace at court.

Servant. On the contrary, he was very rich, and I believe universally esteemed. He cared nothing about love, and was in high favour at court.

Prom. Then why has he done this thing?

Servant. He was weary of life,—so he says in the writing he has left.

Prom. What are these judges doing?

[Pg 57]

Servant. Taking evidence as to whether my master was out of his mind or not. Unless he is proved to have been insane, his goods fall to the crown by law; and really there is nothing to prevent their so doing.

Prom. But had he no friend or relative to whom he could entrust his children instead of killing them?

Servant. Yes, he had; and especially one friend, to whom he has commended his dog.[2]

41

Momus was about to congratulate Prometheus on the good effects of civilisation, and the happiness that seemed to be inseparable from human life. He wished also to remind him that no animal except man voluntarily killed itself, or was impelled by feelings of despair to take the life of its own offspring. But Prometheus anticipated him, and paid the bet at once, without visiting the two remaining parts of the world.

[1] See Robertson's Hist. of America, Book VI.

[2] A fact.

[Pg 58]

DIALOGUE BETWEEN A NATURAL PHILOSOPHER AND A METAPHYSICIAN

Natural Philosopher. Eureka! Eureka!

Metaphysician. What is it? What have you found?

Nat. Phil. The art of long life.[1]

Met. And the book that you carry?

Nat. Phil. Explains my theory. This invention of mine will give me eternal life. Others may live long, but I shall live for ever. I mean that I shall acquire immortal fame.

Met. Follow my advice. Get a leaden casket; enclose therein your book; bury it; and leave in your will directions where it may be found, with instructions to your heirs not to exhume the book until they shall have discovered the art of living a happy life.

Nat. Phil. And meanwhile?

Met. Meanwhile your invention will be good for nothing. It were far better if it taught the art of living briefly.

Nat. Phil. That has already been known a long time. The discovery was not a difficult one. Met. At any rate I prefer it to yours. Nat Phil. Why?

Met. Because if life be not happy, as hitherto it has not been, it were better to endure a short term of it than a long one.

Nat. Phil. No, no. I differ from you. Life is a good in itself, and is naturally desired and loved by every one.

[Pg 59]

Met. So men think. But they are deceived. Similarly people deceive themselves in thinking that colours are attributes of the objects coloured; whereas really they are not qualities of objects, but of light. I assert that man loves and desires nothing but his own happiness. He therefore loves his life only inasmuch as he esteems it the instrument or subject of his happiness. Hence it is happiness that he always loves, and not life; although he very often attributes to the one the affection he has for the other. It is true that this illusion and that relating to colours are both natural. But as a proof that the love of life in men is unnatural, or rather unnecessary, think of the many people that in olden times preferred to die rather than live. In our own time too many people often wish for death, and some kill themselves. Now such things could not occur if man naturally loved life itself. The love of happiness, on the contrary, is innate in every living being; indeed the world would perish before they ceased loving and seeking it in every possible form. And as for your assertion that life in itself is a good thing, I challenge you to prove your words by any arguments you please, whether of physics or metaphysics. Personally I am of opinion that a happy life is undoubtedly a good thing. But this is because of the happiness, not the life. An unhappy life is therefore an evil. And since it is ordained that

42

human life should be inseparable from unhappiness, I leave you to draw your own conclusions.

Nat. Phil. Let us drop the subject, if you please; it is too melancholy. Answer me one question candidly, and without such subtleties. If man had the power to live for ever, I mean in this life and not after death, do you think he would be happy?

Met. Allow me to answer you by a fable. Moreover, as I have never tasted immortality, I cannot reply to you from experience. Besides, I have never by any chance met an immortal, the very existence of whom is[Pg 60] a mere matter of legend. If Cagliostro were alive, he could perhaps enlighten you, since he was said to have lived for several centuries. But he is now dead, like his contemporaries.

To return to the fable. The wise Chiro, who was a god, in time became so wearied of his life, that he asked permission from Jove to die. This was granted to him; so he died.[2] If immortality wrought such an effect on the gods, how would it be with men? The Hyperboreans, an unknown but famous people, whose country is inaccessible by sea or land, were, it is said, rich in all manner of things, and possessed a race of asses of peculiar beauty, which they used to offer as sacrifices. They had the power, unless I am mistaken, of living for ever, and knew nothing of fatigues, cares, wars, discords, or crimes. Yet we learn that after several thousand years of life, they all killed themselves by jumping from a certain rock into the sea, where they were drowned.[3] Here is another legend. The brothers Biton and Cleobus, at a festival, when the mules were not ready, attached themselves to the chariot of their mother, who was a priestess of Juno, and drew her to the temple. Touched by their devotion, the priestess asked Juno to reward her sons for their piety by the greatest gift possible for men to receive. The goddess caused them both to die peacefully within an hour, instead of giving them immortality, as they had expected.

The same happened to Agamede and Trophonius. When these two men had finished the temple of Delphi, they begged Apollo to reward them. The god asked them to wait seven days, at the end of which time he would do so. On the seventh night he sent them a sweet sleep from which they have never awakened. They are so satisfied with their recompense that they have asked nothing more.

[Pg 61]

On the subject of legends, here is one which introduces a question I would have you answer. I know that by you and your colleagues human life is generally considered to be, as a rule, of an uniformly average duration: this in all countries and under all climates. But Pliny relates that the men of some parts of India and Ethiopia do not exceed the age of forty years. They who die at this age are considered very old. Their children marry at seven years of age: and this statement is verified by the custom in Guinea, the Deccan, and elsewhere in the torrid zone. Now, regarding it as true that these people do not live more than forty years (and this as a natural limit, and not due to artificial circumstances), I ask you whether you imagine their lot ought to be considered more or less happy than that of others?

Nat. Phil. Undoubtedly, more miserable, since they die so soon.

Met. I am of the contrary opinion for the very same reason. But that does not matter. Give me your attention for a moment. I deny that life itself, i.e., the mere sensation of existence, has anything pleasurable or desirable in its nature. But we all wish for the other thing, also called life; I mean strength, and numerous sensations. Thus, all activity, and every strong and lively passion, provided it be neither disagreeable nor painful, pleases us simply because it is strong and lively, although it possess no other pleasurable attributes.

43

Now these men, whose life normally lasts only forty years, that is, half the time granted by nature to other men, would experience every moment an intensity of life, twice as strong as ours, because their growth, maturity, and decline are accomplished twice as rapidly as with us. Their energy of life therefore ought to be twice as intense as ours at every moment of their existence. And to this greater intensity there must correspond a more lively activity of the will, more vivacity[Pg 62] and animation. Thus they experience in less time the same quantity of life as we have. And the fewer years that these favoured people spend on the earth are so well filled that there is no sensible vacuum; whereas this same quantity of life is insufficient to vivify a term twice as long. Their actions and sensations, diffused over so limited a space, can duly occupy all their existence; but our longer life is constantly divided by protracted intervals devoid of all activity and lively passion. And since existence itself is in no sense desirable, but only in so far as it is happy; and since good or evil fortune is not measurable by the number of our days; I conclude that the life of these people, though shorter than ours, is much the richer in pleasures, or what are so called. Their life must then be preferable to ours, or even to that of the earliest kings of Assyria, Egypt, China, India, and other countries, who are said to have lived thousands of years. So that, far from being desirous of immortality, I am content to leave it to fishes, which are by Leeuwenhoek believed to be immortal, provided they are neither eaten by us nor their fellows. Instead of delaying the development of the body, in order to lengthen life, as Maupertuis[4] proposed, I would rather accelerate it until the duration of our life was as short as that of the insects called ephemerals; which insects, although the most aged does not live beyond a single day, nevertheless preside over three generations before they die. If it were so, then there would at least be no time for ennui.

What do you think of my reasoning?

Nat. Phil. It does not persuade me. I know that you love metaphysics, whereas I for my part hold to physics. To your subtleties, I oppose simple common sense, which is sufficient for me. Thus, I venture to assert, without appealing to the microscope, that life is better than death. Judging between the two, I would[Pg 63] give the apple to the former, without troubling them to strip for the contest.

Met. And I would do the same. But when I call to mind the custom of those barbarians, who, for every unhappy day of their lives, used to throw a black stone into a quiver, and for every happy day a white one, I cannot help thinking how few white stones compared to the black ones would be found therein on the death of the proprietor of the quiver. Personally, I should like to have now all the stones representing the days of life yet remaining to me, and permission to separate them, throwing away all the black ones and retaining only those that were white; even though the number of the latter was exceedingly small, and their colour a doubtful white.

Nat. Phil. Many people, on the contrary, would be glad to increase the number of their black stones, even though they were blacker than they naturally would be; because they always, in their minds, dread the last as the blackest of all. And such people, of whom I am one, will really be able to add many stones to their normal quantity, if they follow out the instructions contained in my book.

Met. Every one thinks and works in his own way. Death also will not fail to do the same. But if you wish, in prolonging man's life; really to be of service to him, discover an art to increase the number and strength of sensations, and their effects. This would be a genuine augmentation of human life, for it would fill up those long intervals of time, during which we vegetate rather than live. You could then boast of having truly prolonged human life; and without having sought after the impossible, or used violence to natural laws; rather, by having strengthened them. For does it not seem as though the ancients

44

were more full of life than we are, in spite of the many and great dangers by which they were surrounded, and which generally shortened their existence?

[Pg 64]

You will thus render a real service to man, whose life is, I will not say more happy, but certainly less unhappy, when it is better occupied and more violently agitated, without pain or discomfort. When, on the other hand, existence is so full of idleness and ennui as to be justly termed empty, the saying of Pyrrhus, "there is no difference between life and death," is literally realised. Were this saying true, I should be in no slight terror of death.

But finally, unless life be active and vigorous, it is not true life, and death is far preferable to it.

[1] See Instruction in the Art of Long Life, by Hufeland.

[2] See Lucian, Dial. Menip. and Chiro.

[3] See Pindar, Strabo, and Pliny.

[4] See Lettres Philosophiques: let. 11.

[Pg 65]

DIALOGUE BETWEEN TASSO AND HIS FAMILIAR SPIRIT[1]

Spirit. Ah, Torquato. How are you?

Tasso. As well as it is possible to be, when in prison, and up to the neck in misfortunes.

Spirit. Courage! After supper is not the time to be sorrowful. Cheer up, and let us laugh at your griefs.

Tasso. I am little inclined for that. But somehow your presence and conversation always do me good. Come and sit down by me.

Spirit. How can I sit? Such a thing is not easy for a spirit. But what does it matter? Consider that I am seated.

Tasso. Oh, that I could see my Leonora again! Whenever I think of her, I feel a thrill of joy that reaches from the crown of my head to the extremity of my feet, and all my nerves and veins are pervaded with it. My mind, too, becomes inflamed with certain imaginings and longings that seem for the time to transform me. I cannot think that I am the Torquato who has experienced so much misfortune, and I often mourn for myself as though I were dead. Truly, it would seem that worldly friction and suffering are wont to overwhelm and lethargise[Pg 66] our first nature within each of us. This from time to time awakens for a brief space, but less frequently as we grow older, when it always withdraws, and falls into an increasingly sound sleep. Finally, it dies, although our life still continues. In short, I marvel how the thought of a woman should have sufficient power to rejuvenate the mind, and make it forget so many troubles. Had I not lost all hope of seeing Leonora again, I could almost believe I might still succeed in being happy.

Spirit. Which do you consider the more delightful, to see the dear woman, or to think of her?

Tasso. I do not know. It is true when near me she seemed only a woman; at a distance, however, she was like a goddess.

45

Spirit. These goddesses are so amiable that when one approaches you, she instantaneously puts off her divinity, and pockets her halo of greatness for fear of dazzling the mortal to whom she appears.

Tasso. There is only too much truth in what you say. But do you not think it is a great failing in women that they prove really to be so very different from what we imagine?

Spirit. I scarcely think it is their fault that they are, like us, made of flesh and blood, instead of ambrosia and nectar. What in the world has a thousandth part of the perfection with which your fancy endows women? It surprises me that you are not astonished to find that men are men, that is, creatures of little merit and amiability, since you cannot understand why women are not really angels.

Tasso. In spite of all this, I am dying to see her again.

Spirit. Compose yourself. This very night you shall dream of her. I will lead her to you, beautiful as youth, and so kindly disposed that you will be encouraged to speak to her much more freely and readily than in former times. You will be induced at length to take her by the hand, and she, looking intently at you, will surfeit[Pg 67] your soul with sweetness. And to-morrow, whenever you think of the dream, your heart will overflow with affection.

Tasso. What a consolation! A dream instead of the truth.

Spirit. What is truth?

Tasso. I am as ignorant on the subject as Pilate was.

Spirit. Well, I will tell you. Between truth or reality, and a dream there is this difference—the latter is much the finer thing of the two.

Tasso. What! The pleasure of a dream worth more than a real pleasure?

Spirit. It is. As an instance, I know a man who studiously avoids meeting his sweetheart the following day after she has appeared to him in a dream. He knows full well that he would not find in her all the charms with which she was endowed in the dream, and that reality, dispelling the illusion, would deprive him of the pleasure he felt. The ancients too, who were much more diligent and skilful in their search after all the enjoyments possible for man to have, did wisely in endeavouring by various means to realise the sweetness and pleasure of dreams. Pythagoras also was right when he forbad the eating of beans for supper; these vegetables producing a dreamless or troubled sleep.[2] I could also find excuse for those superstitious people who were wont, before going to bed, to invoke the aid of Mercury, the president of dreams. They offered sacrifice to him that he might grant them happy dreams, and used to keep an image of the god at the foot of their bed. Thus it was that being unable to procure any happiness during the day, people sought it in the night-time. I am of opinion that they were in a measure successful, and that Mercury paid more attention to their prayers than was the custom of the other gods.

Tasso. But, since men live for nothing but pleasure,[Pg 68] whether of mind or body, if this pleasure can only be found when we dream, it follows that we live for no other purpose but to dream. Now I really cannot admit that.

Spirit. You already admit it, inasmuch as you live, and are willing to live. But what is pleasure?

Tasso. My acquaintance with it is too slight to enable me to answer you.

Spirit. No one has any real acquaintance with it, because pleasure is not a reality, but a conception. It is a desire, not a fact. A sentiment, imagined not experienced; or, better, it is a conception, and not a sentiment at all. Do you not perceive that even in the very moment of enjoyment, however ardently it may have been longed for or painfully

46

acquired, your mind, not deriving complete satisfaction from the happiness, anticipates at some future time a greater and more complete enjoyment? It is expectation that constitutes pleasure. Thus, you never weary of placing reliance on some pleasure of the future, which melts away just when you expect to enjoy it. The truth is, you possess nothing but the hope of a more complete enjoyment at some other time; and the satisfaction of imagining that you have had some enjoyment, and of talking about it to others, less because you are vain than to persuade yourself that the illusion is a reality. Hence, everyone that consents to live makes this fugitive dream his aim in life. He believes in the reality of past and future enjoyment, both of which beliefs are false and fanciful.

Tasso. Then is it impossible for a man to believe that he is actually happy?

Spirit. If such a belief were possible, his happiness would be genuine. But tell me: do you ever remember having been able at any moment in your life to say sincerely, "I am happy"? Doubtless you have daily been able to say, and have said in all sincerity, "I shall be happy;" and often too, though less sincerely, "I have[Pg 69] been happy." Thus, pleasure is always either a thing of the past, or the future, never the present.

Tasso. You may as well say it is non-existent.

Spirit. So it seems.

Tasso. Even in dreams?

Spirit. Even in dreams, considering pleasure in its true sense.

Tasso. And yet pleasure is the sole object and aim of life! By the term pleasure I mean the happiness which ought to be a consequence of pleasure.

Spirit. Assuredly.

Tasso. Then our life, being deprived of its real aim, must always be imperfect, and existence itself unnatural.

Spirit. Perhaps.

Tasso. There is no perhaps in the matter. But why is it that we live? I mean, why do we consent to live?

Spirit. How should I know? You yourselves ought to know better than I.

Tasso. I assure you I do not know.

Spirit. Ask some one wiser than yourself. Perhaps he may be able to satisfy you.

Tasso. I will do so. But certainly, the life that I lead is an unnatural state, because apart from my sufferings, ennui alone murders me.

Spirit. What is ennui?

Tasso. As to this, I can answer from experience. Ennui seems to me of the nature of atmosphere, which fills up the spaces between material bodies, and also the voids in the bodies themselves. Whenever a body disappears, and is not replaced by another, air fills up the gap immediately. So too, in human life, the intervals between pleasures and pains are occupied by ennui. And since in the material world, according to the Peripatetics, there can be no vacuum, so also in our life there is none, save when for some cause or other the mind loses its power of thought. At all other times[Pg 70] the mind, considered as a separate identity from the body, is occupied with some sentiment. If void of pleasure or pain, it is full of ennui; for this last is also a sentiment like pleasure and pain.

Spirit. And, since all your pleasures are like cobwebs, exceedingly fragile, thin and transparent, ennui penetrates their tissue, and saturates them, just as air penetrates the webs. I believe ennui is really nothing but the desire of happiness, without the illusion of pleasure and the suffering of pain. This desire, we have said, is never completely satisfied, since true pleasure does not exist. So that human life may be said to be interwoven with

47

pain and ennui, and one of these sentiments disappears only to give place to the other. This is the fate of all men, and not of yourself alone.

Tasso. What remedy is there for ennui?

Spirit. Sleep, opium, and pain. The last is the best of the three, because he who suffers never experiences ennui.

Tasso. I would rather submit to ennui for the rest of my life, than take such medicine. But its force and strength may be diminished by action, work, and even other sentiments; though these do not entirely free us from ennui, since they are unable to give us real pleasure. Here in prison however, deprived of human society, without even the means of writing, reduced for an amusement to counting the ticks of the clock, looking at the beams, cracks, and nails of the ceiling, thinking about the pavement stones, and watching the gnats and flies which flit across my cell, I have nothing to relieve for a moment my burden of ennui.

Spirit. How long have you been reduced to this kind of life?

Tasso. For many weeks, as you know.

Spirit. Have you felt no variation in the ennui which oppresses you, from the first day until now?

Tasso. Yes. I felt it more at first. Gradually my[Pg 71] mind is becoming accustomed to its own society; I derive more and more pleasure from my solitude, and by practice I am acquiring so great a readiness in conversation, or rather chattering to myself, that I seem to have in my head a company of talkative people, and the most trifling object is now sufficient to give rise to endless discourse.

Spirit. This habit will grow on you daily to such an extent, that when you are free, you will feel more idle in society than in solitude. Custom has made you bear patiently your kind of life, and the same influence works not only in people who meditate like you, but in everyone. Besides, the very fact that you are separated from men, and even, it may be said, from life itself, will be of some advantage to you. Disgusted and wearied with human affairs, as you are from your sad experience, you will in time begin to look on them, from a distance, with an appreciative eye. In your solitude they will appear to you more beautiful, and worthy of affection. You will forget their vanity and misery, and will take upon yourself to re-create the world as you would have it. Consequently, you will value, desire, and love life. And, provided there be the possibility or certainty of your return to human society some day, your new aspect of life will fill and gladden your mind with a joy like that of childhood.

Solitude does indeed sometimes act like a second youth. It rejuvenates the soul, revives the imagination, and renews in an experienced man those impressions of early innocence that you so ardently desire. But your eyes seem heavy with sleep: I will now therefore leave you to prepare the fine dream I promised you. Thus between dreams and fancies, your life shall pass without other gain than the fact of its passing, which is the sole benefit of life. To hasten it should be the one aim of your existence. You are often obliged to cling to life, as it were with your teeth; happy will be the day when[Pg 72] death releases you from the struggle. But after all, time passes as tediously with your persecutor in his palace and gardens, as with you in your prison chamber. Adieu.

Tasso. Adieu, yet stay a moment. Your conversation always enlivens me. It does not draw me from my sadness, but my mind, which is generally comparable to a dark night, moonless and starless, changes when you are near to a condition like that of a grey dawn, pleasurable rather than otherwise. Now tell me how I can find you in case I want you at some future time.

Spirit. Do you not yet know?—In any generous liquor.

48

[1] Tasso, during his mental hallucinations, used to fancy, like Socrates, that he was visited by a friendly spirit, with which he would hold long conversations. Manso, in his life of Tasso, mentions this, and states that he was once present during such a colloquy or soliloquy between Tasso and his imagined companion.

[2] Apollonius, Hist. Comment., cap. 46, &c.

[Pg 73]

DIALOGUE BETWEEN NATURE AND AN ICELANDER.

An Icelander who had travelled over most of the earth, and had lived in very many different lands, found himself one day in the heart of Africa. As he crossed the equator in a place never before penetrated by man, he had an adventure like that which happened to Vasco di Gama, who, when passing the Cape of Good Hope, was opposed by two giants, the guardians of the southern seas, that tried to prevent his entrance into the new waters.[1] The Icelander saw in the distance a huge bust, in appearance like the colossal Hermes he had formerly seen in the Isle of Pasqua. At first he thought it was made of stone, but as he drew near to it he saw that the head belonged to an enormous woman, who was seated on the ground, resting her back against a mountain. The figure was alive, and had a countenance both magnificent and terrible, and eyes and hair of a jet black colour. She looked fixedly at him for a long time in silence. At length she said:

Nature. Who art thou? What doest thou here, where thy race is unknown?

Icelander. I am a poor Icelander, fleeing from Nature. I have fled from her ever since I was a child, through a hundred different parts of the world, and I am fleeing from her now.

[Pg 74]

Nature. So flees the squirrel from the rattlesnake, and runs in its haste deliberately into the mouth of its tormentor. I am that from which thou fleest.

Icelander. Nature?

Nature. Even so.

Icelander. I am smitten with anguish, for I consider no worse misfortune could befall me.

Nature. Thou mightest well have imagined that I was to be found in countries where my power is supremest. But why dost thou shun me?

Icelander. You must know that from my earliest youth, experience convinced me of the vanity of life, and the folly of men. I saw these latter ceaselessly struggling for pleasures that please not, and possessions that do not satisfy. I saw them inflict on themselves, and voluntarily suffer, infinite pains, which, unlike the pleasures, were only too genuine. In short, the more ardently they sought happiness, the further they seemed removed from it. These things made me determine to abandon every design, to live a life of peace and obscurity, harming no one, striving in nought to better my condition, and contesting nothing with anyone. I despaired of happiness, which I regarded as a thing withheld from our race, and my only aim was to shield myself from suffering. Not that I had the least intention of abstaining from work, or bodily labour; for there is as great a difference between mere fatigue and pain,[2] as between a peaceful and an idle life.

But when I began to carry out my project, I learnt from experience how fallacious it is to think that one can live inoffensively amongst men without offending them. Though I always gave them precedence, and took the smallest part of everything, I found neither[Pg

49

75] rest nor happiness among them. However, this I soon remedied. By avoiding men I freed myself from their persecutions. I took refuge in solitude—easily obtainable in my native island. Having done this, I lived without a shadow of enjoyment; yet I found I had not escaped all suffering. The intense cold of the long winter, and the extreme heat of summer, characteristic of the country, allowed me no cessation from pain. And when, to warm myself, I passed much time by the fire, I was scorched by the flames, and blinded by the smoke. I suffered continuously, whether in the open air, or in the shelter of my cabin. In short, I failed to obtain that life of peace which was my one desire. Terrible storms, Hecla's menaces and rumblings, and the constant fires which occur among the wooden houses of my country, combined to keep me in a state of perpetual disquietude. Such annoyances as these, trivial though they be when the mind is distracted by the thoughts and actions of social and civil life, are intensified by solitude. I endured them all, together with the hopeless monotony of my existence, solely in order to obtain the tranquillity I desired. I perceived that the more I isolated myself from men, and confined me to my own little sphere, the less I succeeded in protecting myself from the discomforts and sufferings of the outer world.

Then I determined to try other climates and countries, to see if anywhere I could live in peace, harming no one, and exist without suffering, if also without pleasure. I was urged to this by the thought that perhaps you had destined for the human race a certain part of the earth (as you have for many animals and plants), where alone they could live in comfort. In which case it was our own fault if we suffered inconvenience from having exceeded our natural boundaries. I have therefore been over the whole earth, testing every country, and always fulfilling my intention of troubling others in the least possible degree, and seeking nothing for myself but a life of[Pg 76] tranquillity. But in vain. The tropical sun burnt me; the Arctic cold froze me; in temperate regions the changeability of the weather troubled me; and everywhere I have experienced the fury of the elements. I have been in places where not a day passes without a storm, and where you, O Nature, are incessantly at war with simple people who have never done you any harm. In other places cloudless skies are compensated for by frequent earthquakes, active volcanoes, and subterranean commotions. Elsewhere hurricanes and whirlwinds take the place of other scourges. Sometimes I have heard the roof over my head groan with the burden of snow that it supported; at other times the earth, saturated with rain, has broken away beneath my feet. Rivers have burst their banks, and pursued me, fleeing at full speed, as though I were an enemy. Wild beasts tried to devour me, without the least provocation on my part. Serpents have sought to poison or crush me; and I have been nearly killed by insects. I make no mention of the daily hazards by which man is surrounded. These last are so numerous that an ancient philosopher[3] laid down a rule, that to resist the constant influence of fear, it were well to fear everything.

Again, sickness has not failed to torment me, though invariably temperate, and even abstemious, in all bodily pleasures. In truth, our natural constitution is an admirably arranged affair! You inspire us with a strong and incessant yearning for pleasure, deprived of which our life is imperfect; and on the other hand you ordain that nothing should be more opposed to physical health and strength, more calamitous in its effects, and more incompatible with the duration of life itself, than this same pleasure. But although I indulged in no pleasures, numerous diseases attacked me, some of which endangered my life, and others the use of my limbs, thus threatening me with even an access of misery. All, during many[Pg 77] days or months, caused me to experience a thousand bodily and mental pangs. And, whereas in sickness we endure new and extraordinary sufferings, as though our ordinary life were not sufficiently unhappy; you do not compensate for this by giving us equally exceptional periods of health and strength, and consequent enjoyment. In regions where the snow never melts, I lost my sight; this is an ordinary occurrence among the Laplanders in their cold country. The sun and air, things necessary for life, and therefore unavoidable, trouble us continually; the latter by its dampness or severity, the former by its heat, and even its light; and to neither of them can man remain exposed without suffering more or less inconvenience or harm. In short, I cannot recollect a single day during which I have not suffered in some way; whereas, on the other hand, the days that have gone by without a shadow of enjoyment are countless. I conclude therefore that we are destined to suffer much in proportion as we enjoy little, and that it is as impossible to live peacefully as happily. I also naturally come to the conclusion that you are the avowed enemy of men, and all other creatures of your creation. Sometimes alluring, at other times menacing; now attacking, now striking, now pursuing, now destroying; you are always engaged in tormenting us. Either by habit or necessity you are the enemy of your own family, and the executioner of your own flesh and blood. As for me, I have lost all hope. Experience has proved to me that though it be possible to escape from men and their persecutions, it is impossible to evade you, who will never cease tormenting us until you have trodden us under foot. Old age, with all its bitterness, and sorrows, and accumulation of troubles, is already near to me. This worst of evils you have destined for us and all created beings, from the time of infancy. From the fifth lustre of life, decline makes itself manifest; its progress we are powerless to stay. Scarce a third of life is spent in the bloom of[Pg 78] youth; but few moments are claimed by maturity; all the rest is one gradual decay, with its attendant evils.

Nature. Thinkest thou then that the world was made for thee? It is time thou knewest that in my designs, operations, and decrees, I never gave a thought to the happiness or unhappiness of man. If I cause you to suffer, I am unaware of the fact; nor do I perceive that I can in any way give you pleasure. What I do is in no sense done for your enjoyment or benefit, as you seem to think. Finally, if I by chance exterminated your species, I should not know it.

Icelander. Suppose a stranger invited me to his house in a most pressing manner, and I, to oblige him, accepted his invitation. On my arrival he took me to a damp and unhealthy place, and lodged me in a chamber open to the air, and so ruinous that it threatened momentarily to collapse and crush me. Far from endeavouring to amuse me, and make me comfortable, he neglected to provide me with even the necessaries of life. And more than this. Suppose my host caused me to be insulted, ridiculed, threatened, and beaten by his sons and household. And on my complaining to him of such ill-treatment, he replied: "Dost thou think I made this house for thee? Do I keep these my children and servants for thy service? I assure thee I have other things to occupy me, than that I should amuse thee, or give thee welcome." To which I answered: "Well, my friend, though you may not have built your house especially for me, at least you might have forborne to ask me hither. And, since I owe it to you that I am here, ought I not to rely on you to assure me, if possible, a life free from trouble and danger?"

Thus I reply to you. I am well aware you did not make the world for the service of men. It were easier to believe that you made it expressly as a place of torment for them. But tell me: why am I here at all? Did I ask to come into the world? Or am I here[Pg 79] unnaturally, contrary to your will? If however, you yourself have placed me here, without giving me the power of acceptance or refusal of this gift of life, ought you not as far as possible to try and make me happy, or at least preserve me from the evils and dangers, which render my sojourn a painful one? And what I say of myself, I say of the whole human race, and of every living creature.

51

Nature. Thou forgettest that the life of the world is a perpetual cycle of production and destruction, so combined that the one works for the good of the other. By their joint operation the universe is preserved. If either ceased, the world would dissolve. Therefore, if suffering were removed from the earth, its own existence would be endangered.

Icelander. So say all the philosophers. But since that which is destroyed suffers, and that which is born from its destruction also suffers in due course, and finally is in its turn destroyed, would you enlighten me on one point, about which hitherto no philosopher has satisfied me? For whose pleasure and service is this wretched life of the world maintained, by the suffering and death of all the beings which compose it?

Whilst they discussed these and similar questions, two lions are said to have suddenly appeared. The beasts were so enfeebled and emaciated with hunger that they were scarcely able to devour the Icelander. They accomplished the feat however, and thus gained sufficient strength to live to the end of the day.

But certain people dispute this fact. They affirm that a violent wind having arisen, the unfortunate Icelander was blown to the ground, and soon overwhelmed beneath a magnificent mausoleum of sand. Here his corpse was remarkably preserved, and in process of time he was transformed into a fine mummy. Subsequently, some travellers discovered the body, and carried it off as a specimen, ultimately depositing it in one of the museums of Europe.

[1] Camoens' Lusiad, canto 5.

[2] Cicero says: "Labour and pain are not identical. Labour is a toil-some function of body or mind—pain an unpleasant disturbance in the body. When they cut Marius' veins, it was pain; when he marched at the head of the troops in a great heat, it was labour."— Tusc. Quæst.

[3] Seneca, Natural. Question: lib. 6, cap. 2.

[Pg 80]

PARINI ON GLORY.

Giuseppe Parini[1] was in our opinion one of the very few Italians who to literary excellence joined depth of thought, and acquaintance with contemporary philosophy. These latter attributes are now so essential to the cultivation of the belles lettres, that their absence would be inconceivable, did we not find an infinite number of Italian littérateurs of the present day, in whom they are wanting.

He was remarkable for his simplicity, his compassion for the unfortunate and his own country, his fidelity, high-mindedness, and the courage with which he bore the adversities of nature and fortune, which tormented him during the whole course of his miserable and lowly life. Death however drew him from obscurity.

He had several disciples, whom he taught, first of all, to gain experience of men and things, and then to amuse themselves with eloquence and poetry. Among his followers was a youth, lately come to him, of wonderful genius and industry, and of very great promise. To him one day Parini spoke as follows:

"You seek, my son, the only avenue to glory which is open to people who lead a private life, such glory as is sometimes the reward of wisdom, and literary and other studies. Now you are not unaware that this glory, though far from being despised, was by our greatest ancestors held in less esteem than that derivable from[Pg 81] other things.

52

Cicero, for instance, though a most ardent and successful follower of glory, frequently and emphatically makes apology for the time and labour he had spent in its pursuit. On one occasion he states that his literary and philosophical studies were secondary to his public life; on another, that being constrained by the wickedness of the age to abandon more important business, he hoped to spend his leisure profitably amid these studies. He invariably rated the glory of his writings at a lower value than that acquired from his consulship and his labours on behalf of the republic.

"Indeed, if human life be the principal subject of literature, and to rule our actions the first lesson of philosophy; there can be no doubt that action itself is as much more important and noble than thoughts and writing, as the end is nobler than the means, or as things and subjects in comparison with words and reasoning. For no man, however clever he be, is naturally created for study, nor born to write. Action alone is natural to him. And we see the majority of fine writers, and especially illustrious poets in the present age (Vittorio Alfieri, for instance), impelled to action in an extraordinary degree. Then, if by chance the deeds of these men prove unacceptable, either from the nature of the times or their own ill-fortune, they take up the pen and write grand things. Nor can people write who have neither the disposition nor power to act. From this you will easily understand why so few Italians gain immortal fame by their writings; it is that they are by nature unfit for noble actions. Antiquity, especially that of the early Greeks or Romans, is, I think, comparable to the design of the statue of Telesilla, who was a poetess, a warrior, and the saviour of her country. She is represented holding her helmet, at which she looks intently and longingly, as though she desired to place it on her head; at her feet lie some books almost disregarded,[Pg 82] as forming but an insignificant part of her glory.[2]

"But men of modern times are differently situated to the ancients. Glory is less open to them. They who make studies their vocation in life show the greatest possible magnanimity; nor need they, like Cicero, apologise to their country for the profession they have chosen. I therefore applaud the nobility of your decision. But since a life of letters, being unnatural, cannot be lived without injury to the body, nor without increasing in many ways the natural infelicity of your mind, I regard it as my duty to explain to you the various difficulties attendant on the pursuit of that glory towards which you aspire, and the results that will follow success should you attain it. You will then be able to estimate, on the one hand, the importance and value of the goal, and your chance of reaching it; and, on the other, the sufferings, exertions, and discomforts inseparable from the pursuit. Thus, you may be better able to decide whether it be expedient to continue as you have begun, or to seek glory by some other road."

[1] Parini lived 1729-1799. As a philosopher and satirist he seems to have exercised no slight influence over the mind of Leopardi.

[2] Pausanias, lib. 2, cap. 20.

CHAPTER II.

"I might first of all say a great deal about the rivalries, envy, bitter censures, libels, injustices, schemes and plots against your character, both in public and private, and the many other difficulties which the wickedness of men will induce them to oppose to you in the path you have chosen. These obstacles, always very hard to overcome and often insuperable, exercise a further influence. It is owing to them that more than one author, not only in life, but even when dead, is robbed of the honour that is due to him. Such an one, not having been famous when alive, because of the hatred or[Pg 83] envy with which he was regarded by others, when dead remains in obscurity, because he is forgotten; for it rarely happens that a man obtains glory after he has ceased writing, when there is no one to excite an interest in him.

"I do not intend to refer to the hindrances which arise from matters personal to the writer, and other more trivial things. Yet it is often owing to these latter that writings worthy of the highest praise, and the fruit of infinite exertions, are for ever excluded from fame, or having been before the world for a short time, fall into oblivion, and disappear entirely from the memory of men. For the same causes other writings, either inferior to or no better than these, become highly honoured. I will merely expose to you the difficulties and troubles which, apart from the malice of men, will stubbornly contest the prize of glory. These embarrassments are of ordinary, not exceptional occurrence, and have been experienced by most great writers.

"You are aware that no one can be called a great writer, nor obtains true and lasting glory, except by means of excellent and perfect works, or such as approach perfection. The following very true utterance of Castiglione is worthy of being engraved on your mind:—It is very seldom that a person unaccustomed to write, however learned he be, can adequately recognise the skill and industry of writers; or appreciate the delicacy and excellence of styles, and those subtle and hidden significations which abound in the writings of the ancients.'

"In the first place, consider how very few people practise or learn the art of composition; and think from how small a number of men, whether in the present or the future, you can in any case look for the magnificent estimation which you hope will be the reward of your life. Consider, too, how much influence style has in securing appreciation for writings. On this, and their degree of perfection, depends the subsequent fate of all[Pg 84] works that come under the heading of 'light literature,' So great is the influence of style, that a book presumably celebrated for its matter often proves valueless when deprived of its manner. Now, language is so interwoven with style that the one can hardly be considered apart from the other. Men frequently confuse the two together, and are often unable to express the distinction between them, if even they are aware of it in the first place. And as for the thousand merits and defects of language and style, with difficulty, if at all, can they be discerned and assigned to their respective properties. But it is certain, to quote the words of Castiglione, that no foreigner is 'accustomed to write' with elegance in your language. It follows therefore that style, which is so great and important a necessity in composition, and a thing of such unaccountable difficulty and labour, both in acquirement and usage, can only properly be judged and appreciated by the persons who in one single nation are accustomed to write. For all other people the boundless exertions attached to the formation of style will be almost useless, and as if entirely wasted. I will not refer to the infinite diversities of opinion, and the various tendencies of readers; owing to which the number of persons adapted to perceive the good qualities of this or that book is still more reduced.

"You must regard it as an undoubted fact that, in order to distinctly recognise the value of a perfect or nearly perfect work, deserving of immortality, it is not enough merely to be accustomed to write. You yourself must be able to accomplish the work in question almost as perfectly as the writer himself. And as experience gradually teaches you what qualities constitute a perfect writer, and what an infinity of difficulties must be surmounted before these can be obtained, you will learn how to overcome the latter, and acquire the former; so that in time knowledge and power will prove to be one and the same thing. Hence a man cannot[Pg 85] discern nor fully appreciate the excellence of perfect writers until he is able to give expression to it in his own writings; because such perfection can only be appreciated by what may be termed a transference of it into oneself. Until this be done, a man cannot really understand what constitutes perfection in writing, and will therefore be unable to duly admire the best writers.

"Now most literary men, because they write easily, think they write well; they therefore regard good writing as a facile accomplishment, even though they assert the contrary. Think, then, how the number will be reduced of those who might appreciate and laud you when, after inconceivable exertions and care, you succeed in producing a noble and perfect work. In the present day there are scarcely two or three men in Italy who have acquired the art of perfect writing; and although this number may appear to you excessively small, at no time nor place has it ever been much greater.

"I often wonder to myself how Virgil, as a supreme example of literary perfection, ever acquired the high reputation in which he is now held. For I am certain that most of his readers and eulogisers do not discover in his poems more than one beauty for every ten or twenty revealed to me by continuous study and meditation. Not that I imagine I have succeeded in estimating him at his proper value, nor have derived every possible enjoyment from his writings. In truth, the esteem and admiration professed for the greatest writers is ordinarily the result of a blind predisposition in their favour, rather than the outcome of an impartial judgment, or the consequence of a due appreciation of their merits.

"When I was young I remember first reading Virgil, being on the one hand unbiassed in my judgment, and careless of the opinion of others (a very rare thing, by the by); and, on the other hand, as ignorant as most boys of my age, though perhaps not more so than is the unchanging condition of many readers. I refused to[Pg 86] admit that Virgil's reputation was merited, since I failed to discover in him much more than is to be found in very ordinary poets. Indeed, it surprises me that Virgil's fame should excel that of Lucan. For we see the mass of readers, at all times, equally when the literature of the day is of a debasing or an elevating tendency, much prefer gross and unmistakable beauties to those that are delicate and half-concealed. They also prefer fervour to modesty; often indeed even the apparent to the real; and usually mediocrity to perfection.

"In reading the letters of a certain prince, exceptionally intelligent, whose writing was remarkable for its wit, pleasantry, smoothness, and acuteness, I clearly discerned that in his heart he preferred the Henriad to the Æneid; although the fear of shocking men's sensibilities might deter him from confessing such a preference.

"I am astonished that the judgment of a few, correct though it be, should have succeeded in controlling that of numbers, and should have established the custom of an esteem no less blind than just. This, however, does not always occur, and I imagine that the fame gained by the best writers is rather a matter of chance than merit. My opinion may be confirmed by what I say as we proceed."

CHAPTER III.

"We have seen how very few people will be able to appreciate you when you succeed in becoming a perfect writer. Now, I wish to indicate some of the hindrances that will prevent even these few from rightly estimating your worth, although they see the signs of it.

"In the first place, there can be no doubt that all writings of eloquence or poetry are judged, not so much on their merits, as by the effect they produce in the mind of the reader. So that the reader may be said[Pg 87] to consider them rather in himself than in themselves. Consequently men who are naturally devoid of imagination and enthusiasm, though gifted with much intelligence, discernment, and no little learning, are almost quite incapable of forming a correct judgment of fanciful writings. They cannot in the least immerse their minds in the mind of the writer, and usually have within themselves a feeling of contempt for his compositions, because unable to discover in what their so great fame consists. Such reading awakens no emotion within them, nor does it arouse their imagination, or create in them any especial sensation of pleasure. And even people who are naturally disposed and inclined to receive the impression of whatever image or fancy a writer has properly signified, very often experience a feeling of coldness, indifference, languor, or dulness; so that for the time they resemble the persons just mentioned. This change is due to divers causes, internal and external, physical and mental, and is either temporary or lasting. At such times no one, even though himself an excellent writer, is a good judge of writings intended to excite the affections or the imagination. Again, there is the danger of satiety due to previous reading of similar writings. Certain passions too, of more or less strength, from time to time invest the mind, leaving no room for the emotions which ought to be excited by the reading. And it often happens that places; spectacles, natural or artificial, music; and a hundred such things, which would ordinarily excite us, are now incapable of arousing or delighting us in the least, although no less attractive than formerly.

"But, though a man, for one or other of these reasons, may be ill disposed to appreciate the effects of eloquence or poetry, he does not for that reason defer judgment of books on both these subjects which he then happens to read for the first time. I myself sometimes take up Homer, Cicero, or Petrarch, and read without feeling the least emotion. Yet, as I am quite aware of the merits of[Pg 88] these writers, both because of their reputation, and my own frequent appreciation of their charms, I do not for a moment think them undeservedly praised simply because I am at present too dull to do them justice. But it is different with books read for the first time, which are too new to have acquired a reputation. There is nothing in such cases to prevent the reader forming a low opinion of the author and the merits of his book, if his mind be indisposed to do justice to the sentiments and imagery contained in the work. Nor would it be easy to induce him to alter his judgment by subsequent study of the same book under better auspices; for probably the disgust inspired by his first reading will deter him from a second; and in any case the strength of first impressions will be almost invincible.

"On the other hand, the mind is sometimes, for one reason or another, in such a state of sensibility, vivacity, vigour, and fervour, that it follows even the least suggestion of the reading; it feels keenly the slightest touch, and as it reads is able to create within itself a thousand emotions and fancies, sometimes losing itself in a sort of sweet delirium, when it is almost transported out of itself. As a natural result of this, the mind, reviewing the pleasures enjoyed in the reading, and not distinguishing between its own predisposition and the actual merits of the book, experiences a feeling of so great admiration, and forms so high a conception of it, as even to rank the book above others of much greater merit, read under less felicitous circumstances. See therefore to what uncertainty is subject even the truth and justice of opinions from the same persons, as to the writings and genius of others, quite apart from any sentiment of malice or favour. So great is this uncertainty that a man varies considerably in his estimation of works of equal value, and even the same work, at different times of life, under different circumstances, and even at different hours of the day."

[Pg 89]
CHAPTER IV.

"Perhaps you may think that these difficulties, due to mental indisposition on the part of readers, are of rare occurrence. Consider, then, how frequently a man, as he grows old, becomes incapable of appreciating the charms of eloquence and poetry, no less than those of the other imitative arts, and everything beautiful in the world. This intellectual decay is a necessity of our nature. In the present day it is so much greater than formerly, begins so much earlier, and progresses so much more rapidly, especially in the studious, as our experience is enlarged in more or less degree by the knowledge begotten of the speculations of so many past centuries. For which reason, and owing to the present condition of civilised life, the phantoms of childhood soon vanish from the imagination of men; with them go the hopes of the mind, and with the hopes most of the desires, passions, and energy of life and its faculties. Whence I often wonder that men of mature age, especially the learned and those inclined to meditate about human affairs, should yet be subject to the influence of poetry and eloquence, which are, however, unable to produce any real effect on them.

"It may be regarded as a fact that, in order to be greatly moved by imagination of the grand and beautiful, one must believe that there is something really grand and beautiful in human life, and that poetry is not mere fable. The young always believe such things, even when they know their fallacy, until personal experience forces them to accept the truth. But it is difficult to put faith in them after the sad discipline of practical life; especially when experience is combined with habits of study and speculation.

"From this it would seem that the young are generally better judges of writings intended to arouse the affections[Pg 90] and the imagination, than men of mature and advanced age. But, on the other hand, the young are novices in literature. They exact from books a superhuman, boundless, and impossible pleasure, and where they fail to experience this they despise the writer. Illiterate people have the same idea of the functions of literature. And youths addicted to reading prefer, both in their own writings and those of others, extravagance to moderation, magnificence or attractiveness of style and ornamentation, to the simple and natural, and sham beauties to real ones. This is partly due to their limited experience, and partly to the impetuosity of their time of life. Consequently, although the young are doubtless more inclined than their elders to applaud what seems good to them, since they are more truthful and candid, they are seldom capable of appreciating the excellences of literary works. As we grow older, the influence exercised over us by art increases, as that of nature diminishes. Nevertheless both nature and art are necessary to produce effect.

"Dwellers in large towns are compelled to sacrifice the beautiful to the useful. Even though of warm and sensitive natures and lively imagination, they cannot experience as an effect of the charms either of nature or literature any tender or noble sentiment, any sublime or delightful fancy; unless indeed, like you, they spend most of their time in solitude. Eor few things are so opposed to the state of mind necessary to appreciate such delights, as the conversation of these men, the riot of these places, and the sight of the tinselled splendour, the falseness, the miserable troubles, and still more miserable idleness which abound there. I also think that the littérateurs of large towns are, as a rule, less qualified to judge books than those of small towns; because, like everything else, the literature of large towns is ordinarily false and pretentious, or superficial.

"And whereas the ancients used to regard literature[Pg 91] and the sciences as a pleasing change from more serious business, in the present day the majority of men who in large towns profess to be students regard literature and writing as merely an agreeable variation of their other amusements.

"I think that works of art, whether painting, sculpture, or architecture, would be much more appreciated if they were disseminated throughout a country in different-sized towns, instead of being, as at present, accumulated in the chief cities. For in the latter places men are so full of thoughts, so occupied with pleasurable pursuits and vain and frivolous excitements, that they are very rarely capable of the profound pleasures of the intellect. Besides, a multitude of fine things gathered together have a distracting influence; the mind bestows but little attention on individual things, and is sensible of no especial gratification; or else it becomes satiated, and regards them all as indifferently as though they were objects of the commonest kind.

"I say the same of music, which is nowhere so elaborate, or brought to such perfection, as in large towns, where men have less appreciation for the wonderful emotions of the art, and are indeed less musical than elsewhere.

"Nevertheless, large towns are a useful home for the fostering and perfecting of the arts; although their inhabitants are less under the influence of their charms than the people of other places. It may be said that artists, who work in solitude and silence, strive laboriously and industriously to please men, who, because accustomed to the bustle and noise of cities, are almost totally incapable of appreciating the fruit of their exertions.

"The fate of writers may in a measure be compared to that of artists."

[Pg 92]

CHAPTER V.

"We will now return to the consideration of authors.

"It is a characteristic of writings approaching perfection that they usually please more when read a second time, than they pleased at first. The contrary effect is produced by many books written carefully and skilfully, but which really possess few merits. These when read a second time are less esteemed than at first. But both kinds of books, when read only once, often deceive even the learned and experienced, so that indifferent books are preferred to excellent ones. In the present day, however, even students by profession can rarely be induced to read new books a second time, especially such as come under the heading of light literature. This was not so in olden times, because then but few books were in existence. Now, it is very different. We possess the literary bequests of all past times. Every nation has its literature, and produces its host of books daily. There are writings in all languages, ancient and modern, relating to every branch of science and learning, and so closely connected and allied that the student must study them all as far as possible. You may therefore easily imagine that a book does not obtain full consideration on a first reading, and that a second reading is out of the question. Yet the first opinion that we form of a new book is seldom changed.

"For the same reasons, even in the first reading of books, especially those of light literature, very rarely sufficient attention and study is given to discover the laborious perfection, the subtle art, and the hidden and unpretentious virtues of the writings. Thus, in the present day the condition of excellent books is really worse than that of indifferent ones. For the charms and qualifications of most of the latter, whether true or false, are so exposed to the eye, that, however trivial they may[Pg 93] be, they are easily discernible at first sight. We may therefore say with truth, that the exertion necessary to produce perfect writing is almost useless for fame. But, on the other hand, books composed, like most modern ones, rapidly and without any great degree of excellence, though perhaps celebrated for a time, cannot fail to be soon forgotten. And many works of recognised value are also lost in the immense stream of new books which pours forth daily, before they have had time to establish their celebrity. They perish for no intrinsic fault of their own, and give place to other books, good and bad, which each in turn live their short spell of life. So that whereas the ancients could acquire glory in a thousand ways, we can only attain it by one single avenue, after much more exertion than formerly.

"The books of the ancients alone survive this universal shipwreck of all later writings. Their fame is established and confirmed; they are diligently and repeatedly read, and are made the subject of careful study. And it is noteworthy that a modern book, if intrinsically equal to any of the ancient writings, would rarely, if ever, give its readers as much pleasure as the ancient work. This for two reasons. In the first place, it would not be read with the care and attention that we bestow on celebrated writings; very few people would read it twice; and no one would study it (for none but scientific books are studied until made venerable by age). In the second place, the world-wide and permanent reputation of writings, whether or not due to their internal excellence, adds to their value, and proportionately increases the pleasure they give; often, indeed, most of the charm of such literature is simply due to its celebrity.

"This reminds me of some remarkable words of Montesquieu about the origin of human pleasures. He says: 'The mind often creates within itself many sources of pleasure, which are intimately dependent on each other. Thus, a thing that has once pleased us,[Pg 94] pleases us again simply because it did so before; we couple together imagination of the present and remembrance of the past. For example, an actress who pleased us on the stage, will probably please us in private life: her voice; her manner; the recollection of the applause she excited; perhaps, too, her rôle of princess joined to her real character,—all combine and form a mixture of influences producing a general feeling of pleasure. Our minds are always full of ideas subordinate to one or more primary ideas. A woman famous for one cause or another, and possessed of some slight inherent defect, is often able to attract by means of this very defect. And women are ordinarily loved less because they inspire affection than because they are well born, rich, or highly esteemed by others.'[1]....

"Often indeed a woman's reputation for beauty and grace, whether well or ill founded, or even the mere fact that others have been under the influence of her charms, suffices to inspire a man with affection for her. And who does not know that most pleasures are due to the imagination rather than to the inherent qualities of the things that please us?

"These remarks refer to writings no less than to all other things. Indeed I will venture to say that were a poem to be published equal or superior to the Iliad, and carefully read by an excellent judge of poetry, it would give less satisfaction and appear less charming than the Greek masterpiece, much less would its fame be comparable with that of the Iliad; for its real merits would not be aided by twenty-seven centuries of admiration, nor the thousand reminiscences and other associations that connect themselves with Homer's poem. Similarly I affirm that if any one were to read carefully either the 'Jerusalem' or the 'Furioso,' without knowing anything of their celebrity, he would be much less pleased than others who were aware of their fame.

[Pg 95]

"In short, it may be accepted as a general rule that the first readers of every remarkable work which in after ages becomes famous, and the contemporaries of the writer, derive less enjoyment from such reading than all other people.

"This fact cannot but be very disadvantageous to the interest of writers."

[1] Ex: Fragment Sur le goût, &c.

CHAPTER VI.

"Such are a few of the obstacles that may prevent you from acquiring glory from the studious, or even from those who excel in knowledge and the art of writing.

"Now there are many people who, though educated sufficiently for the purposes of daily life, are neither writers nor students to any very great extent. They read simply for amusement, and, as you know, are only capable of appreciating certain qualities in literature. The chief reason of this has been already partly explained. There is, however, another cause. It is that they only seek momentary pleasure in what they read. But the present in itself is trivial and joyless to all men. Even the sweetest things, as says Homer,

'Love, sleep, song, and the dance,'

soon weary us, if to the present there be not joined the hope of some pleasure or future satisfaction, dependent on them. For it is contrary to human nature to be greatly pleased with that of which hope does not form a constituent part. And so great is the power of hope that it enlivens and sweetens many exertions, painful and laborious in themselves; whereas, on the other hand, things innately charming, when unaccompanied by hope, are scarce sufficiently attractive to be welcomed. "We see studious people never tired of reading, often even of the driest kind; and they experience a constant delight in their studies, carried on perhaps throughout the greater part of the day. The reason of this is that they have[Pg 96] the future ever before their eyes; they hope in some way, and at some time, to reap the benefit of their labours. Such people always have their interests at heart. They do not take up a book, either to pass time or for amusement, without also distilling from it more or less definite instruction. Others, on the contrary, who seek to learn nothing from books, are satisfied when they have read their first few pages, or those that have the most attractive appearance. They wander wearily from book to book, and marvel to themselves how any one can find prolonged pleasure in prolonged reading.

"It is clear that any skill or industry displayed by the writer is almost entirely wasted on such people, who nevertheless compose the mass of readers. And even men of studious inclinations, having later in life changed the nature of their studies, almost feel a repugnance for books which would formerly have given them intense delight; and though still able to discern their value, are wearied rather than pleased by their merits, because instruction is not at all what they desire."

CHAPTER VII.

"Hitherto we have considered writings in general, and certain things relating to light literature in particular, towards which I see you are more especially attracted. Let us now turn to philosophy, though it must not be supposed that this science is separable from the study of letters.

"Perhaps you will think that because philosophy is derived from reason, which among civilised people is usually a stronger power than the imagination or the affections, the value of philosophical works ought to be more universally recognised than that of poems, and other writings which treat of the pleasurable and the beautiful. It is, however, my opinion that poetry is[Pg 97] better understood and appreciated than philosophy. In the first place, it is certain that a subtle intelligence and great power of reasoning are not sufficient to ensure much progress in philosophy. Considerable imaginative power is also requisite. Indeed, judged from the nature of their intellects, Descartes, Galileo, Leibnitz, Newton, and Vico would have made excellent poets; and, on the other hand, Homer, Dante, and Shakespeare might have been great philosophers. This subject would require much elaboration; I will therefore merely affirm that none but philosophers can perfectly appreciate the value and realise the charm of philosophical books. Of course, I refer to their substance, and not to whatever superficial merit they may have, whether of language, style, or anything else. And, just as men are by nature unpoetical, and consequently rarely catch the spirit of a poem or discern its imagery, although they may follow the meaning of its words; similarly, people unaccustomed to meditate and philosophise within themselves, or who are incapable of deep sustained thought, cannot comprehend the truths that a philosopher expounds, however clear and logical his deductions, arguments, and conclusions may be, although they understand the words that he uses and their signification. Because, being unable or unused to analyse the essence of things by means of thought, or to separate their own ideas into divisions, or to join and bind together a number of these ideas, or simultaneously to grasp with the mind many particulars so as to deduce a single general rule from them, or to follow unweariedly with the mind's eye a long series of truths mutually connected, or to discover the subtle and hidden connection between each truth and a hundred others; they can with difficulty, if at all, grasp and follow his working, or experience the impressions proved by the philosopher. Therefore, they can neither understand nor estimate rightly all the influences that led him to this or that opinion, and made him affirm or deny[Pg 98] this or that thing, and doubt such and such another. Possibly they may understand his ideas, but they neither recognise their truth nor probability; because they are unable to test either the one or the other. They are like those cold and passionless men who are incapable of appreciating the fancies and imagery of the poets. And you know it is common to the poet and the philosopher to penetrate into the depths of the minds of men, and thence to bring into light all their hidden emotions, profundities, and secret working, with their respective causes and effects; thus, men who are incapable of sympathy with the poet and his thoughts, are also incapable of entering into the thoughts of the philosopher.

"This is why we see daily many meritorious works, clear and intelligible to all, interpreted by some people as containing a thousand undoubted truths, and, by others, a thousand patent errors. They are attacked in public and private, not only from motives of malice, interest, and other similar causes, but also because of the incapacity of the readers, and their inability to comprehend the certainty of the principles, the correctness of the deductions and conclusions, and the general fitness, sufficiency, and truth of the reasoning put forward. It often happens that philosophical writings of the most sublime nature are accused of obscurity, not necessarily because they are obscure, but either because their vein of thought is of too profound or novel a nature to be easily intelligible, or because the reader himself is too dense to be a competent judge of such works. Think, then, how difficult it must be to gain praise for philosophical writings, however meritorious they may be. For there can be no doubt that the number of really profound philosophers, who alone can appreciate one another, is in the present day very small, although philosophy is more cultivated than in past times.

"I will not refer to the various sects into which those who profess philosophy are divided. Each sect[Pg 99] ordinarily refuses to allow that there is aught estimable in the others; this is not only from unwillingness, but also because it occupies itself with different principles of philosophy."

CHAPTER VIII.

"If, as the result of your learning and meditation, you chanced to discover some important truth, not only formerly unknown, but quite unlooked for, and even antagonistic to the opinions of the day, you must not anticipate in your lifetime any peculiar commendation for this discovery. You will gain no esteem, even from the wise (except perhaps from a very few), until by frequent and varied reiteration of these truths the ears of men have become accustomed to their sound; then only, after a long time, the intellect begins to receive them.

"For no truth contrary to current opinion, even though demonstrable with almost geometrical certitude, can ever, unless capable of material proof, be suddenly established. Time, custom, and example alone are able to give it a solid foundation. Men accustom themselves to belief, as to everything else; indeed they generally believe from habit, and not from any sentiment of conviction within their minds. At length it happens that the once-questioned truth is taught to children, and is universally accepted. People are then astonished that it was ever unknown to them, and they ridicule their ancestors and contemporaries for the ignorance and obstinacy they manifested in opposing it. The greater and more important the new truths, so much the greater will be the difficulty of procuring acceptance for them; since they will overthrow a proportionately large number of opinions hitherto rooted in the minds of men. For even acute and practised intellects do not easily enter into the spirit of reasonings which demonstrate new truths that exceed the limits of their own knowledge; especially when[Pg 100] these are opposed to beliefs long established within them. Descartes, in his geometrical discoveries, was understood by but very few of his contemporaries. It was the same with Newton. Indeed, the condition of men pre-eminent in knowledge is somewhat similar to that of literary men, and 'savants' who live in places innocent of learning. The latter are not deservedly esteemed by their neighbours; the former fail to be duly appreciated by their contemporaries. Both are often despised for their difference in manner of life and opinions from other men, who neither do justice to their ability nor to the writings they put forth in proof of it.

"There is no doubt that the human race makes continual progress in knowledge. As a body, its march is slow and measured; but it includes certain great and remarkable minds which, having devoted themselves to speculation about the sensible or intelligible phenomena of the universe, and the pursuit of truths, travel, nay sometimes flash, to their conclusions in an immeasurably short space of time. And the rapid progress of these intellects stimulates other men, who hasten their foot-steps so as to reach, later on, the place where these superior beings rested. But not until the lapse of a century or more do they attain to the knowledge possessed by an extraordinary intellect of this kind.

"It is ordinarily believed that human knowledge owes most of its progress to these supreme intellects, which arise from time to time, like miracles of nature.[1] I, on the contrary, think that it owes more to men of common powers than to those who are exceptionally endowed. Suppose a case, in which one of the latter, having rivalled his contemporaries in knowledge, advances independently, and takes a lead of, say ten paces. Most other men, far[Pg 101] from feeling disposed to follow him, regard his progress in silence, or else ridicule it. Meanwhile, a number of moderately clever men, partly aided perhaps by the ideas and discoveries of the genius, but principally through their own endeavours, conjointly advance one step. The masses unhesitatingly follow them, being attracted by the not inordinate novelty, and also by the number of those who are its authors. In process of time, thanks to the exertions of these men, the tenth step is accomplished; and thus the opinions of the genius are universally received throughout the civilised world. But their originator, dead long ago, only acquires a late and unseasonable reputation. This is due partly to the fact that he is forgotten, or to the low esteem in which he was held when living; added to which men are conscious that they do not owe their knowledge to him, and that they are already his equals in erudition, and will soon surpass him, if they have not done so already. They are also his superiors, in that time has enabled them to demonstrate and affirm truths that he only imagined, to prove his conjectures, and give better form and order to his inventions, almost, as it were, maturing them. Perchance, after a time, some student engaged in historical research may justly appraise the influence of this genius, and may announce him to his countrymen with great éclat; but the fame that may ensue from this will soon give way to renewed oblivion.

"The progress of human knowledge, like a falling weight, increases momentarily in its speed; none the less very rarely men of a generation change their beliefs or recognise their errors, so as to believe at one time the opposite of what they previously believed. Each generation prepares the way for its successor to know and believe many things contrary to its own knowledge and belief. But most men are as little conscious of the increasing development of their knowledge, and the inevitable mutation of their beliefs, as they are sensible of the[Pg 102] perpetual motion of the earth. And a man never alters his opinions so as to be conscious of the alteration. But were he suddenly to embrace an opinion totally discordant with his old beliefs, he could not fail to perceive the change. It may therefore be said, that ordinarily no truths, except such as are determinable by the senses, will be believed by the contemporaries of their discoverer."

[1] It is in the order of Providence that the inventive, generative, constitutive mind should come first; and then that the patient and collective mind should follow, and elaborate the pregnant queries and illumining guesses of the former,—S. T. Coleridge, Table Talk, Oct. 8, 1830.

CHAPTER IX.

"Now let us suppose that every difficulty be overcome, and that aided by fortune you have actually in your lifetime acquired not only celebrity, but glory. What will be the fruit of this? In the first place, men will wish to see you, and make your acquaintance; they will indicate you as a distinguished man, and will honour you in every possible way. Such are the best results of literary glory. It would seem more natural to look for such demonstrations in small than in large towns; for these latter are subject to the distracting influence of wealth and power, and all the arts which serve to amuse and enliven the inactive hours of men's lives. But because small towns are ordinarily wanting in things necessary to stimulate literary excellence, they are rarely the abode of men devoted to literature and study. The people of such places esteem learning and wisdom, and even the fame men seek by these means, at a very low value; neither the one nor the other are objects of envy to them. And if a man who is a distinguished scholar take up his residence in a small town, his notability is of no advantage to him. Rather the contrary. For though his fame would secure him high honour in towns not far distant, he is there regarded as the most forlorn and obscure individual in the place. Just as a man who possessed nothing but an abundance of silver and gold would be even poorer than other men in a place where these[Pg 103] metals were valueless; similarly a wise and studious man who makes his abode in a place where learning and genius are unknown, far from being considered superior to other men, will be despised and scornfully treated unless he happen to have some more material possessions. Yet such a man is often given credit for possessing much greater knowledge than he really has, though this reputation does not procure him any especial honour from these people.

"When I was a young man, I used occasionally to return to Bosisio, my native place. Every one there knew that I spent my time in study and writing. The peasants gave me credit for being poet, philosopher, doctor, mathematician, lawyer, theologian, and sufficiently a linguist to know all the languages in the world. They used to question me indiscriminately on any subject, or about any trifle that chanced to enter their minds. Yet they did not hold me in much esteem, and thought me less instructed than the learned people of all other places. But whenever I gave them reason to think my learning was not as extensive as they supposed, I fell vastly in their estimation, and in the end they used to persuade themselves that after all my knowledge was no greater than theirs.

"We have already noticed the difficulties to be overcome in large towns before glory can be acquired, or the fruit of it enjoyed. I will now add that although no fame is more difficult to merit than that of being an excellent poet, writer, or philosopher, nothing is less lucrative to the possessor. You know that the misery and poverty of the greatest poets, both in ancient and modern times, is proverbial. Homer, like his poetry, is involved in mystery; his country, life, and history are an impenetrable secret to men. But, amid this uncertainty and ignorance, there is an unshaken tradition that Homer was poor and unhappy. It is as if time wished to bear witness that the fate of other noble poets was shared by the prince of poetry.

[Pg 104]

"But, passing over the other benefits of glory, we will simply consider what is called honour. No part of fame is usually less honourable and more useless than this. It may be that so many people obtain it undeservedly, or even because of the extreme difficulty of meriting it at all; certain it is that such reputation is scarce esteemed, if regarded as trustworthy. Or perhaps it is due to the fact that most clever half-cultured men imagine they either are, or could easily become, as proficient in literature and philosophy as those who are successful in these studies, and whom they accordingly treat as on an intellectual equality. Possibly both causes combine in their influence. It is certain, however, that the man who is an ordinary mathematician, natural philosopher, philologist, antiquary, artist, sculptor, musician, or who has only a moderate acquaintance with a single ancient or foreign language, is usually more respected, even in large towns, than a really remarkable philosopher, poet, or writer. Consequently, poetry and philosophy, the noblest, grandest, and most arduous of things pertaining to humanity, and the supreme efforts of art and science, are in the present day the most neglected faculties in the world, even in their professed followers. Manual arts rank higher than these noble things; for no one would pretend to a knowledge of them unless he really possessed it, nor could this knowledge be acquired without study and exertion. In short, the poet and the philosopher derive no benefit in life from their genius and studies, except perhaps the glory rendered to them by a very few people. Poetry and philosophy resemble each other in that they are both as unproductive and barren of esteem and honour, as of all other advantages."

CHAPTER X.

"From men you will scarcely derive any advantage whatever from your glory. You will therefore look within[Pg 105] you for consolation, and in your solitude will nerve yourself for fresh exertions, and lay the foundation of new hopes. For like all other human benefits, literary glory is more pleasing in anticipation than in reality, if indeed it can ever be said to be realised. You will therefore at length console yourself with the thought of that last hope and refuge of noble minds, posterity. Even Cicero, richly renowned as he was in life, turned his mind yearningly towards the future, in saying: 'Thinkest thou I should have undertaken so many labours, during day and night, in peace and war, had I imagined my glory was limited to this life? Far better were a life of idleness and peace, devoid of cares and fatigue. No. My soul, in some inexplicable way, used ever to fix its hopes on posterity, and looked for the dawn of its true life from the hour of death.'[1] Cicero here refers to the idea of immortality innate in the minds of men. But the true explanation lies in the fact that all earthly benefits are no sooner acquired than their insignificance becomes apparent; they are unworthy of the fatigues they have cost. Glory is, above all, an example of this; it is a dear purchase, and of little use to the purchaser. But, as Simonides says, I Sweet hope cheers us with its phantom beauties, and with its vain prospect stimulates us to work. Some men await the friendly dawn, others the advance of age, and others more auspicious seasons. Every mortal cherishes within him hopes of coming good from Pluto and the other gods,' Thus, as we experience the vanity of glory, hope, driven and hunted from place to place, finding at length no spot in the whole of life whereon to rest, passes beyond the grave and alights on posterity. For man ever turns instinctively from the present to the future, about which he hopes much in proportion as he knows little. Hence, they who are desirous of glory in life, chiefly nourish themselves on that which they hope to[Pg 106] gain after death. For the lack of enjoyment in the present, man consoles himself with hopes of future happiness, as vain as that of the present."

[1] De Senectute.

CHAPTER XI.

"But what, after all, is this appeal that we make to posterity? The human imagination is such that it forms a more exalted conception of posterity than of the men of past or present times, simply because we are totally ignorant of the people who are yet to be. But, reasonably, and not imaginatively, do we really think our successors will be better than ourselves? I am of a contrary opinion, and for my part put faith in the proverb that says 'the world grows worse as it ages,' It were better for men of genius if they could appeal to their wise ancestors, who, according to Cicero, were not inferior in point of numbers, and far superior in excellence to their successors. But, though such appeal would be sure of a truer judgment, it is certain that the greatest men of our day would be held in little esteem by the ancients.

"It may be allowed that the men of the future, being free from any spirit of rivalry, envy, love, or hatred, not indeed amongst themselves, but towards us, ought to be better qualified than ourselves to pass impartial judgment on our writings. For other reasons, too, they may be better judges. Posterity will perhaps have fewer excellent writers, noble poets, and subtle philosophers. In which case the few followers of these sublime influences will honour us the more. It is also probable that their control over the minds of the people will be still less than that exercised by us. Again, will the affections, imagination, and intellect of men be, as a rule, more powerful than they are at present? If not, we shall gain by the comparison.

"Literature is peculiarly exposed to the influence of[Pg 107] custom. In times of debased literature, we see how firmly this or that barbarism is retained and upheld, as though it alone were reasonable and natural. At such times the best and greatest writers are forgotten or ridiculed. Where, then, is the certainty that posterity will always esteem the kind of writing that we praise? Besides, it is a question whether or not we ourselves esteem what is really praiseworthy. For men have different opinions about what constitutes good writing, and these vary according to the times, the nature of places and people, customs, usages, and individuals. Yet it is to this variety and variability of influences that the glory of writers is subjected.

"Philosophy is even more diverse and changeable than other sciences.[1] At first sight the contrary of this would seem to be true; for whereas the 'belles lettres' are concerned with the study of the beautiful, which is chiefly a matter of custom and opinion, sciences seek the truth, which is fixed and unchangeable. But this truth is hid from mortals, though, as centuries go by, some little of it is revealed. Consequently, on the one hand, in their endeavours to discover it, and their conjectures as to its nature, men are led to embrace this or that resemblance of truth; thereupon opinions and sects multiply. And, on the other hand, it is due to the ever-increasing number of fresh discoveries, and new aspects of truth obtained daily, that even these divisions become subdivided; and opinions which at one time were regarded almost as certainties change shape and substance momentarily. It is owing to the changeability of sciences and philosophy[Pg 108] that they are so unproductive of glory, either at the hands of contemporaries or posterity. For when new discoveries, or new ideas and conjectures, greatly alter the condition of this or that science from its present state, how will the writings and thoughts of men now celebrated in these sciences be regarded? Who, for instance, now reads Galileo's works? Yet in his time they were most wonderful; nor could better and nobler books, full of greater discoveries and grander conceptions, be then written on such subjects. But now every tyro in physics or mathematics surpasses Galileo in his knowledge. Again, how many people in the present day read the writings of Francis Bacon? Who troubles himself about Malebranche? And how much time will soon be bestowed on the works of Locke, if the science almost founded by him progresses in future as rapidly as it gives promise of doing?

"Truly the very intellectual force, industry, and labour, which philosophers and scientists expend in the pursuit of their glory, are in time the cause of its extinction or obscurément. For by their own great exertions they open out a path for the still further advancement of the science, which in time progresses so rapidly that their writings and names fall gradually into oblivion. And it is certainly difficult for most men to esteem others for a knowledge greatly inferior to their own. Who can doubt that the twentieth century will discover error in what the wisest of us regard as unquestionable truths, and will surpass us greatly in their knowledge of the truth?"

[1] Compare the following from H. Rogers' Essay on Leibnitz: "The condition of great philosophers is far less enviable than that of great poets. The former can never possess so large a circle of readers under any circumstances; but that number is still further abridged by the fact that even the truths the philosopher has taught or discovered form but stepping-stones in the progress of science, and are afterwards digested, systematised, and better expounded in other works composed by inferior men."

CHAPTER XII.

"Finally, you would perhaps like to know my opinion, and decided advice to you, about your intended profession. The question is one as to the advisability of your pursuing or abandoning this path to glory, a thing so poor in[Pg 109] usefulness, and so hard and uncertain both to secure and retain, that it may be compared to a shadow which you can neither feel when you hold, nor yet keep from fleeing away. I will tell you then briefly my true opinion. I consider your wonderful genius, noble disposition, and prolific imagination to be the most fatal and lamentable qualities distributed by Fortune to humanity. But since you possess them, you will scarcely be able to avoid their harmful influence. In the present day there is but one possible benefit to be gained from such endowments as yours; viz., the glory that sometimes rewards industry in literature and study. You know those miserable men, who having accidentally lost or injured a limb, try to make as much profit as possible from their misfortune, which they ostentatiously display to excite the pity and consequent liberality of passers-by. In the same way I advise you to endeavour to procure by means of your endowments the only possible advantage, trifling and uncertain though it be. Such qualities as yours are usually regarded as great natural gifts, and are often envied by those who do not possess them. But this feeling is opposed to common sense; as well may the sound man envy those wretched fellows their bodily calamities, or wish to mutilate himself in the same way, for the sake of the miserable profit he might gain. Most men work as long as they can, and enjoy themselves as much as their nature will permit. But great writers are naturally, and by their manner of life, incapable of many human pleasures: voluntarily deprived of many others; often despised by their fellow-men, save perhaps a very few who pursue the same studies; they are destined to lead a life like unto death, and to live only beyond the grave, if even that be granted them.

"But Destiny must be obeyed; duty commands us to follow it courageously and nobly whithersoever it may lead us. Such resignation is especially necessary for you, and those who resemble you."

[Pg 110]

DIALOGUE BETWEEN FREDERIC RUYSCH AND HIS MUMMIES.

Chorus of the dead in Ruysch's laboratory.
O Death, thou one eternal thing,
That takest all within thine arms,
In thee our coarser nature rests
In peace, set free from life's alarms:
Joyless and painless is our state.
Our spirits now no more are torn
By racking thought, or earthly fears;
Hope and desire are now unknown,
Nor know we aught of sorrow's tears.
Time flows in one unbroken stream,
As void of ennui as a dream.
The troubles we on earth endured
Have vanished; yet we sometimes see
Their phantom shapes, as in a mist
Of mingled thought and memory:
They now can vex our souls no more.
What is that life we lived on earth?
A mystery now it seems to be,
Profound as is the thought of death,
To wearers of mortality.
And as from death the living flee,
So from the vital flame flee we.
Our portion now is peaceful rest,
[Pg 111] Joyless, painless. We are not blest
With happiness; that is forbid
Both to the living and the dead.

Ruysch (outside his laboratory, looking through the keyhole). Diamine! Who has been teaching these dead folks music, that they thus sing like cocks, at midnight? Verily I am in a cold sweat, and nearly as dead as themselves. I little thought when I preserved them from decay, that they would come to life again. So it is however, and with all my philosophy I tremble from head to foot. It was an evil spirit that induced me to take these gentry in. I do not know what to do. If I leave them shut in here, they may break open the door, or pass through the keyhole, and come to me in bed. Yet I do not like to show that

67

I am afraid of the dead by calling for help. I will be brave. Let us see if I cannot make them afraid in their turn.

(Entering.)—Children, children, what game are you playing at? Do you not remember that you are dead? What does all this uproar mean? Are you so puffed up because of the Czar's visit,[1] that you imagine yourselves no longer subject to the laws of Nature? I am presuming this commotion is simply a piece of pleasantry on your part, and that there is nothing serious about it. If, however, you are truly resuscitated, I congratulate you, although I must tell you that I cannot afford to keep you living as well as dead, and in that case you must leave my house at once. Or if what they say about vampires be true, and you are some of them, be good enough to seek other blood to drink, for I am not disposed to let you suck mine, with which I have already liberally filled your veins. In short, if you will continue to be quiet and silent as before, we shall get on very well together, and you shall want for nothing in my house. Otherwise, I warn you that I will take hold of this iron bar, and kill you, one and all.

[Pg 112]

A Mummy. Do not put yourself about. I promise you we will all be dead again without your killing us.

Ruysch. Then what is the meaning of this singing freak?

Mummy. A moment ago, precisely at midnight, was completed for the first time that great mathematical epoch referred to so often by the ancients. To-night also the dead have spoken for the first time. And all the dead in every cemetery and sepulchre, in the depths of the sea, beneath the snow and the sand, under the open sky, and wherever they are to be found, have like us chanted the song you have just heard.

Ruysch. And how long will your singing or speaking last?'

Mummy. The song is already finished. We are allowed to speak for a quarter of an hour. Then we are silent again until the completion of the second great year.

Ruysch. If this be true, I do not think you will disturb my sleep a second time. So talk away to your hearts' content, and I will stand here on one side, and, from curiosity, gladly listen without interrupting you.

Mummy. We can only speak in response to some living person. The dead that are not interrogated by the living, when they have finished their song, are quiet again.

Ruysch. I am greatly disappointed, for I was curious to know what you would talk about if you could converse with each other.

Mummy. Even if we could do so, you would hear nothing, because we should have nothing to say to one another.

Ruysch. A thousand questions to ask you come into my mind. But the time is short, so tell me briefly what feelings you experienced in body and soul when at the point of death.

Mummy. I do not remember the exact moment of death.

[Pg 113]

The other Mummies. Nor do we.

Ruysch. Why not?

Mummy. For the same reason that you cannot perceive the moment when you fall asleep, however much you try to do so.

Ruysch. But sleep is a natural thing.

Mummy. And does not death seem natural to you? Show me a man, beast, or plant that shall not die.

Ruysch. I am no longer surprised that you sing and talk, if you do not remember your death.

"A fatal blow deprived him of his breath;
Still fought he on, unconscious of his death "—

as says an Italian poet. I thought that on the subject of death you fellows would at least know something more than the living. Now tell me, did you feel any pain at the point of death?

Mummy. How can there be pain at a time of unconsciousness?

Ruysch. At any rate, every one believes the moment of departure from this life to be a very painful one.

Mummy. As if death were a sensation, and not rather the contrary.

Ruysch. Most people who hold the views of the Epicureans as to the nature of the soul, as well as those who cling to the popular opinion, agree in supposing that death is essentially a pain of the most acute kind.

Mummy. Well, you shall put the question to either of them from us. If man be unaware of the exact point of time when his vital functions are suspended in more or less degree by sleep, lethargy, syncope, or any other cause, why should he perceive the moment-when these same functions cease entirely; and not merely for a time, but for ever? Besides, how could there be an acute sensation at the time of death? Is death itself a sensation? When the faculty of sense is not only weakened and restricted, but so minimised that it[Pg 114] may be termed non-existent, how could any one experience a lively sensation? Perhaps you think this very extinction of sensibility ought also to be an acute sensation? But it is not so. For you may notice that even sick people who die of very painful diseases compose themselves shortly before death, and rest in tranquillity; they are too enfeebled to suffer, and lose all sense of pain before they die.

You may say this from us to whoever imagines it will be a painful effort to breathe his last.

Ruysch. Such reasoning would perhaps satisfy the Epicureans, but not those people who regard the soul as essentially different from the body. I have hitherto been one of the latter, and now that I have heard the dead speak and sing I am more than ever disinclined to change my opinions. We consider death to be a separation of the soul and body, and to us it is incomprehensible how these two substances, so joined and agglutinated as to form one being, can be divided without great force and an inconceivable pang.

Mummy. Tell me: is the spirit joined to the body by some nerve, muscle, or membrane which must be broken to enable it to escape? Or is it a member which has to be severed or violently wrenched away? Do you not see that the soul necessarily leaves the body when the latter becomes uninhabitable, and not because of any internal violence? Tell me also: were you sensible of the moment when the soul entered you, and was joined, or as you say agglutinated, to your body? If not, why should you expect to feel any violent sensation at its departure? Take my word for it, the departure of the soul is as quiet and imperceptible as its entrance.

Ruysch. Then what is death, if it be not pain?

Mummy. It is rather pleasure than anything else. You must know that death, like sleep, is not accomplished in a moment, but gradually. It is true the transition is more or less rapid according to the disease or manner[Pg 115] of death. But ultimately death comes like sleep, without either sense of pain or pleasure. Just before death pain is impossible, for it is too acute a thing to be experienced by the enfeebled senses of a dying person. It were more rational to regard it as a pleasure; because most human joys, far from being of a lively nature, are made up of a sort of languor, in which pain has no part. Consequently, man's senses, even when approaching extinction, are capable of pleasure; since languor is often pleasurable, especially when it succeeds a state of suffering. Hence the languor of death ought to be pleasing in proportion to the intensity of pain from which it frees the sufferer. As for myself, if I cannot recall the circumstances of my death, it may be because the doctors forbade me to exert my brain. I remember, however, that the sensation I experienced differed little from the feeling of satisfaction that steals over a man, as the languor of sleep pervades him.

The other Mummies. We felt the same sensation.

Ruysch. It may be as you say, although every one with whom I have conversed on this subject is of a very different opinion. It is true, however, they have not spoken from experience. Now tell me, did you at the time of death, whilst experiencing this sensation of pleasure, realise that you were dying, and that this feeling was a prelude to death, or what did you think?

Mummy. Until I was dead I believed I should recover, and as long as I had the faculty of thought I hoped I should still live an hour or two. I imagine most people think the same.

The other Mummies. It was the same with us.

Ruysch. Cicero says[2] that, however old and broken-down a man may be, he always anticipates at least another year of life.

But how did you perceive at length that your soul had left the body? Say, how did you know you were[Pg 116] dead?... You do not answer. Children, do you not hear?... Ah, the quarter of an hour has expired. Let me examine them a little. Yes, they are quite dead again. There is no fear that they will give me such another shock. I will go to bed.

NOTE.—Frederic Ruysch (1638-1731) was one of the cleverest anatomists Holland has ever produced. For sixty years he held a professorship of anatomy at Amsterdam, during which time he devoted himself to his art. He obtained from Swammerdam his secret of preserving corpses by means of an injection of coloured wax. Ruysch, it is said, also made use of his own blood for this purpose. His subjects, when prepared, looked like living beings, and showed no signs of corruption. Czar Peter visited Holland in 1698, and was amazed at what he saw in Ruysch's studio. In 1717 the Czar again visited Holland, and succeeded in inducing Ruysch to dispose of his collection of animals, mummies, &c. These were all transported to St. Petersburg. Ruysch formed a second collection as valuable as the first, which after his death was publicly sold.

[1] See note.

[2] De Senectute.

[Pg 117]

REMARKABLE SAYINGS OF PHILIP OTTONIERI.[1]

CHAPTER I.

Philip Ottonieri, a few of whose remarkable sayings I am about to recount, partly heard from his own mouth and partly related to me by others, was born at Nubiana in the province of Valdivento. There he lived most of his life, and died a short time ago, leaving behind him the reputation of having never injured any one either by word or deed. He was detested by the majority of his fellow-citizens, because he took so little interest in the many things that gave them pleasure; although he did nothing to show that he despised those who differed from himself in this respect. He is believed to have been, not only in theory, but also in practice, what so many of his contemporaries professed to be, that is, a

70

philosopher. For this reason other men thought him peculiar, though really he never affected singularity in anything. Indeed, he once said that a man who nowadays practised the greatest possible singularity in dress, manners, or actions, would be far less singular than were those ancients who obtained a reputation for singularity; and that the difference between such a person and his contemporaries would by the ancients have been regarded as scarcely worthy of notice. And, comparing J. J. Rousseau's singularity,[Pg 118] which seemed very striking to the people of his generation, with that of Democritus and the first Cynic philosophers, he said that whoever nowadays lived as differently from his contemporaries as these Greeks lived from theirs, would not merely be regarded as singular, but would be treated as outside the pale of human society. He thought, too, that the degree of civilisation reached by any country might be estimated from observation of the degree of singularity possible in the inhabitants of that country.

Though very temperate in his habits of life, he professed Epicureanism, perhaps lightly rather than from conviction. But he condemned Epicurus, affirming that in his time and nation there was much more pleasure to be obtained from the pursuit of glory and virtue, than from idleness, indifference, and sensuality, which things were considered by that philosopher to represent the greatest good of life. He said also that the Epicureanism of modern times has nothing in common with the Epicureanism of the ancients.

In philosophy, he liked to call himself Socratic. Like Socrates, too, he often spent great part of the day reasoning philosophically with any chance acquaintance, and especially with certain of his friends, on any impromptu subject. But unlike Socrates, he did not frequent the shops of the shoemakers, carpenters, and blacksmiths; for he was of opinion that, though the artisans of Athens may have had time to spend in philosophising, those of Nubiana would starve were they to follow such an example. Nor did he, like Socrates, explain his conclusions by means of endless interrogation and argument; for, he said, although men in the present day may have more patience than their ancestors, they would never consent to reply to a thousand consecutive questions, still less to hear their answers answered. In fact, he only resembled Socrates in his manner of speaking, sometimes ironical, sometimes equivocal.[Pg 119] He analysed the famous Socratic irony in the following way:—

"Socrates was naturally very tender-hearted, and of a most lovable disposition. But he was physically so unattractive that it is probable he despaired from his youth of ever inspiring others with a warmer feeling than that of friendship, far insufficient to satisfy his sensitive and ardent nature, which often felt towards others a much more lively affection. He was courageous in all matters of the intellect, but seems to have been wanting in natural courage, and those other qualities that would have enabled him to hold his own in public life, amid the tumult of wars, the sedition, and the license of all kinds, then characteristic of Athenian affairs. In addition to this, his ridiculous and insignificant figure must have been no slight prejudice to him among people who made little distinction between the good and the beautiful, and who were also much addicted to banter. Thus it happened that in a free city, full of wealth and the bustle and amusements of life, Socrates, poor, rejected by love, incapable of a public career, yet gifted with very great intelligence which doubtless intensified the consciousness of his defects, resigned himself to a life of philosophising on the actions, manners, and thoughts of his fellow-citizens. The irony he used was natural to a man who found himself as it were excluded from participation in the existence of others. But it was due to his inherent nobility and affableness, and perhaps also to the celebrity he gained by his reasonings, and which flattered his self-esteem, that this irony, instead of being bitter and contemptuous, was pleasing, and expressed in a friendly manner.

"Then it was that Philosophy, as Cicero has well said, made her first descent from heaven, and was led by Socrates into the towns and houses of men. Hitherto occupied with speculations as to the nature of hidden things, she now studied the manners and lives of men,[Pg 120] and discussed virtues and vices, things good and useful, and the contrary. But Socrates did not primarily think of introducing this novel feature into philosophy, nor did he propose to teach anything, nor even aspire to the name of philosopher, which then only belonged to those who made physics or metaphysics the study of their lives. He openly proclaimed his ignorance of all things, and in his conversation with others simply discussed the affairs of his neighbours, and the topics of the day. He preferred this amusement to the real study of philosophy, or any other science or art; and being naturally more inclined to act than speculate, he only adopted this manner of life, because shut out from a more congenial employment. He was always more willing to converse with young and handsome persons than with others; in this way he hoped to gain at least esteem, where he would far rather have had love."

And since all the schools of Greek philosophy are traceable directly or indirectly to the Socratic school, Ottonieri asserted that the flat nose and satyr-like visage of a highly intellectual and warm-hearted man were the origin of all Greek philosophy, and, consequently, the philosophy of modern times. He also said that in the writings of his followers, the individuality of Socrates is comparable to those theatrical masks of the ancients, which always retained their name, character, and identity, but the rôle of which varied in each distinct performance.

He left behind him no philosophical or other writings for public benefit. Being asked one day why he did not give written as well as verbal expression to his philosophical views, he replied: "Reading is a conversation held with the writer. Now, as in fêtes and public entertainments, they who take no active part in the spectacle or performance soon become tired, similarly in conversation men prefer to speak rather than listen. And books necessarily resemble those people who take[Pg 121] all the speaking to themselves, and never listen to others. Consequently, to atone for their monopoly of talking, they ought to say many fine and excellent things, expressing them in a remarkable manner. Every book that does not do this inspires the same feeling of aversion as an insatiable chatterer."

[1] A fictitious personage.

CHAPTER II.

Ottonieri made no distinction between business and pleasure. However serious his occupation, he called it pastime. Only once, having been idle temporarily, he confessed he had then experienced no amusement.

He said that our truest pleasures are due to the imagination. Thus, children construct a world out of nothing, whereas men find nothing in the world. He compared those pleasures termed real to an artichoke, all the leaves of which must be masticated in order to reach the pith. He added that such artichokes as these are very rare; and that many others resemble them in exterior, but within are void of kernel. He for his part, finding the leaves unpalatable, determined to abstain from both leaves and kernel.

Being asked what was the worst moment of life, he said: "Except those of pain or fear, the worst moments are, in my opinion, those spent in pleasure. For the anticipation and recollection of these last, which fill up the remainder of life, are better and more delightful than the pleasures themselves." He also made a comparison between pleasures and odours. The latter he considered usually leave behind a desire to experience them again, proportioned to their agreeableness; and he regarded the sense of smell as the most difficult to satisfy of all our senses. Again, he compared odours to anticipations of good things; and said that odoriferous foods are generally more pleasing to the nose than the palate, for their scent[Pg 122] originates savoury expectations which are seldom sufficiently realised. He explained why sometimes he was so impatient about the delay of a pleasure sure to occur sooner or later, by saying that he feared the enjoyment he should derive from it would be of diminished force, on account of the exaggerated anticipation conceived by his mind. For this reason he endeavoured in the meantime to forget the coming good, as though it were an impending misfortune.

He said that each of us in entering the world resembles a man on a hard and uncomfortable bed. As soon as the man lies down, he feels restless and begins to toss from side to side and change his position momentarily, in the hope of inducing sleep to close his eyes. Thus he spends the whole night, and though sometimes he believes himself on the point of falling asleep, he never actually succeeds in doing so. At length dawn comes, and he rises unrefreshed.

Watching some bees at work one day in company with certain acquaintances, he remarked: "Blessed are ye, if ye know not your unhappiness."

He considered the miseries of mortals to be incalculable, and that no single one of them could be adequately deplored.

In answer to Horace's question, "Why is no one content with his lot?" he said: "Because no one's lot is happy. Subjects equally with princes, the weak and the strong, were they happy, would be contented, and would envy no one. For men are no more incapable of being satisfied than other animals. But since happiness alone can satisfy them, they are necessarily dissatisfied, because essentially unhappy."

"If a man could be found," he said, "who had attained to the summit of human happiness, that man would be the most miserable of mortals. For even the oldest of us have hopes and schemes for the improvement of our condition." He recalled a passage in Zenophon, where[Pg 123] a purchaser of land is advised to buy badly cultivated fields, because such as do not in the future bring forth more abundantly than at the time of purchase, give less satisfaction than if they were to increase in productiveness. Similarly, all things in which we can observe improvement please us more than others in which improvement is impossible.

On the other hand, he observed that no condition is so bad that it cannot be worse; and that however unhappy a man may be, he cannot console or boast himself that his misfortunes are incapable of increase. Though hope is unbounded, the good things of life are limited. Thus, were we to consider a single day in the life of a rich or poor man, master or servant, bearing in mind all the circumstances and needs of their respective positions, we should generally find an equality of good throughout. But nature has not limited our misfortunes; nor can the mind scarcely conceive a cause of suffering which is non-existent, or which at some time was not to be found among humanity. Thus, whereas most men vainly hope for an increase of the good things they possess, they never want for genuine objects of fear; and if Fortune sometimes obstinately refuses to benefit us in the least degree, she never fails to afflict us with new torments of such a nature as to crush within us even the courage of despair.

He often used to laugh at those philosophers who think that a man is able to free himself from the tyranny of Fortune, by having a contempt for good and evil things which are entirely beyond his control; as if happiness and the contrary were absolutely in his own power to accept or refuse. On the same subject he also said, amongst other things, that however much a man may act as a philosopher in his relations with others, he is never a philosopher to himself. Again, he said that it is as impossible to take more interest in the affairs of others than in our own, as to regard their affairs as[Pg 124] though they were our own. But, supposing this philosophical disposition of mind were possible, which it is not, and possessed by one of us, how would it stand the test of a thousand trials? Would it not be evident that the happiness or unhappiness of such a person is nevertheless a matter of fortune? Would not the very disposition they boast of be dependent on circumstances? Is not man's reason daily governed by accidents of all kinds? Do not the numberless bodily disturbances due to stupidity, excitement, madness, rage, dullness, and a hundred other species of folly, temporary or continuous, trouble, weaken, distract, and even extinguish it? Does not memory, wisdom's ally, lose strength as we advance in age? How many of us fall into a second childhood! And we almost all decrease in mental vigour as we grow old; or when our mind remains unimpaired, time, by means of some bodily disease, enfeebles our courage and firmness, and not infrequently deprives us of both attributes altogether. In short, it is utter folly to confess that physically we are subject to many things over which we have no control, and at the same time to assert that the mind, which is so greatly dependent on the body, is not similarly controlled by external influences. He summed up by saying that man as a whole is absolutely in the power of Fortune. Being asked for what purpose he thought men were born, he laughingly replied: "To realise how much better it were not to be born."

CHAPTER III.

On the occasion of a certain misfortune, Ottonieri said: "It is less hard to lose a much-loved person suddenly, or after a short illness, than to see him waste away gradually, so that before his death he is transformed in body and mind into quite another being from what he formerly was. This latter is a cruel thing; for the[Pg 125] beloved one, instead of leaving to us the tender recollections of his real identity, remains with us a changed being, in whose presence our old affection slowly but surely fades away. At length he dies; but the remembrance of him as he was at the last destroys the sweeter and earlier image within us. Thus he is lost entirely, and our imagination, instead of comforting, saddens us. Such misfortunes as these are inconsolable."

One day he heard a man lamenting and saying, "If only I were freed from this trouble, all my other troubles would be easy to bear." He replied: "Not so; for then those that are now light would be heavy."

Another person said to him: "Had this pain continued, I could not have borne it." Ottonieri answered: "On the contrary, habit would have made it more bearable."

Touching many things as to human nature, he held opinions not in accordance with those of the multitude, and often different from those of learned men. For instance, he thought it unwise to address a petition to any one when the person addressed is in a state of extraordinary hilarity. "And," he said, "when the petition is such that it cannot be granted at once, I consider occasions of joy and sorrow as equally inopportune to its success. For both sentiments make a man too selfish to trouble himself with the affairs of others. In sorrow our misfortune, in joy our good fortune, monopolises our mind, and erects, as it were, a barrier between us and matters external to ourselves. Both are also peculiarly unsuitable for exciting compassion: when sorrowful, we reserve all pity for ourselves; when joyful, we colour all things with our joy, and are inclined to regard the troubles and misfortunes of others as entirely imaginative, or else we refuse to think of them, as too discordant with the mind's present condition. The best time to ask a favour, or some beneficial promise for others, is when the person petitioned is in a state of quiet,

74

happy good[Pg 126] humour, unaccompanied by any excessive joyfulness; or better still, when under the influence of that keen but indefinite pleasure which results from a reverie of thought, and consists of a peaceful agitation of the spirit. At such times men are most open to pity and entreaty, and are often glad to please others, and give expression to the vague gratifying activity of their thoughts by some good action."

He also denied that an afflicted person ordinarily receives more pity from fellow-sufferers than from other people. For a man's companions in misfortune are always inclined to give their own troubles precedence over his, as being more serious and compassionable. And often, when a man in recounting his sufferings thinks he has excited the sympathy of his auditors, he is interrupted by one of them who expatiates in turn on his misfortunes, and ends by trying to show that he is the more afflicted of the two. He said that in such cases it generally happens as occurred to Achilles when Priam prostrated himself at his feet, with entreaties and lamentations. The tears of Priam excited the tears of Achilles, who began to groan and weep like the Trojan king. This he did, not from sympathy, but because of his own misfortunes, and the thoughts of his dead father and friend. "We compassionate others," he said, "when they suffer from evils we have experienced; but not so when we and they suffer simultaneously."

He said that from carelessness and thoughtlessness we do many cruel or wicked things, which very often have the appearance of genuine cruelty and maliciousness. For example, he mentioned the case of a man who spending his time away from home left his servants in a dwelling scarcely weather proof, not designedly, but simply from thoughtlessness or disregard of their comfort. He considered malice, inhumanity, and the like to be far less common among men than mere thoughtlessness, to which he attributed very many things called by harder names.

[Pg 127]

He once said that it were better to be completely ungrateful towards a benefactor than to make some trifling return for his great kindness. For in the latter case the benefactor must consider the obligation as cancelled, whatever may have been the motive that inspired the donor, and however small the return. He is thus despoiled of the bare satisfaction of gratitude, on which he probably reckoned; and yet he cannot regard himself as treated ungratefully, though he is so in reality.

I have heard the following saying attributed to him:—"We are inclined and accustomed to give our acquaintances credit for being able to discern our true merits, or what we imagine them to be, and to recognise the virtue of our words and actions. We also suppose that they ponder over these virtues and merits of ours, and never let them escape their memory. But, on the other hand, we do not discern similar qualities in them, or else are unwilling to acknowledge the fact."

CHAPTER IV.

Ottonieri observed that irresolute men sometimes persevere in their undertakings in the face of the greatest opposition. This is even a consequence of their irresolution; for were they to abandon their design, it would be evidence that they had for once fulfilled a determination. Sometimes they skilfully and speedily carry out a resolution. To this they are urged by fear lest they should be compelled to cease their task, when they would return to the state of perplexity and uncertainty in which they were formerly. Thus they strenuously hasten the execution of their design, stimulated rather by anxiety and uncertainty as to whether they will conquer themselves, than by the goal or the difficulties to be overcome before it can be reached.

At another time he said, with a smile, that people[Pg 128] accustomed to give expression to their every thought and feeling in conversation with others, cry out when alone if a fly bite them, or if they chance to upset a glass of water; and, on the other hand, they who live solitary lives become so reserved that even the presentiment of apoplexy would not induce them to speak in the presence of others.

He was of opinion that most men reputed great in ancient and modern times have obtained their reputation through a preponderance of one quality over the rest in their character. And a man possessed of the most brilliant but evenly proportioned endowments, would fail to acquire celebrity either with his contemporaries or posterity.

He divided the men of civilised nations into three classes. The first class are they whose individual nature, and partly also their natural human constitution, become transformed under the influence of the arts and customs of urban life. Among these he included all men who are skilful in business, whether private or public, who appreciate society, and make themselves universally agreeable to their fellows. Generally speaking, such men alone inspire esteem and respect. The second class are they who preserve their primitive nature in a greater degree, either from lack of culture or because they are naturally incapable of being influenced by the arts, manners, and customs of others. This is the most numerous of the three classes, and is held in general contempt. It embraces those who are known as the common people, or who deserve to be included with them, be their station in life what it may. The third class, incomparably the smallest in numbers, and often even more despised than the second, consists of those men in whom nature is strong enough to resist and often repulse the civilising influence of the times. They are seldom apt in business, or self-governed in society; nor do they shine in conversation, nor succeed in making themselves agreeable to their fellow-men. This class is[Pg 129] subdivided into two varieties. The one includes those strong and courageous natures that despise the contempt they excite, and often indeed esteem it more than honour. They differ from other men, not only by nature, but also by choice and preference. Having nothing in common with the hopes and pleasures of society, solitary in a crowd, they avoid other men as much as they themselves are avoided. Specimens of this class are rarely met with. The other variety consists of persons whose nature is a compound of strength, weakness, and timidity, and who are therefore in a constant state of agitation. They are as a rule desirous of associating with their fellows, and wishing to emulate the men of the cultivated class, they feel acutely the contempt in which they are held by their inferiors. These men are never successful in life; they fail in ever becoming practical, and in society are neither tolerable to themselves nor others. Not a few of our most gifted men of modern times have belonged to this division in more or less degree. J. J. Rousseau is a famous example, and with him may be bracketed one of the ancients, Virgil. Of the latter it is said, on the authority of Melissus, that he was very slow of speech, and apparently a most ordinary endowed man. And this, together with the probability that owing to his great talents Virgil was little at ease in society, seems likely enough, both from the laboured subtlety of his style, and the nature of his poetry; it is also confirmed by what we read towards the end of the Second Book of the Georgics. There the poet expresses a wish for a quiet and solitary life, as though he regarded it as a remedy and refuge more than an advantage in itself. Now, seeing that with rare exceptions men of these two species are never esteemed until they are dead, and are of little power in the world; he asserted as a general rule, that the only way to gain esteem during life is to live unnaturally. And since the first class, which is the mean of the two extremes, represents the civilisation[Pg 130] of our times; he concluded from this and other circumstances that the conduct of human affairs is entirely in the hands of mediocrity.

He distinguished also three conditions of old age, compared with the other ages of man. When nature and manners were first instituted, men were just and virtuous at all ages. Experience and knowledge of the world did not make men less honest and upright. Old age was then the most venerable time of life; for besides having all the good qualities common to other men, the aged were naturally possessed of greater prudence and judgment than their juniors. But in process of time, the conduct of men changed; their manners became debased and corrupt. Then were the aged the vilest of the vile; for they had served a longer apprenticeship to vice, had been longer under the influence of the wickedness of their neighbours, and were besides possessed of the spirit of cold indifference natural to their time of life. Under such conditions they were powerless to act, save by calumny, fraud, perfidy, cunning, dissimulation, and other such despicable means. The corruption of men at length exceeded all bounds. They despised virtue and well-doing before they knew anything of the world, and its sad truth. In their youth they drained the cup of evil and dissipation. Old age was then not indeed venerable, for few things thence-forward could be so called, but the most bearable time of life. Eor whereas the mental ardour and bodily strength which formerly stimulated the imagination and the conception of noble thoughts, had often given rise to virtuous habits, sentiments, and actions; the same causes latterly increased man's wickedness by enlarging his capacity for evil, to which it lent an additional attractiveness. But this ardour diminished with age, bodily decrepitude, and the coldness incident to age, things ordinarily more dangerous to virtue than vice. In addition to this, excessive knowledge of the world became so dissatisfactory[Pg 131] and wearisome a thing, that instead of conducting men from good to evil, as formerly, it gave them strength to resist wickedness, and sometimes even to hate it. So that, comparing old age with the other periods of life, it may be said to have been as better to good in the earliest times; as worse to bad in the corrupt times; and subsequently as bad to worse.

CHAPTER V.

Ottonieri often talked of the quality of self-love, nowadays called egotism. I will narrate some of his remarks on this subject.

He said that "if you hear a person speak well or ill of another with whom he has had dealings, and term him honest or the contrary; value his opinion not a whit. He speaks well or ill of the man simply as his relationship with him has proved satisfactory or the reverse." He said that no one can love without a rival. Being asked to explain, he replied: "Because the person beloved is a very close rival of the lover."

"Suppose a case," he said, "in which you asked a favour from a friend, who could not grant it without incurring the hatred of a third person. Suppose, too, that the three interested people are in the same condition of life. I affirm that your request would have little chance of success, even though your gratitude to the granter might exceed the hatred he would incur from the other person. The reason of this is as follows: we fear men's anger and hatred more than we value their love and gratitude. And rightly so. For do we not oftener see the former productive of results than the latter? Besides, hatred or vengeance is a personal satisfaction; whereas gratitude is merely a service pleasing to the recipient."

He said that respect and services rendered to others in expectation of some profitable return, are rarely[Pg 132] successful; because men, especially nowadays when they are more knowing than formerly, are less inclined to give than receive. Nevertheless, such services as the young render to the old who are rich or powerful, attain their end more often than not.

The following remarks about modern customs I remember hearing from his own mouth:—

"Nothing makes a man of the world so ashamed as the feeling that he is ashamed, if by chance he ever realises it.

"Marvellous is the power of fashion! For we see nations and men, so conservative in everything else, and so careful of tradition, act blindly in this respect, often indeed unreasonably, and against their own interests. Fashion is despotic. She constrains men to lay aside, change, or assume manners, customs, and ideas, just when she pleases; even though the things changed be rational, useful, or beautiful, and the substitutes the contrary.[1]

"There are an infinite number of things in public and private life which, though truly ridiculous, seldom excite laughter. If by chance a man does laugh in such a case, he laughs alone, and is soon silent. On the other hand, we laugh daily at a thousand very serious and natural things; and such laughter is quickly contagious. Thus, most things which excite laughter are in reality anything but ridiculous; and we often laugh simply because there is nothing to laugh at, or nothing worthy of laughter.

"We frequently hear and say such things as, 'The good ancients,' 'our good ancestors,' &c. Again, 'A man worthy of the ancients,' by which we mean a trustworthy and honest man. Every generation believes, on the one hand, that its ancestors were better than its contemporaries; and on the other hand, that the human race progresses as it leaves the primitive state, to return to which would be a movement for the worse, further and further behind. Wonderful contradiction!

[Pg 133]

"The true is not necessarily the beautiful. Yet, though beauty be preferable to truth, where the former is wanting, the latter is the next best thing. Now in large towns the beautiful is not to be found, because it no longer has a place in the excitement of human life. The true is equally non-existent; for all things there are false or frivolous. Consequently, in large towns one sees, feels, hears, and breathes nothing but falsity, which in time, custom renders even pleasurable. To sensitive minds, what misery can exceed this?

"People who need not work for their bread, and who accordingly leave the care of it to others, have usually great difficulty in providing themselves with one of the chief necessities of life, occupation. This may indeed be called the greatest necessity of life, for it includes all others. It is greater even than the necessity of living; for life itself, apart from happiness, is not a good thing. And possessing life, as we do, our one endeavour should be to endure as little unhappiness as possible. Now, on the one hand, an idle and empty life is very unhappy; and on the other hand, the best way to pass our time is to spend it in providing for our wants."

He said that the custom of buying and selling human beings has proved useful to the race. In confirmation of this, he mentioned the practice of inoculating for small-pox, which originated in Circassia; from Constantinople it passed to England, and thence became disseminated throughout Europe. Its office was to mitigate the destructiveness wrought by true small-pox, which besides endangering the life and comeliness of the Circassian children and youths, was especially disastrous in its effects on the sale of their maidens.

He narrated of himself that on leaving school to enter the world of life, he mentally resolved, inexperienced, and devoted to truth as he was, to praise no person or thing that did not seem really deserving of praise. He kept his determination for a whole year, during which[Pg 134] time he did not utter a single word of praise. Then he broke his vow, fearing lest, from want of practice, he should forget all the eulogistic phraseology he had learnt shortly before, at the School of Rhetoric. From that time he absolutely renounced his intention.

[1] See "Dialogue between Fashion and Death," p. 19.

CHAPTER VI.

Ottonieri was accustomed to read out passages from books taken at hazard, especially those of ancient writers. He would often interrupt himself by uttering some remark or comment on this or that passage.

One day he read from Laertius' "Lives of the Philosophers," the passage where Chilo, being asked how the learned differed from the ignorant, is said to have replied, that the former possess 'hopes,' Ottonieri said: "Now all is changed. The ignorant hope, but the learned do not."

Again, as he read in the same book how Socrates affirmed that the world contains but one benefit, knowledge, and but one evil, ignorance, he said: "I know nothing about the knowledge and ignorance of the ancients; but in the present day I should reverse this saying."

Commenting on this maxim of Hegesias, also from the book of Laertius, "The wise man attends to his own interests in everything," he said: "If all men who carry out this principle be philosophers, Plato may come and establish his republic throughout the civilised world."

He greatly praised the following saying of Bion Borysthenes, mentioned by Laertius: "They who seek the greatest happiness, suffer most." To this he added: "And they on the other hand are happiest who are contented with least, and who are accustomed to enjoy their happiness over again in memory."

From Plutarch he read how Stratocles excited the anger of the Athenians by inducing them on a certain[Pg 135] occasion to sacrifice as though they were victors; and how he then replied by demanding why they blamed him that he had made them happy and joyful for the space of three days. Ottonieri added: "Nature might make the same response to those who complain that she endeavours to conceal the truth beneath a multitude of vain but beautiful and pleasing appearances. How have I injured you, in making you happy for three or four days?"

On another occasion he remarked that Tasso's saying about a child induced to take his medicine under a false belief, "he is nourished on deception," is equally applicable to all our race, in relation to the errors in which man puts faith.

Beading the following from Cicero's "Paradoxes"—"Do pleasures make a person better or more estimable? Is there any one who boasts of the pleasures he enjoys?" he said: "Beloved Cicero, I cannot say that pleasures make men in the present day either more estimable or better; but undoubtedly they cause them to be more esteemed. For in the present day most young men seek esteem by no other way than pleasure. And not only do they boast of these pleasures when they obtain them, but they din the intelligence of their enjoyment into the ears of friends and strangers, willing or unwilling. There are also many pleasures which are eagerly desired and sought after, not as pleasures, but for the sake of the renown, reputation, and self-satisfaction that they bring; and very often these latter things are appropriated when the pleasures have neither been obtained, nor sought, or else have been entirely imaginary."

He noted from Arrian's History of the Wars of Alexander the Great, that at the battle of Issus, Darius placed his Greek mercenaries in the van of his army, and Alexander his Greeks at the wings. He thought that this fact alone was sufficient to determine the result of the battle.

[Pg 136]

He never blamed authors for writing much about themselves. On the contrary, he applauded them for so doing, and said that on such occasions they are nearly always eloquent, and their style, though perhaps unusual and even singular, is ordinarily good and fluent. And this is not surprising; for writers treating of themselves have their heart and soul in the work. They are at no loss what to say; their subject and the interest they take in it are jointly productive of original thought. They confine themselves to themselves, and do not drink at strange fountains; nor need they be commonplace and trite. There is nothing to induce them to garnish their writing with artificial ornamentation, or to affect an unnatural style. And it is an egregious error to suppose that readers are ordinarily little interested in a writer's confessions. For in the first place, whenever a man relates his own experiences and thoughts simply and pleasingly, he succeeds in commanding attention. Secondly, because in no way can we discuss and represent the affairs of others more truthfully and effectively than by treating of our own affairs; seeing that all men have something in common, either naturally or by force of circumstances, and that we are better able to illustrate human nature in ourselves than in others. In confirmation of these opinions, he instanced Demosthenes' Oration for the Crown, in which the speaker, continually referring to himself, is surpassingly eloquent. And Cicero, when he touches on his own affairs, is equally successful; peculiarly so in his Oration for Milo, admirable throughout, but above all praise towards the end, where he himself is introduced. Bossuet also is supremely excellent in his panegyric of the Prince de Condé, where he mentions his own extreme age and approaching death. Again, the Emperor Julian, whose writings are all else trifling, and often unbearable, is at his best in the "Misopogony" (speech against the beard), in which he replies to the ridicule and malice of the people of[Pg 137] Antioch. He is here scarcely inferior to Lucian in wit, vigour, and acuteness; whereas his work on the Cæsars, professedly an imitation of Lucian, is pointless, dull, feeble, and almost stupid. In Italian literature, which is almost devoid of eloquent writings, the apology of Lorenzo de Medici is a specimen of eloquence, grand and perfect in every way. Tasso also is often eloquent where he speaks much of himself, and is nearly always excessively so in his letters, which are almost occupied with his own affairs.

CHAPTER VII.

Many other famous sayings of Ottonieri are recorded. Amongst them is a reply he gave to a clever, well-read young man, who knew little of the world. This youth said that he learned daily one hundred pages of the art of self-government in society. "But," remarked Ottonieri, "the book has five million pages."

Another youth, whose thoughtless and impetuous behaviour constantly got him into trouble, used to excuse himself by saying that life is a comedy. "May be," replied Ottonieri, "but even then it is better for the actor to gain applause than rebuke; often, too, the ill-trained or clumsy comedian ends by dying of starvation."

One day he saw a murderer, who was lame, and could not therefore escape, being carried off by the police. "See, friends," he said, "Justice, lame though she be, can bring the doer of evil to account, if he also be lame."

During a journey through Italy he met a courtier, who, desirous of acting the critic to Ottonieri, began: "I will speak candidly, if you will allow me." "I will listen attentively," said the other, "for, as a traveller, I appreciate uncommon things."

Being in need of money, he once asked a loan from[Pg 138] a certain man, who, excusing himself on the plea of poverty, added that were he rich, the necessities of his friends would be his first thought. "I should be truly sorry were you to bestow on us such a valuable moment," replied Ottonieri: "God grant you may never become rich!"

When young, he wrote some verses, using certain obsolete expressions. At the request of an old lady he recited them to her. She professed ignorance of their meaning, and said that in her day such words were not in use. Ottonieri replied: "I thought they might have been, simply because they are very ancient."

Of a certain very rich miser who had been robbed of a little money, he said: "This man behaved in a miserly manner even to thieves."

He said of a man who had a mania for calculating on every possible occasion: "Other men make things; this fellow counts them."

Being asked his opinion about a certain old terra-cotta figure of Jove, over which some antiquaries were disputing, he said: "Do you not see that it is a Cretan Jove?"

Of a foolish fellow, who imagined himself to be an admirable reasoner, yet was illogical whenever he spoke two words, he said: "This person exemplifies the Greek definition of man, as a 'logical animal.'"

When on his deathbed, he composed this epitaph, which was subsequently engraved on his tomb:

HERE LIE
THE BONES OF
PHILIP OTTONIERI.
BORN FOR VIRTUE AND GLORY,
HE LIVED IDLE AND USELESS,
AND DIED IN OBSCURITY;
NOT WITHOUT A KNOWLEDGE OF NATURE
AND HIS OWN DESTINY.
[Pg 139]
DIALOGUE BETWEEN CHRISTOPHER COLUMBUS AND PIETRO GUTIERREZ.

Columbus. A fine night, friend.

Gutierrez. Fine indeed; but a sight of land would be much finer.

Col. Decidedly. So even you are tired of a life at sea.

Gut. Not so. But I am rather weary of this voyage, which turns out to be so much longer than I expected. Do not, however, think that I blame you, like the others. Rather, consider that I will, as hitherto, do all I can to help you in anything relating to the voyage. But just for the sake of some talk I wish you would tell me candidly and explicitly, whether you are as confident as at first about finding land in this part of the world; or if, after spending so much time to no purpose, you begin at all to doubt.

Col. Speaking frankly as to a friend who will not betray me, I confess I am a little dubious; especially because certain evidences during the voyage, which filled me with hope, have turned out deceitful; for instance, the birds which dew over us from the west, soon after we left Gomera, and which I considered a sure sign of land not far distant. Similarly, more than one conjecture and anticipation, made before setting out, regarding different things that were to have taken place during the voyage, have failed of realisation. So that at length I cannot[Pg 140] but say to myself, "Since these predictions in which I put the utmost faith have not been verified, why may not also my chief conjecture, that of finding land beyond the ocean, be also unfounded?" It is true this belief of mine is so logical, that if it be false, on the one hand it would seem as if no human judgment could be reliable, except such as concern things actually seen, and touched; and on the other hand, I remember how seldom reality agrees with expectation. I ask myself, "What ground have you for believing that both hemispheres resemble each other, so that the western, like the eastern, is part land and part water? Why may it not be one immense sea? Or instead of land and water, may it not contain some other element? And, supposing it to have land and water like the other, why may it not be uninhabited? or even uninhabitable? If it be peopled as numerously as our hemisphere, what proof have you that rational beings are to be found there, as in ours? And if so, why not some other intelligent animals instead of men? Supposing they be men, why not of a kind very different from those you are acquainted with; for instance, with much larger bodies, stronger, more skilful, naturally gifted with much more genius and intelligence, more civilised, and richer in sciences and arts?"

These thoughts occur to me. And in truth, we see nature endowed with such power, so diverse and manifold in her effects, that we not only are unable to form a certain opinion about her works in distant and unknown parts of the world, but we may even doubt whether we do not deceive ourselves in drawing conclusions from the known world, and applying them to the unknown. Nor would it be contrary to probability to imagine that the things of the unknown world, in whole or part, were strange and extraordinary to us. For do we not see with our own eyes that the needle in these seas falls away from the Pole Star not a little towards the west? Such a thing is perfectly novel, and hitherto unheard of by[Pg 141] all navigators; and even after much thought I can arrive at no satisfactory explanation of it. I do not infer that the fables of the ancients regarding the wonders of the undiscovered world and this ocean are at all credible. Annonus, for instance, said of these parts, that the nights were illumined by flames, and the glow of fiery torrents, which emptied themselves into the sea. We observe also, how foolish hitherto have been all the fears of miraculous and terrible novelties felt by our fellow-sailors during the voyage; as when, on coming to that stretch of seaweed, which made as it were a meadow in the sea, and impeded us so greatly, they imagined we had reached the verge of navigable waters.

I say this simply because I wish you to see that although this idea of mine about undiscovered land may be founded on very reasonable suppositions, in which many excellent geographers, astronomers, and navigators, with whom I conversed on the subject in Spain, Italy, and Portugal, agree with me, it might yet be fallacious. In short, we often see many admirably drawn conclusions prove erroneous, especially in matters about which we have very little knowledge.

Gut. So that in fact you have risked your own life, and the lives of your companions, on behalf of a mere possibility.

Col. I cannot deny it. But, apart from the fact that men daily endanger their lives for much frailer reasons, and far more trifling things, or even without thinking at all, pray consider a moment.

If you, and I, and all of us were not now here in this ship, in the middle of this ocean, in this strange solitude, uncertain and hazardous though it be, what should we be doing? How should we be occupied? How should we be spending our time? More joyfully perhaps? More probably, in greater trouble and difficulty; or worse, in a state of ennui?

For what is implied in a state of life free from[Pg 142] uncertainty and danger? If contentment and happiness, it is preferable to all others; if weariness and misery, I know nothing so undesirable.

I do not wish to mention the glory and useful intelligence that we shall take back with us, if our enterprise succeed, as we hope. If the voyage be of no other use to us, it is very advantageous, inasmuch as it for a time frees us from ennui, endears life to us, and enhances the value of many things that we should not otherwise esteem.

You remember perhaps what the ancients say about unfortunate lovers. These used to throw themselves from the rock of St. Maur (then called Leucadia) into the sea; being rescued therefrom, they found themselves, thanks to Apollo, delivered from their love passion. Whether or not this be credible, I am quite sure that the lovers, having escaped their danger, for a short time even without Apollo's assistance, loved the life they previously hated; or loved and valued it increasedly. Every voyage is, in my opinion, comparable to the leap from the Leucadian rock, producing the same useful results, though these are of a more durable kind.

It is ordinarily believed that sailors and soldiers, because incessantly in danger of their lives, value existence more lightly than other people. Eor the same reason, I come to a contrary conclusion, and imagine few persons hold life in such high estimation as soldiers and sailors. Just as we care nothing for many benefits as soon as we possess them; so sailors cherish and value, very greatly, numerous things that are far from being good, simply because they are deprived of them. Who would think of including a little earth in the catalogue of human benefits? None but navigators; and especially such as ourselves, who, owing to the uncertain nature of our voyage, desire nothing so much as the sight of a tiny piece of land. This is our first thought on awaking, and our last before we fall asleep. And if at some future[Pg 143] time we chance to see in the distance the peak of a mountain, the tops of a forest, or some such evidence of land, we shall scarcely be able to contain ourselves for joy. Once on terra firma, the mere consciousness of being free to go where we please will suffice to make us happy for several days.

Gut. That is all very true; and if your conjecture only prove to be as reasonable as your justification of it, we shall not fail to enjoy this happiness sooner or later.

Col. Personally, I think we shall soon do so; though I dare not actually promise such a thing. You know we have for several days been able to fathom; and the quality of the matter brought up by the lead seems to me auspicious. The clouds about the sun towards evening are of a different form and colour to what they were a few days ago. The atmosphere, as you can feel, is warmer and softer than it was. The wind no longer blows with the same force, nor in so straightforward and unwavering a manner; it is inclined to be hesitating and changeable, as though broken by some impediment. To these signs add that of the piece of cane we discovered floating in the sea, which bore marks of having been recently severed; and the little branch of a tree with fresh red berries on it; besides, the swarms of birds that pass over us, though they have deceived me before, are now so frequent and immense, that I think there must be some special reason for their appearance, particularly because we see amongst them some which do not resemble sea birds. In short, all these omens together make me very hopeful and expectant, however diffident I may pretend to be.

Gut. God grant your surmises may be true.

[Pg 144]

PANEGYRIC OF BIRDS.

Amelio, a lonely philosopher, was seated, reading, one spring morning in the shade of his country house. Being distracted by the songs of the birds in the fields, he gradually resigned himself to listening and thinking. At length he threw his book aside, and taking up a pen wrote as follows:—

Birds are naturally the most joyful creatures in the world. I do not say this because of the cheerful influence they always exercise over us; I mean that they themselves are more light-hearted and joyful than any other animal. For we see other animals ordinarily stolid and grave, and many even seem melancholy. They rarely give signs of joy, and when they do, these are but slight and of brief duration. In most of their enjoyments and pleasures they do not express any gratification. The green fields, extensive and charming landscapes, noble planets, pure and sweet atmosphere, if even a cause of pleasure to them, do not excite in them any joyful demonstrations; save that on the authority of Zenophon, hares are said to skip and frolic with delight when the moon's radiance is at its brightest.

Birds, on the other hand, show extreme joy, both in motion and appearance; and it is the sight of this evident disposition for enjoyment on their part that gladdens us as we watch them. And this appearance must not be regarded as unreal and deceptive. They[Pg 145] sing to express the happiness they feel, and the happier they are, the more vigorously do they sing. And if, as it is said, they sing louder and more sweetly when in love than at other times, it is equally certain that other pleasures besides love incite them to sing. For we may notice they warble more on a quiet and peaceful day, than when the day is dark and uncertain. And in stormy weather, or when frightened, they are silent; but the storm passed, they reappear, singing and frolicking with one another. Again, they sing in the morning when they awake; being partly incited to this by a feeling of joy for the new day, and partly by the pleasure generally felt by every animal when refreshed and restored by sleep. They also delight in gay foliage, rich valleys, pure and sparkling water, and beautiful country....

It is said that birds' voices are softer and sweeter, and their songs more refined, with us than among wild and uncivilised people. This being so, it would seem that birds are subject to the influence of the civilisation with which they associate. Whether or not this be true, it is a remarkable instance of the providence of nature that they should have capacity for flight, as well as the gift of song, so that their voices might from a lofty situation reach a greater number of auditors. It is also providential that the air, which is the natural element of sound, should be inhabited by vocal and musical creatures.

Truly the singing of birds is a great solace and pleasure to us, and all other animals. This fact is not, I believe, so much due to the sweetness of the sounds, nor to their variety and harmony, as to the joyful signification of songs generally, and those of birds in particular. Birds laugh, as it were, to show their contentment and happiness. It may therefore be said that they partake in a degree of man's privilege of laughter, unpossessed by other animals. Now some people think that man may[Pg 146] as well be termed a laughing animal, as an animal possessed of mind and reason; for laughter seems to them quite as much peculiar to man as reason. And it is certainly wonderful that man, the most wretched and miserable of all creatures, should have the faculty of laughter, which is wanting in other animals. Marvellous also is the use we make of this faculty! We see people suffering from some terrible calamity or mental distress, others who have lost all love of life, and regard every human thing as full of vanity, who are almost incapable of joy, and deprived of hope, laugh nevertheless. Indeed, the more such men realise the vanity of hope, and the misery of life, the fewer their expectations and pleasures, so much the more do they feel inclined to laugh. Now it is scarcely possible to explain or analyse the nature of laughter in general, and its connection with the human mind. Perhaps it may aptly be termed a species of momentary folly or delirium. For men can have no reasonable and just cause for laughter, because nothing really satisfies nor truly pleases them. It would be curious to discover and trace out the history of this faculty. There is no doubt that in man's primitive and wild state, it was expressed by a peculiar gravity of countenance, as in other animals, who show it even to the extent of melancholy. For this reason I imagine that laughter not only came into the world after tears, which cannot be questioned, but that a long time passed before it appeared. During that time, neither the mother greeted her child with a smile, nor did the child smilingly recognise her, as Virgil says. And the reason why, in the present day, among civilised people, children smile as soon as they are born, is explainable by virtue of example: they see others smile, therefore they also smile. It is probable that laughter originated in drunkenness,[1][Pg 147] another peculiarity of the human race. This vice is far from being confined to civilised nations, for we know that scarcely any people can be found that do not possess an intoxicating liquor of some kind, which they indulge in to excess. And this cannot be wondered at, when we remember that men, the most unhappy of all animals, are above all pleased with anything that easily alienates their minds, such as self-forgetfulness, or a suspension of their usual life; from which interruption and temporary diminution of the sense and knowledge of their peculiar evils they receive no slight benefit. And whereas savages have ordinarily a sad and grave countenance, yet, when in a state of drunkenness, they laugh immoderately, and talk and sing incessantly, contrary to their custom. But I will discuss this matter more in detail in a history of laughter which I think of composing. Having discovered its origin, I will trace its history and fortune to the present day, when it is more valued than at any previous time. It occupies among civilised nations a place, and fills an office somewhat similar to the parts formerly played by virtue, justice, honour, and the like, often indeed frightening and deterring men from the committal of evil.

But to return to the birds. From the effect their singing produces in me, I conclude that the sight and recognition of joy in others, of which we are not envious, gratifies and rejoices us. We may therefore be grateful to Nature for having ordained that the songs of birds, which are a demonstration of joy and a species of laughter, should be in public, differing from the private nature of the singing and laughter of men, who represent the rest of the world. And it is wisely decreed that the earth and air should be enlivened by creatures that seem to applaud universal life with the joyful harmony of their sweet voices, and thus incite other living beings to joy, by their continual, though false, testimony to the happiness of things.

[Pg 148]

It is reasonable that birds should be, and show themselves, more joyful than other creatures. For, as I have said, they are naturally better adapted for joy and happiness. In the first place, apparently, they are not subject to ennui. They change their position momentarily, and pass from country to country, however distant, and from the lowest regions of the air to the highest, quickly and with wonderful ease. Life to them is made up of an infinite variety of sights and experiences. Their bodies are in a continuous state of activity, and they themselves are full of vital power. All other animals, their wants being satisfied, love quietude and laziness; none, except fishes and certain flying insects, keep long in motion simply for amusement. The savage, for instance, except to supply his daily wants, which demand little and brief exertion, or when unable to hunt, scarcely stirs a step. He loves idleness and tranquillity above everything, and passes nearly the whole day sitting in silence and indolence within his rude cabin, or at its opening, or in some rocky cave or place of shelter. Birds, on the contrary, very rarely stay long in one place. They fly backwards and forwards without any necessity, simply as a pastime, and often having gone several hundred miles away from the country they usually frequent, they return thither the same evening. And even for the short time they are in one place, their bodies are never still. Ever turning here and there, they are always either flocking together, pecking, or shaking themselves, or hopping about in their extraordinarily vivacious and active maimer. In short, from the time a bird bursts its shell until it dies, save intervals of sleep, it is never still for a moment. From these considerations it may reasonably be affirmed that whereas the normal state of animals, including even man, is quietude, that of birds is motion.

We find also that birds are so endowed that their natural qualities harmonise with the exterior qualities[Pg 149] and conditions of their life; this again makes them better adapted for happiness than other animals. They have remarkably acute powers of hearing, and a faculty of vision almost inconceivably perfect. Owing to this last they can discern simultaneously a vast extent of country, and are daily charmed by spectacles the most immense and varied. From these things it may be inferred that birds ought to possess an imagination, vivid and powerful in the highest degree,. Not the ardent and stormy imagination of Dante or Tasso; for this is a disastrous endowment, and the cause of endless anxieties and sufferings. But a fertile, light, and childish fancy, such as is productive of joyful thoughts, sweet unrealities, and manifold pleasures. This is the noblest gift of Nature to living creatures. And birds have this faculty in a great; measure for their own delight and benefit, without experiencing any of its hurtful and painful consequences. For their prolific imagination, as with children, combines, with their bodily vigour, to render them happy and contented, instead of being injurious, and productive of misery, as with most men. Thus, birds may be said to resemble children equally in' their vivacity and restlessness, and the other attributes of their nature. If the advantages of childhood were common to other ages, and its evils not exceeded later in life, man might perhaps be better able to bear patiently the burden of existence.

To me it seems that the nature of birds, considered aright, is manifestly more perfect than that of other animals. For, in the first place, birds are superior to other animals in sight and hearing, which are the principal senses of life. In the second place, birds naturally prefer motion to rest, whereas other creatures have the contrary preference. And since activity is a more living thing than repose, birds may be said to have more life than other animals. It follows therefore that birds are physically, and in the exercise of their faculties, superior to other creatures.

[Pg 150]

Now, if life be better than its contrary, the fuller and more perfect the life, as with birds, the greater is the superiority of creatures possessing it, over less endowed animals.

We must not forget also that birds are adapted to bear great atmospheric changes. Often they rise instantaneously from the ground far up into the air, where the cold is extreme; and others in their travels fly through many different climates.

In short, just as Anacreon wished to be changed into a mirror that he might be continually regarded by the mistress of his heart, or into a robe that he might cover her, or balm to anoint her, or water to wash her, or bands that she might draw him to her bosom, or a pearl to be worn on her neck, or shoes that she might at least press him with her feet; so I should like temporarily to be transformed into a bird, in order to experience their contentment and joyfulness of life.

[1] Compare Shakespeare's Henry IV., Part 2, Act 4, sc. 3. Falstaff: " ... nor a man cannot make him laugh;—but that's no marvel, he drinks no wine."

[Pg 151]

THE SONG OF THE WILD COCK.

86

Certain Hebrew savants and writers affirm, that between heaven and earth, or rather, partly in one and partly on the other, lives a wild cock which stands with its feet resting on the earth, and touching the sky with its crest and beak. This gigantic cock, besides possessing other peculiarities mentioned by these writers, has the use of reason; or else, like a parrot, it has been taught, I know not by whom, to express itself in human fashion. In proof of this, an old parchment manuscript has been discovered, containing a canticle written in Hebrew characters, and in a language compounded of Chaldean, Targumic, Rabbinical, Cabalistic and Talmudic, entitled "Morning Song of the Wild Cock." (Scir detarnegòl bara letzafra.) This, not without great exertion, and the interrogation of more than one Rabbi, Cabalist, theologian, jurist, and Hebrew philosopher, has been interpreted and translated as follows. I have not yet been able to ascertain whether this song is still uttered by the cock on certain occasions, or every morning, or whether it was sung but once, or who is said to have heard it, or if this language be the proper tongue of the cock, or whether the canticle was translated from some other language. In the following translation I have used prose rather than verse, although it is a poem, in order to ensure as literal a rendering as possible. The broken style and occasional bombast must not be imputed to[Pg 152] me, for it is a reproduction of the original; and in this respect the composition partakes of the characteristics of Oriental languages, and especially of Oriental poems.

"Mortals, awake! The day breaks; truth returns to the earth and vain fancies flee away. Arise; take up again the burden of life; forsake the false world for the true.

"Now is the time when each one takes again to his mind all the thoughts of his real life. He recalls to memory his intentions, aims, and labours; and thinks of the pleasures and cares that must occur during the new day. And every one at this time eagerly seeks to discover in his mind joyful hopes and sweet thoughts. Few, however, are satisfied in this desire; for all men it is a misfortune to awake. The miserable man is no sooner aroused than he falls again into the clutches of his unhappiness. Very sweet a thing is that sleep induced by joy or hope. These preserve themselves in their entirety until the following morning, when they either vanish or decrease in force.

"If the sleep of mortals were continuous and identical with life; if under the star of day all living beings languished on the earth in utter rest, and no work was wrought; if the oxen ceased bellowing in the meadows, the beasts roaring in the forests, the birds singing in the air, the bees buzzing, and the butterflies skimming over the fields; if no voice nor motion except that of the waters, winds, and tempests anywhere existed, the universe would indeed be useless; but would there be less happiness or more misery than there is to-day?

"I ask of thee, O Sun, author of day, and guardian of eve; in the course of the centuries measured out and consummated by thee, thus rising and setting, hast thou ever at any time seen one living being possessed of happiness? Of the numberless works of mortals which hitherto thou hast seen, thinkest thou that a single one was successful in its aim of procuring satisfaction, durable[Pg 153] or temporary, for its originator? And seest thou, or hast thou ever seen, happiness within the boundaries of the world? Where does it dwell? In what country, forest, mountain, or valley; in what land, inhabited or uninhabited; in which planet of the many that thy flames illumine and cherish? Does it perchance hide from thee in the bowels of the earth, or the depths of the sea? What living being, what plant, or other thing animated by thee, what vegetable or animal participates in it? And thou thyself, like an indefatigable giant, traversing swiftly, day and night, sleepless and restless, the vast course prescribed to thee; art thou content or happy?

87

"Mortals, arouse yourselves! Not yet are you free from life. The time will come when no eternal force, no internal agitation, shall awaken you from the repose of sleep, in which you shall ever and insatiably rest. For the present, death is not granted to you; only from time to time you are permitted to taste briefly its resemblance, because life would fail were it not often suspended. Too long abstention from this short and fleeting sleep is a fatal evil, and causes eternal sleep. Such thing is life, that to secure its continuance it must from time to time be laid aside; man then in sleep refreshes himself with a taste, and, as it were, a fragment of death.

"It seems as though death were the essential aim of all things. That which has no existence cannot die; yet all that exists has proceeded from nothing. The final cause of existence is not happiness, for nothing is happy. It is true, living creatures seek this end in all their works, but none obtain it; and during all their life, ever deceiving, tormenting, and exerting themselves, they suffer indeed for no other purpose than to die.

"The earliest part of the day is ordinarily the most bearable for living beings. Few, when they awake, find again in their minds delightful and joyful thoughts, but almost all people give birth to them for the time being.[Pg 154] For then the minds of men, being free from any special concentration, are predisposed to joy fulness, and inclined to bear evils more patiently than at other times. Thus a man who falls asleep in the anguish of despair is filled anew with hope when he awakes, though it can profit him nothing, Many misfortunes and peculiar hardships, many causes of fear and distress, then seem less formidable than they appeared the previous evening. Often, also, the pangs of yesterday are remembered with contempt, and are ridiculed as follies and vain fancies.

"The evening is comparable to old age; and on the other hand, the dawn of the morning resembles youth; the one full of comfort and hope, and then sad evening with its discouragement and tendencies to look on the dark side of things. But, just as the time of youth in life is very short and fleeting, so is the infancy of each new day, which quickly ages towards its evening.

"Youth, if indeed it be the best of life, is a very wretched thing. Yet even this poor benefit is so soon over, that when by many signs man is led to perceive the decline of his existence, he has scarcely experienced its perfection, or fully realised its peculiar strength, which, once diminished, the best part of life is gone with every race of mortals. Thus, in all her works, Nature turns and points towards death: for old age reigns universally. Every part of the world hastens untiringly; with diligence and wonderful celerity, towards death. The world itself alone seems exempt from decay; for although in autumn and winter it appears as it were sick and aged, nevertheless in the spring it ever rejuvenates. But just as mortals in the first part of each day regain some portion of their youth, yet grow old as the day progresses, and are at length extinguished in sleep; so although in the beginning of the year the world becomes young again, none the less it perpetually ages. The time will come when this world, and Nature herself, shall die. And as at the present day there[Pg 155] remains no trace nor record of many very great kingdoms and empires, so in the whole world there shall not he left a vestige of the infinite changes and catastrophes of created things. A naked silence and an utter calm shall fill the vast space. Thus, this wonderful and fearful mystery of universal existence shall be unloosed, and shall melt away before it be made manifest or be comprehended."[1]

[1] This is a poetical not philosophical conclusion. Speaking philosophically, existence, which has had no beginning, will have no ending.

[Pg 156]

Timandro. I am very anxious to have some conversation with you. It is about the matter and tendency of your writings and words, which seem to me most blamable.

Meandro. So long as you find no fault with my actions, I confess I do not much care; because words and writings are of little consequence.

Tim. There is nothing in your actions, as far as I can see, for which I need blame you. I am aware that you benefit no one because you cannot do so, and I observe that you injure no one because you are unwilling to do so. But I consider your speech and writings very reprehensible, and I do not agree with you that they are of little importance. Our life may almost be said to consist of nothing else. For the present we will disregard the words, and simply consider the writings. In the first place, the incessant vituperation and continuous satire that you bestow on the human race are out of fashion.

Mean. My brain also is out of fashion. It is quite natural for a child to resemble its father.

Tim. Then you must not be surprised if your books, like everything contrary to the custom of the day, are ill received.

Mean. That is a small misfortune. They were not[Pg 157] written for the purpose of begging a little bread at the doors of the rich.

? Tim. Forty or fifty years ago, philosophers used to say hard things about the human race, but now they do just the contrary.

Mean. Do you believe that forty or fifty years ago the philosophers were right or wrong in their statements?

Tim. More often right than wrong.

Mean. Do you think that in these forty or fifty years the human race has changed to the opposite of what it then was?

Tim. Not at all. But that has nothing to do with the question.

Elean. Why not? Has humanity progressed in strength and perfection, that the writers of to-day should be constrained to flatter, and compelled to reverence it?

Tim. What have such pleasantries to do with so grave a matter?

Elean. Then seriously. I am not unaware that the people of this century, although continuing to ill-treat their fellow-men as their ancestors did, have yet a very high opinion of themselves, such as men of the past century did not possess. But I, who ill-treat no one, do not see that I am obliged to speak well of others against my conscience.

Tim. You must, however, like all men, endeavour to serve your race.

Elean. If my race, on the contrary, does its best to injure me, I do not see that this obligation holds, as you say. But supposing you are right, what ought I to do, if I cannot be useful to my race?

Tim. By actions, perhaps, you may be unable to be of much use. Such power is in the hands of but few people. But by your writings you can, and indeed ought to serve it. And the race is not benefited by books which snarl incessantly at men in general. Such behaviour is, on the contrary, extremely injurious.

[Pg 158]

Elean. I admit that it does no good, but I also imagine it does no harm. Do you, however, think books are able to help the human race?

Tim. Not I only, but all the world think so.

Elean. What kind of books?

Tim. Many kinds; but especially books treating of morals.

Elean. All the world does not think so, because I, amongst others, do not, as a woman once said to Socrates. If books of morals could be useful to men, I should place poetry above all others. I use the word poetry in its widest sense, as including all writings, the aim of which is to excite the imagination, whether in prose or verse. Now I hold in little esteem that sort of poetry which, when read and meditated over, does not leave in the mind of the reader a sufficiently elevating sentiment to deter him for half an hour from giving way to a single base thought or unworthy action. If, however, the reader commits, for example, a breach of faith towards his best friend an hour after such reading, I do not condemn the poetry for that, because then the finest, most stirring, and noblest poetry the world possesses would come under condemnation. Exceptions to this influence are readers who live in great cities. These people, however great their concentration, cannot forget themselves for even half an hour, nor are they much pleased, or moved, by any sort of poetry.

Tim. You speak, as usual, maliciously, and so as to leave an impression that you are habitually ill-treated by others. This, in most instances, is the true cause of the ill-humour and contempt exhibited by certain people towards their race.

Elean. Indeed, I cannot say that men have treated, or do treat me very well. If I could say so, I imagine I should be unique in my experience. But neither have they done me any serious harm, because in demanding nothing from men, and having nothing in common with[Pg 159] them, I scarcely give them a chance of offending me. I must confess, however, that recognising clearly, as I do, how ignorant I am of the simplest means of making myself agreeable to others, both in conversation and the daily intercourse of life, whether from a natural defect or fault of my own, I should esteem men less if they treated me better.

Tim. Then you are so much the more to blame. For, had you even a mistaken ground of complaint, your hatred and desire for revenge against men would be in a measure justifiable. But your hatred, from what you say, is based on nothing in particular, except perhaps an extraordinary and wretched ambition of becoming famous as a misanthrope like Timon—a desire abominable in itself, and especially out of place in a century like the present, so peculiarly devoted to philanthropy.

Elean. I need not reply to your remark about ambition, because I have already said that I want nothing from men. Does that seem incredible to you? You will at least grant that it is not ambition which urges me to write books, such as on your own showing are more likely to bring me reproaches than glory. Besides, I am so far from hating the human race, that I neither can nor wish to hate even those who particularly offend me. Indeed, the fact that hatred is so completely foreign to me, goes far to explain my inability to do as other men do. But I cannot change this, because I always think that whenever a man displeases or injures another, he does so in the hope of procuring some pleasure or advantage for himself. His aim is not to injure others (which can never be the motive of any action, nor the object of any thought), but to benefit himself,—a natural desire, and undeserving of odium. Again, whenever I notice a particular vice or fault in my neighbour, I carefully examine myself, and as far as circumstances will allow, I put myself in his place. Thereupon I invariably find that I should have done the same as he, and been guilty of the[Pg 160] same faults. Consequently my mind loses what irritation it previously felt. I reserve my wrath for occasions when I might see some wickedness of which my nature is incapable; but so far I have never met with such a case. Finally, the thought of the vanity of human things is so constantly in my mind that I am unable to excite myself about any one of them. Hatred and anger seem to me great and strong passions, out of harmony with the insignificance of life. Thus you see there is a great difference between

90

Timon and myself. Timon hated and shunned all men except Alcibiades, for whom he reserved all his affection, because he saw in him the initiator of innumerable evils for their common country. I, on the other hand, without hating Alcibiades, would have especially avoided him. I would have warned my fellow-citizens of their danger, exhorting them at the same time to take the requisite steps to preserve themselves from it. Some say that Timon did not hate men, but beasts in the likeness of men. As for me, I neither hate men nor beasts.

Tim. Nor do you love any one.

Mean. Listen, my friend. I am born to love. I have loved; and perhaps with as deep a passion as is possible for human soul to feel. To-day, although, as you see, I am not sufficiently old to be naturally devoid of passion, nor even of a lukewarm age, I am not ashamed to say that I love no one except myself, by the necessity of nature, and that as little as possible. Nevertheless, I would always rather bear suffering myself than be the cause of it to others. I believe you can bear witness to the truth of this, little as you know about my habits.

Tim. I do not deny it.

Mean. I try to procure for men, even at my own expense, that greatest possible good, which alone I seek for myself, viz., a state of freedom from suffering.

Tim. But do you distinctly confess that you do not love the human race in general?
[Pg 161]

Elean. Yes, absolutely. But in such a way that if it depended on me, I would punish those who deserved punishment, without hating them, as also I would benefit my race to the utmost, although I do not love it.

Tim. Well, it may be so. But then, if you are not incited by injuries received, nor by hatred, nor ambition, why do you write in such a manner?

Mean. For many reasons. First, because I cannot tolerate deceit and dissimulation. I may sometimes have to give way to these in conversation, but never in my writings; because I am often obliged to speak unwillingly, but I never write unless I please. I should derive no satisfaction from puzzling my brains, and expressing the result on paper, unless I could write what I really think. All sensible people laugh at those who now-a-days write Latin, because no one speaks, and few understand, the language. I think it is equally absurd to take for granted, whether in conversation or writing, the reality of certain human qualities no longer extant, and the existence of certain rational beings, formerly considered as divinities, but now really regarded as non-existent equally by those who mention them, and those who hear them mentioned. I could understand men using masks and disguises in order to deceive other men, or to avoid being recognised. But it seems childish for them all to conceal themselves behind the same kind of mask, and use the same disguise, whereby they deceive no one, but recognise each other perfectly, in spite of it. Let them lay aside their masks, and retain merely their clothes. The effect will be precisely the same, and they will be more at ease. Besides, this perpetual simulation, though useless, and this eternal acting of a part between which and oneself there is nothing in common, cannot be carried on without fatigue and weariness. If men had passed suddenly, instead of gradually, from the savage condition to their present state of civilisation, would the names of the things just mentioned be found in general[Pg 162] usage, with the custom of deducing from them a thousand philosophical conclusions? In truth, this custom seems to me like one of those ceremonies and ancient practices so incompatible with our present habits, which nevertheless continue to exist by force of usage. I for my part cannot submit to these ceremonies; and I write in the language of modern times, not that of the Trojan era. In the second place, I do not so much, in my writings, find fault with the human race, as grieve over its destiny. There is nothing I think more clear and palpable than the necessary unhappiness of all living beings. If this unhappiness be not a fact, then all my arguments are wrong, and we may abandon the discussion. If it be true, why may I not lament openly and freely, and say that I suffer? Doubtless, if I did nothing but weep incessantly (this is the third cause which moves me), I should become a nuisance to others as well as myself, without profiting any one. But in laughing at our misfortunes, we do much to remedy them. I endeavour therefore to persuade others to profit in this way, as I have done. Whether I succeed or not, I feel assured that such laughter is the only solace and remedy that can be found. The poets say that despair has always a smile on its lips.

But you must not think that I am devoid of compassion for the unhappiness of humanity. Its condition is incurable by art, industry, or anything else, therefore I consider it far more manly and consistent with a magnanimous despair to laugh at our common woes, than to sigh, weep, and moan with others, thereby encouraging them in their lamentations.

Lastly, permit me to say that I desire as much as you, or any one else, the welfare of my race in general, but I am hopeless of its attainment; nor can I, like so many philosophers of this century, nourish and soothe my mind with anticipations of good. My despair is absolute, unchangeable, and so based on firm judgment[Pg 163] and conviction, that I cannot imagine such a thing as a joyous future, nor can I undertake anything with the hope of bringing it to completion. And you are well aware that man is never inclined to attempt what he knows or thinks cannot succeed; or if he does, he acts feebly and without confidence. Similarly a writer, who expresses himself contrary to his real opinion, though this be erroneous, utters nothing worthy of consideration.

Tim. But when his judgment is, like yours, a false one, he should rectify it.

Elean. My judgment is of myself alone, and I am quite sure I do not err in announcing my unhappiness. If other men are happy, I congratulate them with all my heart. I know also that death alone can deliver me from my misfortune. If others are more hopeful, I rejoice once again.

Tim. We are all unhappy, and have always been so. I scarcely think you can take credit for the novelty of your idea. But man's present condition, superior as it is to his past, will be greatly improved in the future. You forget, or seem to disregard the fact, that man is perfectible.

Elean. Perfectible he may be. But that he is capable of perfection, which is of more importance, I know not who can convince me.

Tim. He has not yet had time to reach perfection. Ultimately he will no doubt attain to it.

Elean. I do not doubt it. The few years that have passed since the world began are, I agree with you, quite insufficient to complete our education. We cannot judge from what seem to us the nature and capabilities of man. Besides, humanity hitherto has been too occupied with other business to give itself up to the task of attaining perfection. But in future all its endeavours will be towards this one aim.

Tim. Yes, the whole civilised world is working zealously towards this end. And, taking into consideration[Pg 164] the number and sufficiency of the means employed, which have indeed recently increased in an astounding manner, we have every reason to think that the goal will be reached, sooner or later. This conviction itself is by no means one of the least stimulants to progress, because it gives birth to a host of undertakings and labours useful for the common welfare. If, then, at any time it was fatal and blâmable to manifest despair like yours, and to teach men such doctrines as the absolute necessity of their wretchedness, the vanity of life, the insignificance of their race, and the evil of their nature, much more is it so in the present day. Such conduct can only result in depriving us of courage, and that feeling of self-esteem which is the foundation of an honest, useful, and glorious life; it will also divert us from the path of our own welfare.

Elean. Kindly say distinctly, whether or not you regard as true what I have said about the unhappiness of mankind.

Tim. You return to your old argument. Well, supposing I admit the truth of what you say, how does that alter the matter? I would remind you that it is not always well to preach truth simply because it is truth.

Elean. Answer me another question. Are these truths, which I merely express, without any pretence of preaching, of primary or secondary importance in philosophy?

Tim. In my opinion they are the very essence of all philosophy.

Elean. In that case, they greatly deceive themselves who affirm that man's perfection consists in complete knowledge of the truth; that his misfortunes are the consequence of his ignorance and prejudices; and that the human race will be happy when men have discovered the truth, and conform their lives to its teaching. Yet such doctrines are taught by most philosophers, ancient and modern. But you are of opinion that these truths,[Pg 165] though confessedly the substance of all philosophy, ought to be concealed from the majority of men. You would rather that they were unknown or disregarded by all men, because of the baneful influence they exercise over the mind. And this is equivalent to an admission that philosophy ought to be banished from the earth. I grant you, however, that the final conclusion to be drawn from true and perfect philosophy is that it were better to dispense with philosophy. It would therefore seem that, first of all, philosophy is superfluous, since its conclusions are attainable without its assistance; secondly, it is extremely injurious, because its conclusion is a very painful one to be accepted, and when accepted is useless: nor is it in man's power to disregard truths once recognised. Besides, the habit of philosophising is one of the most difficult habits to throw off. Thus, philosophy which at first inspires hope as a possible remedy for the ills of humanity, ends by seeking in vain a cure for itself. And now I would ask you why you imagine we are nearer perfection than our ancestors were? Is it that we are better acquainted with the truth? This cannot be, since we have seen that such knowledge is extremely prejudicial to man's happiness. Perhaps, however, it is because some few men in the present day have learnt that the truest philosopher is he who abstains from philosophy? But in what then are we superior to the men of primitive times, who were perfectly unacquainted with philosophy? And even in the present day savages abstain from philosophy, without feeling the least inconvenience.

In what, therefore, are we more advanced than our ancestors; and what means of attaining perfection do we possess, which they had not?

Tim. We have many of great importance. To explain them would be a work of considerable time.

Elean. Put them aside for the moment, and reconsider my theory. I say that if, on the one hand, I[Pg 166] express in my writings certain hard and bitter truths, whether to relieve my mind, or console myself in laughing at them, I do not fail at the same time to deplore and disadvise the search after that cold and miserable truth, acquaintance with which reduces us to a state of either indifference and hypocrisy, or baseness of soul, moral corruption, and depravity. And, on the other hand, I praise and exalt those noble, if false ideas, which give birth to high-minded and vigorous actions and thoughts, such as further the welfare of mankind, or individuals; those glorious illusions, vain though they be, which give value to life, and which are natural to the soul; in short, the superstitions of antiquity, distinct from the errors of barbarism. These latter should be rooted out, but the former respected. Civilisation and philosophy having exceeded their natural bounds, as is usual with all things pertaining to humanity, have drawn us from one state of barbarism only to precipitate us into another, no better than the first. This new barbarism, born of reason and science instead of ignorance, manifests itself more in the mind than the body. Yet I imagine, that though these superstitions become daily more necessary for the well-being of civilised nations, the possibility of their re-introduction diminishes daily.

And as for man's perfection, I assure you if I had perceived any signs of it, I would have written a volume in praise of the human race. But since I have not yet seen it, and as it is improbable I ever shall see it, I think of leaving in my will a certain sum of money for the purpose of procuring an annual panegyric of the human race, to be publicly recited from the time of its perfection, and to pay for the erection of a temple, statue, or monument, as may be judged best, to commemorate the event.

[Pg 167]
COPERNICUS:

A DIALOGUE IN FOUR SCENES.

Scene I.—The First Hour and the Sun.
First Hour. Good day, Excellency.
Sun. Thanks; good-night as well.
First Hour. The horses are waiting, your Excellency.
Sun. Very well.
First Hour. And the Morning Star has been up some time.
Sun. All right. Let it rise and set, just as it pleases.
First Hour. What do I hear your Excellency say?
Sun. I wish you would leave me alone.
First Hour. But, Excellency, the night has already lasted so long, that it can last no longer; and if we delay, imagine, Excellency, the confusion that will ensue.
Sun. I don't mean to stir, whatever happens.
First Hour.0 Excellency! what is this? Does your Excellency feel ill?
Sun. No, no; I feel nothing, except that I don't wish to move. So you can go and attend to your own affairs.
First Hour. How can I go unless your Excellency comes? I am the first Hour of the day, and how can the day exist, if your Excellency does not deign to go forth as usual?
Sun. If you will not be of the day, you shall be of the night; or better, the hours of the night shall do[Pg 168] double duty, and you and your companions shall be idle. For you must know I am tired of this eternal going round to give light to a race of little animals that live far away in a ball of clay, so small that I, who have good sight, cannot see it. During the night I have decided not to trouble myself any more in this fashion. If men want light, let them make their own fires for the purpose, or provide it in some other way.
First Hour. But, Excellency, how can the little fellows manage that? It will be a very great expense for them to keep lanterns or candles burning all day long. If only they could now discover a certain atmosphere to warm and illumine their streets, rooms, shops, taverns, and everything else at little expense, then they would not be so badly off. But men will have to wait some three hundred years, more or less, before they discover this; and meanwhile, all the oil, wax, pitch, and tallow of the earth will be exhausted, and they will have nothing more to burn.

94

Sun. Let them hunt the will-o-the-wisp, and catch those shining things called glow-worms.

First Hour. And how will they protect themselves against the cold? For without the assistance of your Excellency, all the forests together will not make a fire large enough to warm them. Besides, they will also die of hunger, since the earth will no longer bring forth its fruits. And so, after a few years, the seed of the poor little folk will be lost. They will go groping about the earth, seeking food and warmth, until having consumed every possible thing, and used up the last flicker of fire, they will all die in the darkness, frozen like pieces of rock-crystal.

Sun. What is this to do with me? Am I the nurse of the human race; or the cook, that I should look after the preparation of their food? And why need I care if a few invisible little creatures, millions of miles away from me, are unable to see, or bear the cold, when[Pg 169] deprived of my light and warmth? Besides, even supposing, as you say, that I ought to act the part of stove or fireplace to this human family, surely it is more reasonable, if men want to warm themselves, that they should come to the stove, than that the stove should go whirling round them. Therefore, if the Earth requires me, let it come hither to satisfy its needs. I want nothing from the Earth, that I should thus trouble myself to rotate round it.

First Hour. Your Excellency means, if I understand rightly, that henceforth the Earth must do for itself that which hitherto you have done on its behalf.

Sun. Yes: now and for the future.

First Hour. Well, your Excellency knows best what is right, and can do as it pleases you. But nevertheless, will your Excellency deign to think what a number of beautiful and useful things will be destroyed by this new decree. The day will be deprived of its handsome gilded chariot, and beautiful horses, which bathe themselves in the sea. Amongst other changes, we poor Hours must suffer; we shall no longer have a place in heaven, but shall have to descend from our position as celestial children to that of terrestrials, unless, as is more probable, we dissolve into thin air instead. But be that as it may, the difficulty will be to persuade the Earth to go round, necessarily a hard thing, because it is unaccustomed to do so; and the experience of rotating and exerting itself incessantly will be all the more strange, seeing that hitherto it has never stirred from its present position. If, then, your Excellency now begins to think of idleness, I fear the Earth will be as little desirous of bestirring itself as ever it was.

Sun. In that case, it must be pricked, and made to bestir itself as much as is necessary. But the quickest and surest way is to find a poet, or, better, a philosopher, who will persuade the Earth to move itself, or persuasion being unsuccessful, will use force. Eor philosophers and[Pg 170] poets ordinarily manage these affairs. When I was younger I used to have a great esteem for the poets, though they rather caricatured me in representing me racing madly, great and stout as I am, round and round a grain of sand, simply for the sake of amusement or exercise. But now that I am older, I am more partial to philosophy. I study to discern the utility, not the beauty of things, and poetry seems to me either absurd or wearisome. I wish, also, to have good substantial reasons for whatever I do. Now, I see no reason why I should value a life of activity more than a life of ease and idleness. I have determined, therefore, in future, to leave the fatigues and discomforts to others, and for my own part to live quietly at home, without undertaking business of any kind. This change in me is partly due to my age, but has chiefly been brought about by the philosophers, a race of people whose power and influence increase daily. Consequently, to induce the Earth to rotate in my place, a poet would intrinsically be better than a philosopher: because the poets are accustomed to give a fictitious value

95

to things by exaggerating the truth, beauty, and utility of subjects about which they treat, and because by raising a thousand pleasurable hopes, they often incite people to fatigues they would else have avoided; whereas philosophers weary them. But, now that the power of philosophers is so predominant, I doubt whether a poet would be of much use, if even the Earth gave him a hearing. Therefore, we had better have recourse to a philosopher. It is true, philosophers are usually little suited, and still less inclined, to stimulate other people to exertions; but possibly in so extreme a case, they may be induced to act contrary to custom. The Earth has, however, one alternative; it has the option of declining to undertake all this hard labour. Its destruction will then ensue, and I am far from sure that this would not be the best thing for it. But enough of this: we shall see what will take place. Now, either you or[Pg 171] one of your companions had better go at once to the Earth. If there you discover any one of these philosophers in the open air, regarding the heavens, and wondering about the cause of this protracted night, as well he may, take charge of him, and bring him hither on your back. Do you clearly understand?

First Hour. Yes, Excellency. You shall be obeyed.

Scene II.—Copernicus pacing the terrace of his house, with his eyes anxiously directed towards the eastern horizon. A roll of paper in his hand, which ever and anon he uses as a telescope.

This is a marvellous thing. Either the clocks are all wrong, or else the sun should have risen more than an hour ago. Yet not a gleam of light is to be seen in the east, though the sky is as bright and clear as a mirror. All the stars shine as if it were midnight. I must go and consult the Almagest and Sacrobosco, and see what they say about this event. I have often heard talk of the night Jove passed with the wife of Amphitryon, and I also remember reading a little while ago, in a modern Spanish book, that the Peruvians record a very long night, at the end of which the sun proceeded forth from a certain lake called Titicaca. Hitherto I have regarded these as mere tales, and have never wavered in my belief. Now, however, that I perceive reason and science to be absolutely useless, I am determined to believe the truth of these, and similar things. I will also visit the lakes and puddles in the neighbourhood, and see if I can fish out the sun.

Ha! what is this that I hear? It is like the flapping of the wings of some huge bird.
[Pg 172]
Scene III.—The Last Hour and Copernicus.

Last Hour. Copernicus, I am the Last Hour.

Copernicus. The Last Hour! Well, I suppose I must be resigned. But I beg of you, if possible, to give me enough time to make my will, and put my things in order, before I die.

Last Hour. Die! What do you mean? I am not the last hour of your life.

Copernicus. Oh, then, what are you? The last hour of the office of the breviary?

Last Hour. I can quite imagine you prefer that one to the others, when you are in your stall.

Copernicus. But how do you know I am a Canon? And how is it you know my name?

Last Hour. I procured my information about you, from certain people in the street. I am, in fact, the Last Hour of day.

Copernicus. Ah! now I understand. The First Hour is unwell; and that is why day is not yet visible.

Last Hour. I have news for you. There will never be any more daylight unless you provide it yourself.

Copernicus. You would throw on me the responsibility of making daylight? A fine thing, indeed!

Last Hour. I will tell you how. But first of all, you must come with me at once to the house of the Sun, my father. You shall hear more when we set out. His Excellency will explain everything when we arrive.

Copernicus. I trust it is all right. But the journey, unless I am mistaken, must be a very long one. And how can I take enough food to prevent my dying of hunger a few years before reaching the Sun? Besides, I doubt if his Excellency's lands produce the where-withal to supply me with even a single meal.

Last Hour. Do not trouble yourself with these doubts. You will not stay long in my father's house, and the journey will be completed in a moment. For you must know that I am a spirit.

[Pg 173]

Copernicus. Maybe. But I am a body.

Last Hour. Well, well: you are not a metaphysician that you need excite yourself about these matters. Come now, mount on my shoulders, and leave all the rest to me.

Copernicus. Courage. There, it is done! I will pursue this novelty to its issue.

Scene IV.—Copernicus and the Sun.

Copernicus. Most noble Lord.

Sun. Forgive me, Copernicus, if I do not offer you a chair: one does not use such things here. But we will soon despatch our business. My servant has already explained the matter to you; and from what the child tells me, I imagine you will do very well for our purpose.

Copernicus. My lord, I discern great difficulties in the matter.

Sun. Difficulties ought not to frighten such a man as yourself. They are even said to make the brave man still more courageous. But tell me briefly of what these difficulties consist.

Copernicus. In the first place, although philosophy is a great power, I doubt whether it can persuade the Earth to change its comfortable sitting posture for a state of restless activity; especially in these times, which are not heroic.

Sun. And if persuasion be ineffectual, you must try force.

Copernicus. Willingly, Illustrious, if I were a Hercules, or even an Orlando, instead of a mere Canon of Varmia.

Sun. What has that to do with it? Did not one of your ancient mathematicians say, that if he had standing room given him outside the world, he would undertake to move heaven and earth? Now, you are not required to move heaven, and behold, you are already in a place outside the earth. Therefore, unless you are not so clever as that ancient, you will no doubt be able to move the Earth, whether it be willing, or not.

[Pg 174]

Copernicus. My lord, such a thing might be possible. But a lever would be necessary, of such dimensions that neither I nor even your Illustrious Lordship could pay half the cost of its materials and manufacture. There are, however, other and far more serious difficulties, which I will now mention.

You know the Earth has hitherto occupied the principal position in the Universe, that is the centre. Motionless, it has had nothing to do but regard all the other spheres, great and small, brilliant and obscure, continuously gyrating around and on all sides of it with a marvellous regularity and speed. All things seem to be occupied in its service; so that the Universe may be likened to a court, in the midst of which the Earth sits as on a throne, surrounded by attendant globes, like courtiers, guards, and servants, each of which

97

fulfils its respective office. Consequently, the Earth has always regarded itself as Empress of the Universe. So far, indeed, little fault can be found with its control, and I do not think your design an improvement on the old state of affairs. But what shall I say to you about men? We esteem ourselves (and shall always do so) to be in the same relation to the rest of created beings as the Earth is to the Universe. And more than this. Supreme among terrestrial creatures, we all, including the ragged beggar who dines on a morsel of black bread, have a most exalted idea of ourselves. We are each of us emperors, and our empire is only bounded by the Universe, for it includes all the stars and planets, visible and invisible. Man is, in his own > estimation, the final cause of all things, including even your Illustrious Lordship.

Now, if we remove the Earth from its place in the centre, and make it whirl round and round unremittingly, what will be the consequence? Simply, that it will act like all the other globes, and be enrolled in the number of the planets. Then all its terrestrial majesty will vanish, and the Earth will have to abdicate its imperial throne.[Pg 175] Men, too, will lose their human majesty, and be deprived of their supremacy; they will be left alone with their rags, and miseries, which are not insignificant.

Sun. In short, Don Nicolas, what do you wish to prove by this discourse? Is it that you have scruples of conscience lest the deed should be treasonable?

Copernicus. No, it is not that, Illustrious. For, to the best of my knowledge neither the Codes, nor the Digest, nor the books of public, imperial, international, or natural law, make any mention of such treason. What I wanted to show was, that this action, subverting our planetary relationships, will not only work alteration in the order of nature; for it will change the position of things inter se, and the ends for which created beings now exist; it will also necessarily make a great revolution in the science of metaphysics, and everything connected with the speculative part of knowledge. The result will be that men, even if they are able and willing to critically examine into the why and wherefore of life, will discover themselves and their aims to be very different from what they are now, or from what they imagine them to be.

Sun. My dear child, the thought of these things does not disturb me much; so little respect have I for metaphysics, or physics, or even alchemy, necromancy, or any such things. Besides, men will in time become content with their position; or, if they do not like it, they may argue the matter to their hearts' content, and will doubtless succeed in believing just what they please. In this way they may still deceive themselves under the names of Barons, Dukes, Emperors, or anything else. If, however, they are inconsolable, I confess it will not give me much uneasiness.

Copernicus. Well, then, apart from men and the Earth, consider, Illustrious, what may reasonably be expected to happen in regard to the other planets. These, when they see the Earth reduced to their condition, and doing precisely what they do, just like one of themselves, will be[Pg 176] jealous of its apparent superiority. They will be dissatisfied with their own naked simplicity and sad loneliness, and will desire to have their rivers, mountains, seas, plants, animals, and men; for they will see no reason why they should be in the smallest degree less endowed than the Earth. Thereupon will ensue another great revolution in the Universe: an infinite number of new races and people will instantaneously proceed from their soil, like mushrooms.

Sun. Well, let them come, and the more the merrier. My light and heat will suffice for them all without any extra expense. The Universe shall have food, clothes, and lodging amply provided gratis.

Copernicus. But, if your Illustrious Lordship will reflect a moment, yet another objection may be discerned. The stars, having rivalled the Earth, will turn their attentions to you. They will notice your fine throne, noble court, and numerous planetary satellites. Consequently, they also will wish for thrones. And more, they will desire to rule, as you do, over inferior planets, each of which must of course be peopled and ornamented like the Earth. It is needless to mention the increased unhappiness of the human race. Their insignificance will be greater than ever. They will burst out in all these millions of new worlds, so that even the tiniest star of the milky way will be provided with its own race of mortals. Now, looking at this, solely as affecting your interests, I affirm that it will be very prejudicial. Hitherto you have been, if not the first, certainly the second in the Universe; that is, after the Earth; nor have the stars aspired to rival you in dignity. In this new state, however, you will have as many equals as stars, each with their respective stars. Beware then lest this change be ruinous to your supremacy.

Sun. You remember Cæsar's remark, when, crossing the Alps, he happened to pass a certain miserable little barbarian village. He said that he would rather be the[Pg 177] first in that village, than the second in Rome. Similarly I would rather be first in this my own world than second in the Universe. But you must not think it is ambition that makes me desirous of changing the present state of things; it is solely my love of peace, or, more candidly, idleness. Therefore it is a small matter to me whether I am first or last in the Universe: unlike Cicero, I care more for ease than dignity.

Copernicus. I also, Illustrious, have striven my utmost to obtain this ease. But, supposing your Lordship is successful in your endeavour, I doubt whether it will be of long duration. For, in the first place, I feel almost sure that before many years have elapsed you will be impelled to go winding round and round like a windlass, or a wheel, without however varying your locality. Then, after a time, you will probably be desirous of rotating round something—the Earth for instance. Ah! well, be that as it may; if you persist in your determination, I will try to serve you, in spite of the great difficulties necessarily to be overcome. If I fail, you must attribute the failure to my inability, not unwillingness.

Sun. That is well, my Copernicus. Do your best.

Copernicus. There is however yet another obstacle.

Sun. What is it?

Copernicus. I fear lest I should be burnt alive for my pains. In which case, it would be improbable that I, like the Phoenix, should rise from my ashes. I should therefore never see your Lordship's face again.

Sun. Listen, Copernicus. You know that once upon a time I was a prophet, when poetry ruled the world, and philosophy was scarcely hatched. I will now utter my last prophecy. Put faith in me on the strength of my former power. This is what I say. It may be that those who come after you, and confirm your deeds, shall be burnt, or killed in some other way; but you shall be safe, nor shall you suffer at all on account of this undertaking. And to make your safety certain, dedicate to[Pg 178] the Pope the book[1] you will write on the subject. If you do this, I promise that you will not even lose your canonry.

[1] Copernicus did in effect dedicate his book on the "Revolution of the Celestial Bodies," the printing of which was only completed a few days before his death, to Pope Paul III. The system expounded therein was condemned by a decree of Paul V. in 1616. This condemnation remained in force until 1821, when it was revoked by Pius VII. The sun is supposed to be in the centre, and motionless; the earth and the rest of the planets move round it in elliptical orbits. The heavens and stars are supposed to be stationary, and their apparent diurnal motion from east to west is imputed to the earth's motion from west to east.

DIALOGUE BETWEEN AN ALMANAC SELLER AND A PASSER-BY.

Almanac Seller. Almanacs! New Almanacs! New Calendars! Who wants new Almanacs?

Passer-by. Almanacs for the New Year?

Alm. Seller. Yes, Sir.

Passer. Do you think this New Year will be a happy one?

Alm. Seller. Yes, to be sure, Sir.

Passer. As happy as last year?

Alm. Seller. Much more so.

Passer. As the year before?

Alm. Seller. Still more, Sir.

Passer. Why? Should you not like the New Year to resemble one of the past years?

Alm. Seller. No, Sir, I should not.

Passer. How many years have gone by since you began to sell almanacs?

Alm. Seller. About twenty years, Sir.

Passer. Which of the twenty should you wish the New Year to be like?

Alm. Seller. I do not know.

Passer. Do you not remember any particular year which you thought a happy one?

Alm. Seller. Indeed I do not, Sir.

Passer. And yet life is a fine thing, is it not?

Alm. Seller. So they say.

Passer. Would you not like to live these twenty years, and even all your, past life from your birth, over again?

Alm. Seller. Ah, dear Sir, would to God I could!

Passer. But if you had to live over again the life you have already lived, with all its pleasures and sufferings?

Alm. Seller. I should not like that.

Passer. Then what other life would you like to live? Mine, or that of the Prince, or whose? Do you not think that I, or the Prince, or any one else, would reply exactly as you have done; and that no one would wish to repeat the same life over again?

Alm. Seller. I do believe that.

Passer. Then would you recommence it on this condition, if none other were offered you?

Alm. Seller. No, Sir, indeed I would not.

Passer. Then what life would you like?

Alm. Seller. Such an one as God would give me without any conditions.

Passer. A life at hap-hazard, and of which you would know nothing beforehand, as you know nothing about the New Year?

Alm. Seller. Exactly.

Passer. It is what I should wish, had I to live my life over again, and so would every one. But this proves that Fate has treated us all badly. And it is clear that each person is of opinion that the evil he has experienced exceeds the good, if no one would wish to be re-born on condition of living his own life over again from the beginning, with just its same proportion of good and evil. This life, which is such a fine thing, is not the life we are

100

acquainted with, but that of which we know nothing; it is not the past life, but the future. With the New Year Fate will commence treating you, and me, and every one well, and the happy life will begin. Am I not right?

Alm. Seller. Let us hope so.

[Pg 181]

Passer. Show me the best almanac you have.

Alm. Seller. Here it is, Sir. This is worth thirty soldi.

Passer. Here are thirty soldi.

Alm. Seller. Thank you, Sir. Good day, Sir.—Almanacs! New Almanacs! New Calendars!

[Pg 182]

DIALOGUE BETWEEN PLOTINUS AND PORPHYRIUS.

"One day when I, Porphyrius, was meditating about taking my own life, Plotinus guessed my intention. He interrupted me, and said that such a design could not proceed from a healthy mind, but was due to some melancholy indisposition, and that I must have change of air" (Ex. Life of Plotinus, by Porphyrius).

The same incident is recounted in the life of Plotinus by Eunapius, who adds that Plotinus recorded in a book the conversation he then held with Porphyrius on the subject.

Plotinus. You know, Porphyrius, how sincerely I am your friend. You will not wonder therefore that I am unquiet about you. For some time I have noticed how sad and thoughtful you are; your expression of countenance is unusual, and you have let fall certain words which make me anxious. In short, I fear that you contemplate some evil design.

Porphyrius. How! What do you mean?

Plotinus. I think you intend to do yourself some injury; it were a bad omen to give the deed its name. Listen to me, dear Porphyrius, and do not conceal the truth. Do not wrong the friendship that has so long existed between us. I know my words will cause you displeasure, and I can easily understand that you would rather have kept your design hid. But I could not be silent in such a matter, and you ought not to refuse to confide in one who loves you as much as himself. Let us[Pg 183] then talk calmly, weighing our words. Open your heart to me. Tell me your troubles, and let me be auditor of your lamentations. I have deserved your confidence. I promise, on my part, not to oppose the carrying out of your resolution, if we agree that it is useful and reasonable.

Porphyrius. I have never denied a request of yours, dear Plotinus. I will therefore confess to you what I would rather have kept to myself; nothing in the world would induce me to tell it to anyone else. You are right in your interpretation of my thoughts. If you wish to discuss the subject, I will not refuse, in spite of my dislike to do so; for on such occasions the mind prefers to encompass itself with a lofty silence, and to meditate in solitude, giving itself up for the time to a state of complete self-absorption. Nevertheless, I am willing to do as you please.

In the first place, I may say that my design is not the consequence of any special misfortune. It is simply the result of an utter weariness of life, and a continuous ennui which has long possessed me like a pain. To this may be added a feeling of the vanity and nothingness of all things, which pervades me in body and soul. Do not say that this disposition of mind is unreasonable, though I will allow that it may in part proceed from physical causes. It is in itself perfectly reasonable, and therein differs from all our other dispositions; for everything which makes us attach some value to life and human things, proves on analysis to be contrary to reason, and to proceed from some illusion or falsity.

101

Nothing is more rational than ennui.[1] Pleasures are all unreal. Pain itself, at least mental pain, is equally false, because on examination it is seen to have scarcely any foundation, or none at all. The same may be said of fear and[Pg 184] hope. Ennui alone, which is born from the vanity of things, is genuine, and never deceives. If, then, all else be vain, the reality of life is summed up in ennui.

Plotinus. It may be so. I will not contradict you as to that. But we must now consider the nature of your project. You know Plato refused to allow that man is at liberty to escape, like a fugitive slave, from the captivity in which he is placed by the will of the gods, in depriving himself of life.

Porphyrius. I beg you, dear Plotinus, to leave Plate alone now, with his doctrines and dreams. It is one thing to praise, explain, and champion certain theories in the schools and in books, but quite another to practically exemplify them. School-teaching and boots constrain us to admire Plato, and conform to him, because such is the custom in the present day. Bat in real life, far from being admired, he is even detested. It is true Plato is said to have spread abroad by his writings the notion of a future life, thus leaving men in doubt as to their fate after death, and serving a good purpose in deterring men from evil in this life, through fear of punishment in the next. If I imagined Plato to have been the inventor of these ideas and beliefs, I would speak thus to him:—

"You observe, O Plato, how inimical to our race the power which governs the world has always been, whether known as Nature, Destiny, or Fate. Many reasons contradict the supposition that man has that high rank in the order of creation which we are pleased to imagine; but by no reason can he be deprived of the characteristic attributed to him by Homer—that of suffering. Nature, however, has given us a remedy for all evils. It is death, little feared by those who are not fully intelligent, and by all others desired.

"But you have deprived us of this dearest consolation of our life, full of suffering that it is. The doubts raised by you have torn this comfort from our minds, and[Pg 185] made the thought of death the bitterest of all thoughts. Thanks to you, unhappy mortals now fear the storm less than the port. Driven from their one place of repose, and robbed of the only remedy they could look for, they resign themselves to the sufferings and troubles of life. Thus, you have been more cruel towards us than Destiny, Nature, or Fate. And since this doubt, once conceived, can never be got rid of, to you is it due that your fellow-men regard death as something more terrible than life. You are to blame that rest and peace are for ever banished from the last moments of man, whereas all other animals die in perfect fearlessness. This one thing, O Plato, was wanting to complete the sum of human misery.

"True, your intention was good. But it has failed in its purpose. Violence and injustice are not arrested, for evil-doers only realise the terrors of death in their last moments, when quite powerless to do more harm. Your doubts trouble only the good, who are more disposed to benefit than injure their fellow-men, and the weak and timid, who are neither inclined by nature nor disposition to oppress anyone. Bold and strong men, who have scarcely any power of imagination, and those who require some other restraint than mere law, regard these fears as chimerical, and are undeterred from evil doing. We see daily instances of this, and the experience of all the centuries, from your time down to the present, confirms it. Good laws, still more, good education, and mental and social culture,—these are the things that preserve justice and mildness amongst men. Civilisation, and the use of reflection and reason, make men almost always hate to war with each other and shed one another's blood, and render them disinclined to quarrel, and endanger their lives by lawlessness. But such good results are never due to threatening fancies, and bitter expectation of terrible chastisement; these, like the multitude and cruelty of the punishments used in certain states, only serve to increase the baseness and[Pg 186] ferocity of men, and are therefore opposed to the well-being of human society.

"Perhaps, however, you will reply that you have promised a reward in the future for the good. What then is this reward? A state of life which seems full of ennui, even less tolerable than our present existence! The bitterness of your punishments is unmistakable; but the sweetness of your rewards is hidden and secret, incomprehensible to our minds. How then can order and virtue be said to be encouraged by your doctrine? I will venture to say that if but few men have been deterred from evil by the fear of your terrible Tartarus, no good man has been led to perform a single praiseworthy action by desire of your Elysium. Such a Paradise does not attract us in the least. But, apart from the fact that your heaven is scarcely an inviting place, who among the best of us can hope to merit it? What man can satisfy your inexorable judges, Minos, Eacus, and Rhadamanthus, who will not overlook one single fault, however trivial? Besides, who can say that he has reached your standard of purity? In short, we cannot look for happiness in the world to come; and however clear a man's conscience may be, or however upright his life, in his last hour he will dread the future with its terrible incertitude. It is due to your teaching that fear is a much stronger influence than hope, and may be said to dominate mankind.

"This then is the result of your doctrines. Man, whose life on earth is wretched in the extreme, anticipates death, not as an end to all his miseries, but as the beginning of a condition more wretched still. Thus, you surpass in cruelty, not only Nature and Destiny, but the most merciless tyrant and bloodthirsty executioner the world has ever known.

"But what cruelty can exceed that of your law, forbidding man to put an end to his sufferings and troubles by voluntarily depriving himself of life, thereby[Pg 187] triumphing over the horrors of death? Other animals do not desire to put an end to their life, because their unhappiness is less than ours; nor would they even have sufficient courage to face a voluntary death. But if they did wish to die, what should deter them from fulfilling their desire? They are affected by no prohibition, nor fear of the future. Here again you make us inferior to brute beasts. The liberty they possess, they do not use; the liberty granted also to us by Nature, so miserly in her gifts, you take away. Thus, the only creatures capable of desiring death, have the right to die refused them. Nature, Destiny, and Fortune overwhelm us with cruel blows, that cause us to suffer fearfully; you add to our sufferings by tying our arms and enchaining our feet, so that we can neither defend ourselves, nor escape from our persecutors.

"Truly, when I think over the great wretchedness of humanity, it seems to me that your doctrines, above all things, O Plato, are guilty of it, and that men may well complain of you more than of Nature. For the latter, in decreeing for us an existence full of unhappiness, has left us the means of escaping from it when we please. Indeed, unhappiness cannot be called extreme, when we have in our hands the power to shorten it at will. Besides, the mere thought of being able to quit life at pleasure, and withdraw from the miseries of the world, is so great an alleviation of our lot, that in itself it suffices to render existence supportable. Consequently, there can be no doubt that our chief unhappiness proceeds from the fear, that in abbreviating our life we might be plunged into a state of greater misery than the present. And not only will our misery be greater in the future, but it will be so full of the refinement of cruelty, that a comparison of these unexperienced tortures with the known sufferings of this life, reduces the latter almost to insignificance.

"You have easily, O Plato, raised this question of[Pg 188] immortality; but the human species will become extinct before it is settled. Your genius is the most fatal thing that has ever afflicted humanity, and nothing can ever exist more disastrous in its effects."

That is what I would say to Plato, had he invented the doctrine we are discussing; but I am well aware he did not originate it. However, enough has been said. Let us drop the subject, if you please.

Plotinus. Porphyrius, you know how I revere Plato; yet in talking to you on such an occasion as this, I will give you my own opinion, and will disregard his authority. The few words of his that I spoke were rather as an introduction than anything else. Returning to my first argument, I affirm that not only Plato and every other philosopher, but Nature herself, teaches us that it is improper to take away our own life. I will not say much on this point, because if you reflect a little, I am sure you will agree with me that suicide is unnatural. It is indeed an action the most contrary possible to nature. The whole order of things would be subverted if the beings of the world destroyed themselves. And it is repugnant and absurd to suppose that life is given only to be taken away by its possessor, and that beings should exist only to become non-existent. The law of self-preservation is the strictest law of nature. Its maintenance is enjoined in every possible way on man and all creatures of the universe. And, apart from anything else, do we not instinctively fear, hate, and shun death, even in spite of ourselves? Therefore, since suicide is so utterly contrary to our nature, I cannot think that it is permissible.

Porphyrius. I have already meditated on the subject from all points of view; for the mind could not design such a step without due consideration. It seems to me that all your reasoning is answerable with just as much counter reasoning. But I will be brief.

You doubt whether it be permissible to die without[Pg 189] necessity. I ask you if it be permissible to be unhappy? Nature, you say, forbids suicide. It is a strange thing that since she is either unable or unwilling to make me happy, or free me from unhappiness, she should have the power to force me to live. If Nature has given us a love of life, and a hatred of death, she has also given us a love of happiness, and a hatred of suffering; and the latter instincts are much more powerful than the former, because happiness is the supreme aim of all our actions and sentiments of love or hatred. For to what end do we shun death, or desire life, save to promote our well-being, and for fear of the contrary?

How then can it be unnatural to escape from suffering in the only way open to man, that is, by dying; since in life it can never be avoided? How, too, can it be true, that Nature forbids me to devote myself to death, which is undoubtedly a good thing, and to reject life, which is undoubtedly an evil and injurious thing, since it is a source of nothing but suffering to me?

Plotinus. These things do not persuade me that suicide is not unnatural. Have we not a strong instinctive horror of death? Besides, we never see brute beasts, which invariably follow the instincts of their nature (when not contrarily trained by man), either commit suicide, or regard death as anything but a condition to be struggled against, even in their moments of greatest suffering. In short, all men who commit this desperate act, will be found to have lived out of conformity to nature. They, on the contrary, who live naturally, would without exception reject suicide, if even the thought proposed itself to them.

Porphyrius. Well, if you like, I will admit that the action is contrary to nature. But what has that to do with it, if we ourselves do not conform to nature; that is, are no longer savages? Compare ourselves, for instance, with the inhabitants of India or Ethiopia, who are said to have retained their primitive manners and[Pg 190] wild habits. You would scarcely think that these people were even of the same species as ourselves.

This transformation of life, and change of manners and customs by civilisation, has been accompanied, in my opinion, by an immeasurable increase of suffering. Savages never wish to commit suicide, nor does their imagination ever induce them to regard death as a desirable thing; whereas we who are civilised wish for it, and sometimes voluntarily seek it.

Now, if man be permitted to live unnaturally, and be consequently unhappy, why may he not also die unnaturally? For death is indeed the only way by which he can deliver himself from the unhappiness that results from civilisation. Or, why not return to our primitive condition, and state of nature? Ah, we should find it almost impossible as far as mere external circumstances are concerned, and in the more important matters of the mind, quite impossible. What is less natural than medicine? By this I mean surgery, and the use of drugs. They are both ordinarily used expressly to combat nature, and are quite unknown to brute beasts and savages. Yet, since the diseases they remedy are unnatural, and only occur in civilised countries, where people have fallen from their natural condition, these arts, being also unnatural, are highly esteemed and even indispensable. Similarly, suicide, which is a radical cure for the disease of despair, one of the outcomes of civilisation, must not be blamed because it is unnatural; for unnatural evils require unnatural remedies. It would indeed be hard and unjust that reason, which increases our misery by forcing us to go contrary to nature, should in this matter join hands with nature, and take from us our only remaining hope and refuge, and the only resource consistent with itself, and should force us to continue in our wretchedness.

The truth is this, Plotinus. Our primitive nature has departed from us for ever. Habit and reason have given[Pg 191] us a new nature in place of the old one, to which we shall never return. Formerly, it was unnatural for men to commit suicide, or desire death. In the present day, both are natural. They conform to our new nature, which however, like the old one, still impels us to seek our happiness. And since death is our greatest good, is it remarkable that men should voluntarily seek it? For our reason tells us that death is not an evil, but, as the remedy for all evils, is the most desirable of things.

Now tell me: are all other actions of civilised men regulated by the standard of their primitive nature? If so, give me a single instance. No, it is our present, and not our primitive nature, that interprets our actions; in other words, it is our reason. Why then should suicide alone be judged unreasonably, and from the aspect of our primitive nature? Why should this latter, which has no influence over our life, control our death? Why should not the same reason govern our death which rules our life? It is a fact, whether due to reason or our unhappiness, that in many people, especially those who are unfortunate and afflicted, the primitive hatred of death is extinguished, and even changed into desire and love, as I have said. Such love, though incompatible with our early nature, is a reality in the present day. We are also necessarily unhappy because we live unnaturally. It were therefore manifestly unreasonable to assert that the prohibition which forbade suicide in the primitive state should now hold good. This seems to me sufficient justification of the deed. It remains to be proved whether or not it be useful.

Plotinus. Never mind that side of the question, my dear Porphyrius, because if the deed be permissible, I have no doubt of its extreme utility. But I will never admit that a forbidden and improper action can be useful. The matter really resolves itself into this: which is the better, to suffer, or not to suffer? It is certain that most men would prefer suffering mixed with enjoyment,[Pg 192] to a state devoid of both suffering and enjoyment, so ardently do we desire and thirst after joy. But this is beside the question, because enjoyment and pleasure, properly speaking, are as impossible as suffering is inevitable. I mean a suffering as continuous as our never satisfied desire for pleasure and happiness, and quite apart from the peculiar and accidental sufferings which must infallibly be experienced by even the happiest of men. In truth, were we certain that in continuing to live, we should continue thus to suffer, we should have sufficient reason to prefer death to life; because existence does not contain a single genuine pleasure to compensate for such suffering, even if that were possible.

Porphyrius. It seems to me that ennui alone, and the fact that we cannot hope for an improved existence, are sufficiently cogent reasons to induce a desire for death, even though our condition be one of prosperity. And it is often a matter of surprise to me that we have no record of princes having committed suicide through ennui and weariness of their grandeur, like other men in lower stations of life. We read how Hegesias, the Cyrenaic, used to reason so eloquently about the miseries of life, that his auditors straightway went and committed suicide; for which reason he was called the "death persuader," and was at length forbidden by Ptolemy to hold further discourse on the subject. Certain princes, it is true, have been suicides, amongst others Mithridates, Cleopatra, and Otho. But these all put an end to themselves to escape some peculiar evils, or from dread of an increase of misfortune. Princes are, I imagine, more liable than other men to feel a hatred of their condition, and to think favourably of suicide. For have they not reached the summit of what is called human happiness? They have nothing to hope for, because they have everything that forms a part of the so-called good things of this life. They cannot anticipate greater pleasure to-morrow than they have enjoyed to-day.[Pg 193] Thus they are more unfortunately situated than all less exalted people. For the present is always sad and unsatisfactory; the future alone is a source of pleasure.

But be that as it may. We see then that there is nothing to prevent men voluntarily quitting life, and preferring death, save the fear of another world. All other reasons are palpably ill-founded. They are due to a wrong estimate, in comparing the advantages and evils of existence; and whoever at any time feels a strong attachment to life, or lives in a state of contentment, does so under a mistake, either of judgment, will, or even fact.

Plotinus. That is true, dear Porphyrius. But nevertheless, let me advise, nay implore, you to listen to the counsels of Nature rather than Reason. Follow the instincts of that primitive Nature, mother of us all, who, though she has manifested no affection for us in creating us for unhappiness, is a less bitter and cruel foe than our own reason, with its boundless curiosity, speculation, chattering, dreams, ideas, and miserable learning. Besides, Nature has sought to diminish our unhappiness by concealing or disguising it from us as much as possible. And although we are greatly changed, and the power of nature within us is much lessened, we are not so altered but that much of our former manhood remains, and our primitive nature is not quite stifled within us. In spite of all our folly, it will never be otherwise. So, too, the mistaken view of life that you mention, although I admit that it is in reality palpably erroneous, will continue to prevail. It is held not only by idiots and the half-witted, but by clever, wise, and learned men, and always will be, unless the Nature that made us—and not man nor his reason—herself puts an end to it. And I assure you that neither disgust of life, nor despair, nor the sense of the nullity of things, the vanity of all anxiety, and the insignificance of man, nor hatred of the world and oneself, are of long duration;[Pg 194] although such dispositions of mind are perfectly reasonable, and the contrary unreasonable. For our physical condition changes momentarily in more or less degree; and often without any especial cause life endears itself to us again, and new hopes give brightness to human things, which once more seem worthy of some attention, not indeed from our understanding, but from what may be termed the higher senses of the intellect. This is why each of us, though perfectly aware of the truth, continues to live in spite of Reason, and conforms to the behaviour of others; for our life is controlled by these senses, and not by the understanding.

Whether suicide be reasonable, or our compromise with life unreasonable, the former is certainly a horrible and inhuman action. It were better to follow Nature, and remain man, than act like a monster in following Reason. Besides, ought we not to give some thought to the friends, relatives, acquaintance, and people with whom we have been accustomed to live, and from whom we should thus separate for ever? And if the thought of such separation be nothing to us, ought we not to consider their feelings? They lose one whom they loved and respected; and the atrocity of his death enhances their grief. I know that the wise man is not easily moved, nor yields to pity and lamentation to a disquieting extent; he does not abase himself to the ground, shed tears immoderately, nor do other similar things unworthy of one who clearly understands the condition of humanity. But such fortitude of soul should be reserved for grievous circumstances that arise from nature, or are unavoidable; it is an abuse of fortitude to deprive ourselves for ever of the society and conversation of those who are dear to us. He is a barbarian, and not a wise man, who takes no account of the grief experienced by his friends, relations, and acquaintances. He who scarcely troubles himself about the grief his death would cause to his friends and family[Pg 195] is selfish; he cares little for others, and all for himself. And truly, the suicide thinks only of himself. He desires nought but his personal welfare, and throws away all thought of the rest of the world. In short, suicide is an action of the most unqualified and sordid egotism, and is certainly the least attractive form of self-love that exists in the world.

Finally, my dear Porphyrius, the troubles and evils of life, although many and inevitable, when, as in your case, unaccompanied by grievous calamity or bodily infirmity, are after all easy to be borne, especially by a wise and strong man like yourself. And indeed, life itself is of so little importance, that man ought not to trouble himself much either to retain or abandon it; and, without thinking greatly about it, we ought to give the former instinct precedence over the latter.

If a friend begged you to do this, why should you not gratify him?

Now I earnestly entreat you, dear Porphyrius, by the memory of our long friendship, put away this idea. Do not grieve your friends, who love you with such warm affection, and your Plotinus,[2] who has no dearer nor better friend in the world. Help us to bear the burden of life, instead of leaving us without a thought. Let us live, dear Porphyrius,[3] and console each other. Let us not[Pg 196] refuse our share of the sufferings of humanity, apportioned to us by destiny. Let us cling to each other with mutual encouragement, and hand in hand strengthen one another better to bear the troubles of life. Our time after all will be short; and when death comes, we will not complain. In the last hour, our friends and companions will comfort us, and we shall be gladdened by the thought that after death we shall still live in their memory, and be loved by them.

[1] "Ennui is a state only experienced by the intelligent. The greater the mind, the more constant, painful, and terrible is the ennui it suffers. Ennui is in some respects the sublimest of human sentiments" (Leopardi's "Pensieri" Nos. lxvii. and lxviii.)

[2] Plotinus was born 204 A.D. He began teaching philosophy in Rome, and was highly esteemed at court. Eunapius says of him, "The heavenly elevation of his mind, and his perplexed style, made him very tiresome and unpleasant." He was ascetic in his habits; disparaged patriotism; depreciated material things; purposely forgot his birthday; and acted altogether rather as a spectator of other men's lives than as a living man himself.

[3] Porphyrius was born 233 A.D. He was a pupil of Plotinus, and like him established a school of philosophy at Rome. From study of the writings of Plotinus he fell into a state of disgust with life, and retiring from Rome, lived alone in a solitary and wild part of Sicily. Here he determined to put an end to his life by starvation. He was found by Plotinus, who had followed him from Rome, in a state of extreme weakness, and was, by his wise counsels, dissuaded from completing his intention.

[Pg 197]

COMPARISON OF THE LAST WORDS OF MARCUS BRUTUS AND THEOPHRASTUS.

I think, in all ancient history there can be found no words more lamentable and terrifying, yet withal, speaking humanly, more true, than those uttered by Marcus Brutus shortly before death, in disparagement of virtue. This is what, according to Dionysius Cassius, he is reported to have said:—

"O miserable virtue! Thou art but a mere phrase, and I have followed thee, as though thou wert a reality. Fate is stronger than thee."

Plutarch, in his life of Brutus, makes no mention of this, which has induced Pier Vettori to conclude that Cassius has here taken licence in prose often accorded to poetry. But its truth is confirmed by the witness of Florus, who states that Brutus, when at the point of death, exclaimed, that virtue was "an expression, and not a reality."

Many people are shocked at those words of Brutus, and blame him for uttering them. They infer from their meaning, either that virtue is a sealed book to them, or else that they have never experienced ill-fortune. The former inference alone is credible. In any case, it is certain they but slightly understand, and still less realise the unhappiness of human affairs, or else they stupidly wonder why the doctrines of Christianity were not in force before the time of Christ.

[Pg 198]

Other people interpret these words as demonstrating that Brutus was not after all the noble and pious man he was supposed to have been. They imagine that just before death he threw off the mask. But they are wrong; and if they give Brutus credit for sincerity in uttering these words in repudiation of virtue, let them consider how it were possible for him to abandon what he never possessed, or to disassociate himself from that with which he never had any association. If they think he was insincere, and spoke designedly and with ostentation, let them explain what object he could have in speaking vain and fallacious words, and immediately afterwards acting in accordance with them? Are facts deniable, simply because they are not in harmony with words?

Brutus was a man overwhelmed by a great and unavoidable catastrophe. He was disheartened, and wearied with life and fortune, and having abandoned all desires and hopes, the deceitfulness of which he had experienced, he determined to take his destiny into his own hands, and to put an end to his unhappiness. Why should he, at the very moment of eternal separation from his fellows, trouble to hunt the phantom of glory, and study to give forth words and thoughts to deceive those around him, and to gain human esteem, when he was about to leave humanity for ever? What was it to him that he might gain a reputation on that earth which appeared so hateful and contemptible to him?

These words of Brutus are well known to most of us. The following utterance of Theophrastus at the point of death is, I believe, less known, though very worthy of consideration. It forms a parallel with that of Brutus, both as to its substance and time of delivery. Diogenes Laertius mentions it, not, in my opinion, as original to himself, but as an extract from some more ancient and important work. He says that Theophrastus, just before death, being asked by his disciples whether he would leave them any token or words of advice, replied:

[Pg 199]

"None, except that man despises and rejects many pleasures for the sake of glory. But no sooner does he begin to live than death overtakes him. Hence the love of glory is as fatal a thing as possible. Strive to live happily: abandon studies, which are a weariness; or cultivate them only so that they may bring you fame. Life is more vain than useful. As for me, I have no time to think more about it; you must study what is most expedient." So saying, he died.

Other sayings of Theophrastus on this occasion are mentioned by Cicero and St. Jerome. These are better known, but have nothing to do with our subject.

It would seem that Theophrastus lived to the age of more than a hundred, having devoted all his lifetime to study and writing, and having been an unwearied pursuer of glory. Suidas says that his death was due to the excess of his studies, and that he died surrounded by about two thousand of his disciples and followers, reverenced for his wisdom throughout the whole of Greece, regretting his pursuit of glory, just as Brutus repented of virtue. These two words, glory and virtue, were by the ancients regarded as almost synonymous in meaning, though it is not so in the present day. Theophrastus did not indeed say that glory is more frequently a matter of fortune than merit, which is oftener true now than in former times; but had he said so, there would have been no difference between his idea and that of Brutus.

Such abjurations, or rather apostasies, of those noble errors which beautify, nay compose our very life, are of daily occurrence. They are due to the fact that the human intelligence in process of time discovers, not only the nakedness, but even the skeleton of things: wisdom also, which was regarded by the ancients as the consolation and chief cure for our unhappiness, has been obliged to impeach our condition, and almost requires a consolation for itself, since had not men followed it, they would not have known the greatness of their misfortune, or at[Pg 200] least would have been able to remedy it with hope. But the ancients used to believe, according to the teaching of Nature, that things were things, and not appearances, and that human life was destined to partake of happiness as well as unhappiness. Consequently, such apostasies as these were very rare, and were the result not of passions and vices, but of a sentiment and realisation of the truth of things. Therefore they deserve careful and philosophical consideration.

The words of Theophrastus are the more surprising when we think of the circumstances in which he died. He was prosperous and successful; and it would seem as though he could not have a single cause for regret. His chief aim, glory, he had succeeded in acquiring long ago. The utterance of Brutus, on the other hand, was one of those inspirations of misfortune which sometimes open out a new world to our minds, and persuade us of truths that require a long time for the mere intelligence to discover. Misfortune may indeed be compared in its effect to the frenzy of lyric poets, who at a glance, as if situated in a lofty place, take in as much of the domain of human knowledge as requires many centuries before it be discerned by philosophers. In almost all ancient writings (whether philosophical, poetical, historical, or aught else), we meet with many very sorrowful expressions, common enough to us nowadays, but strange to the people of those times. These sentences, however, were mostly due to the innate or accidental misfortune of the writer, or the persons who spoke them, whether imaginary or real. And rarely we find on the monuments of the ancients any expression of the sadness or ennui which they felt because of the unreality of happiness, or their misfortunes, whether natural, or due to force of circumstances. For when they suffered, they lamented their sufferings as the only hindrance to their happiness, which they not only considered it possible to obtain, but even man's right, although Fate proved sometimes too strong.

[Pg 201]

Now, let us seek what could have placed in the mind of Theophrastus this sentiment about the vanity of glory and life, which, considering his epoch and nation, is an extraordinary one. In the first place, we find that the studies of this philosopher were not limited to one or two branches of science. The record of his writings, which are mostly lost, informs us that his knowledge included little less than everything then knowable. And this universal science was not like that of Plato, subordinated to his imagination, but conformed to the teaching of Aristotle in being the result of experience and reason; its aim, too, was not the discovery of the beautiful, but that which is its especial contrary, the useful. This being so, it is not wonderful that Theophrastus should attain to the height of human wisdom,—that is, a knowledge of the vanity of life, and wisdom itself. For it is a fact that the numerous discoveries made recently by philosophers about the nature of men and things, are chiefly the result of a comparison and synthesis of the different sciences and studies, whereby the mutual connection between the most distant parts of nature is demonstrated.

Besides, from his book of "Characters" we learn how clearly Theophrastus discerned the qualities and manners of men; indeed, with the exception of the poets, very few ancient writers equal him in this respect. And this faculty is the sure sign of a mind capable of numerous, diverse, and powerful sensations. For, to produce a keen representation of the moral qualities and passions of men, the writer relies less on what actual facts he may have collected, or observations made, about the manners of others, than on his own mind, even though his personal habits be very different from those of his subjects.

Massillon was asked one day what enabled him to describe so naturally the habits and feelings of men, who, like himself, lived more in solitude than society. He[Pg 202] replied: "I contemplate myself." Dramatists and other poets do the same thing. Now a many-sided mind, subtle in discernment, cannot but feel the nakedness and absolute unhappiness of life; it acquires a tendency to sadness after meditation excited by numerous studies, especially such as are concerned with the very essence of things, like the speculative sciences.

It is certain that Theophrastus, who loved study and glory above everything, and was master or rather founder of a very numerous school, knew and formally announced the uselessness of human exertions, including his own teaching and that of others; the little affinity existing between virtue and happiness of life; and the superior power of fortune to merit in the acquirement of happiness, equally among the wise and others. In this respect, perhaps, he was superior to all the Greek philosophers, especially those preceding Epicurus, from whom both in manners and thought he was essentially different. This is owing partly to circumstances already mentioned, and is also due to other things referred to by ancient writers on the subject of his teaching It would seem as though his own fate has proved the truth of his doctrine. For he is not esteemed by modern philosophers as he ought to be, since all his moral writings are lost, with the exception of his "Characters." His writings, too, on the subjects of politics and laws, and almost all those relating to metaphysics, are also missing. Besides, the ancient philosophers were little inclined to give him credit for keener perception than they possessed; on the contrary, many of them, especially such as were shallow and conceited, blamed and ill-treated him. These men taught that the wise man is essentially happy, and that virtue and wisdom suffice to procure happiness; although they were only too well aware of the contrary, even supposing they had any real knowledge of either the one or the other. Philosophers will never be cured of this idea. Even the philosophy of[Pg 203] the present day teaches the same thing; whereas, correctly speaking, it can only say that everything beautiful, delightful, and great, is mere falsity and nothingness.

But to return to Theophrastus. Most of the ancients were incapable of the profound and sorrowful sentiment that inspired him. "Theophrastus is roughly handled by all the philosophers in their writings and schools for having praised this saying of Callisthenes: 'Fortune, not wisdom, is the mistress of life.' They consider that no philosopher ever gave expression to a weaker sentiment." So says Cicero, who in another place remarks that Theophrastus in his book about "The Happy Life," attributed much influence to fortune, which he considered a most important factor of happiness. Again, he adds, "Let us make much use of Theophrastus; but give virtue more reality and value than he gave to it."

Perhaps it may be imagined from these remarks that Theophrastus had little sympathy with the weaknesses of human nature, and that he waged war against their influence in public and private life, both by his writings and actions. It might also be thought that he would restrict the empire of the imagination in favour of that of reason. As a matter of fact, he did just the contrary. Concerning his actions, we read in Plutarch's book against Colotes that our philosopher twice freed his country from a tyranny. As for his teachings, Cicero says that Theophrastus in a writing on the subject of "Wealth," dilated at considerable length on the advantages of magnificence and pomp at the shows and national festivals; indeed he considered the chief usefulness of riches to lie in the consequent power of expenditure that accompanied them. This idea is blamed and ridiculed by Cicero, with whom, however, I will not discuss the question, for his superficial knowledge of philosophy might have easily led him to a wrong conclusion. I imagine Cicero to have been a man rich in civil and domestic virtues, but ignorant of the greatest stimulants and bulwarks of virtue that the world[Pg 204] possesses, namely, those things that are peculiarly adapted to excite and arouse the mind, and exercise the powers of the imagination.

I will merely say that those men among, the ancients and moderns who knew best and realised most strongly and deeply the nullity of everything, and the force of truth, have not only refrained from endeavouring to lead others to their condition, but have even laboured hard to conceal and disguise it from themselves. They acted like men who had learnt from experience the wretchedness that resulted from wisdom and knowledge. Many celebrated examples of this are furnished, especially in recent times. Truly, if our philosophers fully understood what they endeavour to teach, and realised in their own persons the consequences of their philosophy, instead of welcoming their knowledge, they would hate and abhor it. They would strive to forget what they know, and to shut' their eyes to that which they see. They would take refuge, as their best resource, in those sweet unrealities, which Nature herself has placed in all our minds; nor would they think it well to enforce on others the doctrine of the nothingness of all things. If, however, desire of glory should incite them to do this last, they will admit that in this part of the universe we can only live by putting faith in things that are non-existent.

There is another considerable difference between the circumstances of Theophrastus and Brutus, that of time. When Theophrastus lived, the influence of those fictions and phantoms which ruled the thoughts and actions of the ancients, had not departed. The epoch of Brutus, on the other hand, may be termed the last age of the imagination. Knowledge and experience of the truth prevailed amongst the people. Had it not been so, Brutus need not have fled from life as he did, and the Roman republic would not have died with him. And not only the republic, but also the whole of antiquity, that is, the[Pg 205] old customs and characteristics of the civilised world, were at the point of death, together with the opinions which gave birth to, and supported them. Life had already lost its value, and wise men sought to console themselves not so much for their fate as for existence itself; because they regarded it as incredible that man should be born essentially and solely for misery. Thus they arrived at the conception of another life, which might explain the reason of virtue and noble actions. Such explanation had hitherto been found in life itself, but was so no longer, nor was it ever again to be found there.

To these ideas of futurity are due the noble sentiments often expressed by Cicero, especially in his oration for Archias.

[Pg 206]
DIALOGUE BETWEEN TRISTANO AND A FRIEND.

Friend. I have read your book. It is as melancholy as usual.

Tristano. Yes, as usual.

Friend. Melancholy, disconsolate, hopeless. It is clear that this life appears to you an abominable thing.

Tristano. How can I excuse myself? I was then so firmly convinced of the truth of my notion about the unhappiness of life.

Friend. Unhappy it may be. But even then, what good ...

Tristano. No, no; on the contrary, it is very happy. I have changed my opinion now. But when I wrote this book I had that folly in my head, as I tell you. And I was so full of it, that I should have expected anything rather than to doubt the truth of what I wrote on the subject. For I thought the conscience of every reader would assuredly bear witness to the truth of my statements. I imagined there might be differences of opinion as to the use or harm of my writings, but none as to their truth. I also believed that my lamentations, since they were aroused by misfortunes common to all, would be echoed in the heart of every one who heard them. And when I afterwards felt impelled to deny, not merely some particular observation, but the whole fabric of my book, and to say that life is not unhappy, and that[Pg 207] if it seemed so to me, it must have been the effect of illness, or some other misfortune peculiar to myself, I was at first amazed, astonished, petrified, and for several days as though transported into another world. Then I began to think, and was a little irritated with myself. Finally I laughed, and said to myself that the human race possesses a characteristic common to husbands. For a married man who wishes to live a quiet life, relies on the fidelity of his wife, even when half the world knows she is faithless. Similarly, when a man takes up his abode in any country, he makes up his mind to regard it as one of the best countries in the world, and he does so. For the same reason, men, desiring to live, agree to consider life a delightful and valuable thing; they therefore believe it to be so, and are angry with whoever is of the contrary opinion. Hence it follows, that in reality people always believe, not the truth, but what is, or appears to be, best for them. The human race, which has believed, and will continue to put faith in so many absurdities, will never acknowledge that it knows nothing, that it is nothing, and that it has nothing to hope. No philosopher teaching any one of these three things would be successful, nor would he have followers, and the populace especially would refuse to believe in him. For, apart from the fact that all three doctrines have little to recommend them to any one who wishes to live, the two first offend man's pride, and they all require courage and strength of mind in him who accepts them. Now, men are cowards, of ignoble and narrow minds, and always anticipating good, because always ready to vary their ideas of good according to the necessities of life. They are very willing, as Petrarch says, to surrender to fortune; very eager and determined to console themselves in any misfortune; and to accept any compensation in exchange for what is denied them, or for that which they have lost; and to accommodate themselves to any condition of life, however wicked and barbarous. When deprived of any[Pg 208] desirable thing, they nourish themselves on illusions, from which they derive as much satisfaction as if their conceptions were the most genuine and real things in the world. As for me, I cannot refrain from laughing at the human race, enamoured of life, just as the people in the south of Europe laugh at husbands enamoured of faithless wives. I consider men show very little courage in thus allowing themselves to be deceived and deluded like fools; they are not only content to bear the greatest sufferings, but also are willing to be as it were puppets of Nature and Destiny. I here refer to the deceptions of the intellect, not the imagination. Whether these sentiments of mine are the result of illness, I do not know; but I do know that, well or ill, I despise men's cowardice, I reject every childish consolation and illusive comfort, and am courageous enough to bear the deprivation of every hope, to look steadily on the desert of life, to hide no part of our unhappiness, and to accept all the consequences of a philosophy, sorrowful but true. This philosophy, if of no other use, gives the courageous man the proud satisfaction of being able to rend asunder the cloak that conceals the hidden and mysterious cruelty of human destiny.

This I said to myself, almost as though I were the inventor of this bitter philosophy, which I saw rejected by every one as a new and unheard-of thing. But, on reflection, I found that it dated from the time of Solomon, Homer, and the most ancient poets and philosophers, who abound with fables and sayings which express the unhappiness of human life. One says that "man is the most miserable of the animals." Another that, "it were better not to be born, or, being born, to die in the cradle." Again, "whom the gods love, die young;" besides numberless other similar sayings. And I also remembered that from then even until now, all poets, philosophers, and writers, great and small, have in one way or another echoed and confirmed the same doctrines.

[Pg 209]

Then I began to think again, and spent a long time in a state of wonder, contempt, and laughter. At length I turned to study the matter more deeply, and came to the conclusion that man's unhappiness is one of the innate errors of the mind, and that the refutation of this idea, through the demonstration of the happiness of life, is one of the greatest discoveries of the nineteenth century. Now, therefore, I am at peace, and confess I was wrong to hold the views I previously held.

Friend. Then have you changed your opinion?

Tristano. Of course. Do you imagine I should oppose the discoveries of the nineteenth century?

Friend. Do you believe all the century believes?

Tristano. Certainly. Why not?

Friend. You believe then in the infinite perfectibility of the human race, do you not?

Tristano. Undoubtedly.

Friend. Do you also believe that the human race actually progresses daily?

Tristano. Assuredly. It is true that sometimes I think one of the ancients was physically worth four of us. And the body is the man; because (apart from all else) high-mindedness, courage, the passions, capacity for action and enjoyment, and all that ennobles and vivifies life, depend on the vigour of the body, without which they cannot exist. The weak man is not a man, but a child, and less than a child, because it is his fate to stand aside and see others live. All he can do is to chatter. Life is not for him. Hence in

113

olden times, and even in more enlightened ages, weakness of body was regarded as ignominious.

But with us, it is very long since education deigned to think of such a base and abject thing as the body. The mind is its sole care. Yet, in its endeavours to cultivate the mind, it destroys the body without perceiving that the former is also necessarily destroyed. And even if it were possible to remedy this false system of education, it[Pg 210] would be impossible to discover, without a radical change in the state of modern society, any cure for the other inconveniences of life, whether public or private.

Everything that formerly tended to preserve and perfect the body, seems to-day to be in conspiracy for its destruction. The consequence is, that, compared with the ancients, we are little better than children, and they in comparison with us may indeed be termed perfect men. I refer equally to individuals in comparison with individuals, as to the masses (to use this most expressive modern term) compared to the masses.

I will add also that the superior vigour of the ancients is manifested in their moral and metaphysical systems.

But I do not allow myself to be influenced by such trifling objections, and I firmly believe that the human race is perpetually in a state of progression.

Friend. You believe also, if I rightly understand you, that knowledge, or, as, it is called, enlightenment, continually increases.

Tristano. Assuredly. Although I observe that the desire of knowledge grows in proportion as the appreciation for study diminishes. And, astonishing to say, if you count up the number of truly learned men who lived contemporaneously a hundred and fifty years ago, or even later, you will find them incomparably more numerous than at present. It may perhaps be said that learned people are rare nowadays because knowledge is more universally disseminated, instead of being confined to the heads of a few; and that the multitude of educated people compensate for the rarity of learned people. But knowledge is not like riches, which whether divided or accumulated, always make the same total. In a country where every one knows a little, the total knowledge is small; because knowledge begets knowledge, but will not bear dispersion. For superficial instruction cannot indeed be divided amongst many, though it may be common to many unlearned men. Genuine knowledge belongs only[Pg 211] to the learned, and depth in knowledge to the few that are very learned. And, with rare exceptions, only the man who is very learned, and possessed of an immense fund of knowledge, is able to add materially to the sum of human science. Now, in the present time, it is daily more difficult to discover a really learned man, save perhaps in Germany, where science is not yet dethroned.

I utter these reflections simply for the sake of a little talk and philosophising, not because I doubt for a single moment the truth of what you say. Indeed, were I to see the world quite full of ignorant impostors on the one hand, and presumptuous fools on the other, I should still hold to my present belief that knowledge and enlightenment are on the increase.

Friend. Of course, then, you believe that this century is superior to all the preceding ones?

Tristano. Decidedly. All the centuries have had this opinion of themselves; even those of the most barbarous ages. The present century thinks so, and I agree with it. But if you asked me in what it is superior to the others, and whether in things pertaining to the body or the mind, I should refer you to what I said just now on the subject of progress.

Friend. In short, to sum it up in two words, do you agree with what the journals say about nature, and human destiny? We are not now talking of literature or politics, on which subjects their opinion is indisputable.

Tristano. Precisely. I bow before the profound philosophy of the journals, which will in time supersede every other branch of literature, and every serious and exacting study. The journals are the guides and lights of the present age. Is it not so?

Friend. Very true. Unless you are speaking ironically, you have become one of us.

Tristano. Yes. Certainly I have.

Friend. Then what shall you do with your book? Will[Pg 212] you allow it to go down to posterity, conveying doctrines so contrary to the opinions you now hold?

Tristano. To posterity? Permit me to laugh, since you are no doubt joking; if I thought otherwise, I should laugh all the more. For it is not a personal matter, but one relating to the individuals and individual things of the nineteenth century; about whom and which there is no fear of the judgment of posterity, since they will know no more about the matter than their ancestors knew. "Individuals are eclipsed in the crowd," as our modern thinkers elegantly say; which means, that the individual need not put himself to any inconvenience, because, whatever his merit, he can neither hope for the miserable reward of glory, in reality, nor in his dreams.

Leave therefore the masses to themselves; although I would ask the wiseacres who illumine the world in the present day, to explain how the masses can do anything without the help of the individuals that compose them.

But to return to my book, and posterity. Books now are generally written in less time than is necessary for reading them. Their worth is proportioned to their cost, and their longevity to their value. It is my opinion that the twentieth century will make a very clean sweep of the immense bibliography of the nineteenth. Perhaps however it will say something to this effect: "We have here whole libraries of books which have cost some twenty, some thirty years of labour, and some less, but all have required very great exertion; let us read these first, because it is probable there is much to be learnt from them. These at an end, we will pass to lighter literature."

My friend, this is a puerile age, and the few men remaining are obliged to hide themselves for very shame, resembling, as they do, a well-formed man in a land of cripples. And these good youths of the century are desirous of doing all that their ancestors did. Like children they wish to act on the spur of the moment,[Pg 213] without any laborious preparation. They would like the progress of the age to be such as to exempt them and their successors from all fatiguing study and application in the acquirement of knowledge. For instance, a commercial friend of mine told me the other day that even mediocrity has become very rare. Scarcely any one is fit to fulfil properly the duty which devolves upon him, either by necessity or choice. This seems to me to mark the true distinction between this century and the preceding ones. At all times greatness has been rare; but in former centuries mediocrity prevailed, whereas in our century nullity prevails. All people wish to be everything. Hence, there is such confusion and riot, that no attention is paid to the few great men who are still to be found, and who are unable to force a way through the vast multitude of rivals. Thus, whilst the lowest people believe themselves illustrious, obscurity and success in nothing is the common fate both of the highest and lowest.

But, long live statistics! Long live the sciences, economical, moral, and political; the pocket encyclopædias; the manuals of everything; and all the other fine creations of our age! And may the nineteenth century live for ever! For though poor in results, it is yet very rich and great in promise, which' is well known to be the best of signs. Let us therefore console ourselves that for sixty-six[1] more years this admirable century will have the talking to itself, and will be able to utter its own opinions.

Friend. You speak, it seems, somewhat ironically. But you ought at least to remember that this is a century of transition.

Tristano. What do you infer from that? All centuries have been, and will be, more or less transitional; because human society is never stationary, and will never at any time attain to a fixed condition. It follows therefore[Pg 214] that this fine word is either no excuse for the nineteenth century, or is one common to all the centuries. It remains to be seen whether the transition now in progress is from good to better, or from bad to worse.

But perhaps you mean to say that the present age is especially transitional, inasmuch as it is a rapid passage from one state of civilisation to another, absolutely different. In which case I would ask your permission to laugh at this rapidity. Every transition requires a certain amount of time, and when too rapidly accomplished, invariably relapses, and the progress has to recommence from the very beginning. Thus it has always been. For nature does not advance by leaps; and when forced, no durable result is obtained. In short, precipitous transitions are only apparent transitions, and do not represent genuine progress.

Friend. I advise you not to talk in this fashion with every one, because if you do you will gain many enemies.

Tristano. What does it matter? Henceforth, neither enemies nor friends can do me much harm.

Friend. Very probably you will be despised as one incapable of comprehending the spirit of modern philosophy, and who cares little for the progress of civilisation and the sciences.

Tristano. I should be very sorry for that; but what can I do? If I am despised, I will endeavour to console myself.

Friend. But have you, or have you not, changed your opinions? And what is to be done about your book?

Tristano. It would be best to burn it. If it be not burnt, it may be preserved as a book full of poetic dreams, inventions, and melancholy caprices; or better, as an expression of the unhappiness of the writer. Because, I will tell you in confidence, my dear friend, that I believe you and every one else to be happy. As for myself, however, with your permission, and that of[Pg 215] the century, I am very unhappy, and all the journals of both worlds cannot persuade me to the contrary.

Friend. I do not know the cause of this unhappiness of which you speak. But a man is the best judge of his own happiness or unhappiness, and his opinion cannot be wrong.

Tristano. Very true. And more, I tell you frankly that I do not submit to my unhappiness, nor bow the head, and come to terms with Destiny, like other men. I ardently wish for death above everything, with such warmth and sincerity as I firmly believe few have desired it.

I would not speak to you thus, if I were not sure that when the time came I should not belie my words. I may add that although I do not yet foresee the end of my life, I have an inward feeling that almost assures me the hour of which I speak is not far distant. I am more than ripe for death, and it seems to me too absurd and improbable, that being dead spiritually, as I am, and the tale of my life being told in every part, I should linger out the forty or fifty years with which Nature threatens me. I am terrified at the mere thought of such a thing. But, like all evils that exceed the power of imagination, this seems to me a dream and illusion, devoid of truth. So that if any one speaks to me about the distant future, as though I were to have a part in it, I cannot help smiling to myself, so sure am I

116

that I have not long to live. This thought, I may say, alone supports me. Books and studies, which I often wonder I ever loved, great designs, and hopes of glory and immortality, are things now undeserving of even a smile. Nor do I now laugh at the projects and hopes of this century. I cordially wish them every possible success, and I praise, admire, and sincerely honour their good intentions. But I do not envy posterity, nor those who have still a long life before them. Formerly I used to envy fools, imbeciles, and people with a high opinion of themselves,[Pg 216] and I would willingly have changed my lot with any one of them. Now, I envy neither fools, nor the wise, the great, the small, the weak, the powerful. I envy the dead, and with them alone would I exchange my lot. Every pleasurable fancy, every thought of the future that comes to me in my solitude, and with which I pass away the time, is allied with the thought of death, from which it is inseparable. And in this longing, neither the remembrance of my childish dreams, nor the thought of having lived in vain, disturbs me any more as formerly. When death comes to me, I shall die as peacefully and contentedly as if it were the only thing for which I had ever wished in the world. This is the sole prospect that reconciles me to Destiny.

If, on the one hand, I were offered the fortune and fame of Cæsar or Alexander, free from the least stain; and, on the other hand, death to-day, I should unhesitatingly choose to die to-day.

[1] Written in 1834.

THE END.

26175640R00068

Printed in Great Britain
by Amazon